EARTH 2.0

Published in Great Britain in 2023
by Big White Shed, Nottingham
www.bigwhiteshed.co.uk
Printed and bound by Imprint Digital, Devon

ISBN 978-1-915021-17-5
Copyright © Nottingham Writers Studio
individual copyright remains with the authors
Cover Design by Raphael Achache

A CIP catalogue record of this book is available
from the British Library.

Dedicated to Thom Seddon.

Without his tireless energy this book wouldn't have been finished, without his boundless humour the process wouldn't have been as fun.

Foreword

Firstly, thank you for taking a chance on a little-known anthology and doubly thank you for taking the time to read the foreword! I'm well aware that there are thousands of other books you could be reading right now, so I'm humbled and honoured you chose ours.

Thankfully for both of us, *Earth 2.0* is a cracking collection of some of the greatest environmentally-themed stories written in 2022. Authors from all around the globe worked to create this collection, spanning a variety of genres. I'm certain you're going to find a story you love (or five) and plenty which will make you laugh, cry and in one or two cases possibly squirm. To say more though, of course, would make us wander into spoiler territory.

You may not know that this anthology came about be due to a competition run by a small organisation with a lot of heart, *The Nottingham Writers' Studio*. In 2020, just as the pandemic was going into full swing many of us watched another horror take place – the murder of George Floyd. While I will not re-cap those terrible events, it left many of us at the Studio soul searching about what we could do to make the world a more just place, even if only in a tiny way.

Ultimately, this resulted in *The George Floyd Short Story Competition*' a free-to-enter event open to all, but specifically targeting authors of colour, inviting them to write about today's most topical social issues. In 2021, this led to our first anthology *Black Lives*, which if you haven't had the good fortune to pick up, I thoroughly recommend you do, with all proceeds going to the Stephen Lawrence Day Foundation.

Earth 2.0 continues this trend, but rather than focusing on the issue of race we now have turned our gaze to the world around us.

Each entrant was invited to consider where they think the planet is going and while it won't take a particularly cynical mind to expect a lot of negative stories, you might be surprised how much heart and laughter there is on the road to hell. Or maybe not. I wouldn't want to spoil the show before it even gets started.

Before I sign off, I'd like to personally thank Thom Seddon who was not only an incredibly valuable reader and judge on this anthology, he also edited the entire book! I'd also like to thank Alan Walker, our fearless leader, and my colleagues Tracey Hylton and Nick Sturgeon, all of whom gracefully dedicated their time to help curate this book. Finally, it would be unfair not to mention my gratitude to Anne Holloway at *Big White Shed* for putting it all together!

Now, if you've made it this far it seems only fair to reward you with a couple of hidden nuggets of trivia. The title *Earth 2.0* was not just chosen because we asked writers to imagine a future earth. It's also because the current scientific consensus is that the planet can only handle another 2° C temperature increase before things start to go catastrophically bad for us, ergo – Earth 2.0.

This last bit is a little hidden secret snaking through the book. It's a mild spoiler so if you'd rather go in completely blind, please feel free to flick on a couple of pages and come back later.

Still here?

Well, purely coincidentally we discovered during the editing process that virtually all the stories when put together actually create a workable timeline. The first story *How We Got Here* starts off at the very beginning with the next several stories set in modern times and then move into distinctive stages of a near future, before the fall, the fall and a rebuilding - creating a rather beautiful, rather accidental mosaic novel. The one exception outside this timeline is *When the World Froze* which we've decided to think of as a dreamlike interlude.

I hope you enjoyed a little peak behind the curtain and once again my sincere thanks for picking up this anthology, I hope you enjoy reading it as much as I was honoured to curate it.

Adam O'Connell
Vice-chair NWS

Contents

How We Got Here
Jeremy Morton

Monday, 2nd September

I look in the mirror. The uniform itches.

Mum is calling.

I've done my best. I'm not proud.

I always think about Bobby, more than me. He can't protect himself.

I try to retrace this summer's main events, like hot rocks on the beach. Imagining time reversing, putting everything back together. I could climb out of the bath and not be wet. The bath water would be clear and still. My pyjamas would rise to me from the floor.

The collapsed cliffs would form themselves again. A gathering cloud of dust, a soft rumbling, earth drawn up to the cliff top like salmon returning to spawn. Someone's house rebuilds itself, high on the edge. A rusting car is revealed on the beach. An old couple pick themselves up, looking around and above their heads in mystical wonder, before strolling backwards along the shore. Weird stuff like that.

Saturday, 31st August

I watched a vast expanse of cliffs shear off, heard the echoing thud. Felt it in my chest. I thought I could hear Kirk laughing, but it was Saturday and he was miles away, visiting his father in prison. It was like a sign, that I'd be punished.

I got back and told Mum about the cliff, and she said thank God Lawrence's place had all the land you could want between us and the edge. She said I needed a bath.

The grime all lifted off in the hot water. I lay there thinking about the cliffs. About Dad. And how long could Mum pretend to be so keen on Lawrence? Earlier, I'd been googling on Mum's phone: *When will I see my father again?* But there were just a lot of people asking the same thing, all over the world probably, about their dead dads, with no real answers. No one had anything definite to say.

I slapped the surface of the foamy water, shifting my body, imagining the waves pounding the cliffs. Then I started crying like a maniac.

Tuesday, 27th August

Newtown:
Bowling alley.
Multiplex cinema.
Multi-storey car park.
Newtown Leisure Centre
      (gym, indoor swimming pool, indoor tennis).
Radio Newtown.

Whittard:

I pressed the pen to my lips, like adults do. It helps you think.

Sheila was out. She spent a lot of her time on errands, or in the back room where she could count batches of postcards in glorious isolation. I hoped she'd get back soon. I didn't want to be alone with my thoughts.

It had been such a slow morning. I had finished reading Rev. T.W. Plunkett V.C.'s *Whittard - Past and Present*, from the library, and was taking another look at my list of things Newtown had, compared to here, when the automatic door buzzer sounded. I didn't leap up or do anything dramatic, not wanting to fawn and put them

11

off. I turned my list over, sitting up and forming an arch with my fingertips. I'd admit my heart was racing.

On Tuesdays it's always quiet, even though it's summertime. Pretty much anyone coming in on a Tuesday makes me sit up and pay attention. I go in with a sense of dread, because it can be so dull. And hope, in case a miraculous busload of Japanese OAPs spews out onto the esplanade. No one starts their holiday on a Tuesday, and nothing happens in town. Someone should make the council organise an event, to attract visitors on Tuesdays. A big music festival. Or a fireworks display. It could be set up on the land behind the Co-op Minimart, if they cleared the debris.

He wasn't a tourist.

I'd seen him before somewhere, but I couldn't say for sure. All I knew was, he was someone official. A teacher, or a bus inspector. His hair sat like coils of mangled, dirty wire discarded on the beach, and one of his eyes obviously wasn't real – it looked in a different direction to the other one, I mean.

He pressed his knuckles onto my desk and leaned forward, like he was inspecting me. Then he tilted his head and said, 'You seen Kirk Henderson?'

I felt a queasy gathering in my stomach. Word gets around in a place like this. People see things they aren't supposed to. It hadn't burned like we thought it would. But that was ages ago. Weeks ago.

My palms were sweating. I put my pen to my lips again, trying to evoke calm attention and a degree of efficient concern.

'You know him,' he said. 'Don't pretend you don't. I've seen the pair of you. Round my restaurant.'

I could smell pickles and wafts of sweat off of him. I realised who he was then. The boss at the chippy, up on the cliff. He didn't fry anything himself, just sat in the back room doing paperwork with a stubby pencil, emerging every so often to order the staff around. They kept their heads down. He wore the same gear as them, a greasy apron and paper hat, but never got his hands dirty.

12

'I – not really,' I said. 'I don't think so.'

One of his eyes stared right at me while the other scanned the carousel where we display the excursion leaflets. I wondered if he was planning a visit to the old lighthouse.

'You tell Kirk Henderson,' he said, 'you see him – if that car's not back where it belongs in the morning, he'll bloody –'

His real eye roamed the room, perhaps seeking the right word, or perhaps he thought Kirk might be hiding somewhere.

I'd told Kirk not to use the car again. He was meant to push it off the cliffs like we'd discussed.

'You tell him,' he said. 'What's your name, you little prick?'

I noticed him attempting to train his eye on my lanyard. Why wasn't he speaking to Kirk himself? Or the police?

'Hold on,' I said. 'Bit of an emergency?'

I said 'emergency' like a question, which is an annoying habit I've acquired.

I got up and walked slowly to the office, and once I was inside with the door shut I lit a cigarette under the smoke alarm, my hand shaking badly all of a sudden. I could see Sheila through the back window, returning from her lunchtime shopping, empty-handed and oblivious. I left as calmly as I could through the fire escape.

I knew Kirk and I were friends now. We could protect each other.

Tuesday night, 13th August

I'll never forget the sound of Beast's skull crushing under Kirk's boot.

Scoop it all up and put it in the box, he said. Don't leave any of that fucking mess there.

I was thinking, what would archaeologists say in a thousand years from now, finding Beast's remains, inside Kirk's dad's ammo tin? Its nameless collar, the decayed remnants of its chew ball. That is, if Earth still had humans in a thousand years. If it still existed at all.

13

Kirk did all the digging, with a shovel we'd found on the farm, really deep. You'd think he was a professional gravedigger. He had muscles like a grown man.

We sat on the ground and leaned back against the wheel of a rusted tractor, smoking. Kirk wiped the sweat off his face with his arm. The light was fading.

'Newt,' he said, quietly. I didn't like him calling me that, but I didn't dare say anything. 'You ever seen a ghost?'

I wanted to impress him. I'd heard ghosts, plenty of times, not always at night either. I hadn't seen them. They were like a sudden rushing of soft noise in my head. I suppose it began after what happened to Dad. I'd have to run out of the house, but the sounds would follow. Like a murmuring of prayers.

I couldn't say that to Kirk.

I told him I'd been down on the shore once when it was getting dark. Kirk had never been on the beach, even though he'd lived here all his life and could have pretty much walked down there in an hour or so.

'It was midnight,' I said. 'This thing came up out of the sea underneath the old arcades, in the moonlight.' What else should I say? 'All clanking with chains, and kind of moaning. I'll admit I shat myself.'

'Fuck off,' he said. 'Give us another cig.'

He filled his lungs and let it out through his teeth, tapping his finger on the cigarette while he thought about something. About the ghost, maybe. The fire was dying out.

'Do you think there are ghosts of dogs, like?'

I thought for a while. It was a good question.

'Yeah,' I said. 'I think I've seen them.'

'What, on the beach?'

He looked at me expectantly. I didn't say anything for what seemed like a long time.

'I don't know,' I said.

'We should never have burnt him', Kirk said. His face crumpled and he wiped his eyes with his sleeves. 'I wish we'd never taken him.'

His voice was strange, different. I let my head drop, sitting in silence as his shoulders jerked next to me. His emotions were boiling over, and it was my fault. I didn't know what to say. I wasn't going to find him another dog. Should I say it would be OK? I was waiting for those murmuring prayers to start up again in my head.

Tuesday afternoon, 13th August

The rain had cleared, and Kirk got the fire going good. He knew how to build it. He'd had a brilliant idea. We would bury Beast's ashes, not its body. I hoped the fire wouldn't attract attention. We'd gone to the waste ground behind the deserted farm. Where it had died. All around us were rusted machines and collapsing sheds. There was a chronic smell like some kind of corrosive glue. I'd brought two cans of Carlsberg from Lawrence's stash. He keeps booze all over the place, in his hidey-holes.

Kirk squirted paraffin onto Beast's stiff corpse. He was reciting some kind of poem.

'Half a league, half a league,
Half a league onward,
All in the valley of Death
Rode the six hundred.'

He surprised me sometimes.

Beast didn't look too sparkling now, you would have to admit. It just looked like some sort of condemned meat. Two days, gathering flies in the hiding place, waiting for the storm to end. According to Mum, Jim Hammond had gone nuts and got into a fight in the pub. Poor Jim, she said, it was all 'rather unfortunate'. I'd also brought a box of pamphlets about the funicular railway that didn't exist any more, on account of its falling into the sea.

It just fitted in my backpack. I thought they'd burn well, and we could bury the ashes in the box. Kirk said the box was too big. He had an ammo tin that was his dad's, and we'd put the ashes in that, and bury it. I couldn't deny that was the better plan, though less biodegradable and not that much smaller than my box.

I put a dog biscuit and the remains of Beast's chew ball in the tin. 'For the journey,' I said.

Let these safeguard him on his way, I thought. I really did. This life had to be just one stage of the journey, I knew that, even for a dog. There had to be more for this animal than waiting on its leash for Jim Hammond outside the chippy, and dying alone in the dark.

Kirk was kneeling and staring into the flames, repeating his poem. I don't think he knew all the lines.

He told me to take Beast's collar off its neck and put that in the box. I had a drink first. I was nearly sick, touching the fur. Kirk wiped his nose, smoke rising into his face, and clipped the lid on, like he was forgetting we still had a dog to put in there.

'God speed ya, Beast, to the afterlife, you daft bastard.'

It was the strangest sentence I'd ever heard anyone say.

The ancient Egyptians believed the mind was in your heart. They thought the brain was junk. For a few moments I sent my head round in circles wondering if I thought my mind – my soul – was in my brain, or whether I could make myself believe it was somewhere else. In my feet, for example.

'The Egyptians were mental for the afterlife,' I said, softly. 'Them and the Aztecs.'

Kirk poked at the flames with his stick. I couldn't tell if he was taking in what I said.

I imagined a bright ray of light, pointing the way to dog heaven. And Beast, looking like it used to, like a dog, sort of floating up along it, serene and forgiving, spinning slowly, to the sound of eerie music. I wanted Kirk to see it too.

I was watching Kirk poke at the blaze, when he threw down his stick and grabbed me by the wrist, pulling our hands over the flames. He was staring at me. I couldn't get my hand away.

'Kirk, please don't. *Please*, Kirk.'

All I could think to do was to start howling like a wolf. *A-ooh!* *A-ooh!* Kirk must have thought I was enjoying myself. I really went for it, no matter who might hear.

He released me, sniggering and rubbing his hand on his chin.

'Crazy bastard,' I said, though not very loud.

'Shouldn't we do a sacrifice, then?' He was looking around the place, perhaps for a handy squirrel or God knew what. 'Like in ancient times?'

To be honest, I was keen to get home.

'Maybe,' I said, the embers flying up to the darkening sky. 'But… him being an animal, he won't thank us for sacrificing anything that's, you know, of the animal world.'

'We can't sacrifice a human, you fucking psycho.'

The idea seemed to tickle him something chronic. He started to laugh, his face lit up all orange. He got hold of Beast and dropped it on top of the fire, sending sparks glinting in the air and making a foul smoke. We never did sacrifice anything, apart from Beast itself that is, and he was already dead.

Monday, 12ᵗʰ August

Sheila had popped out to the post office in the morning. She said she didn't mind the rain.

I helped myself to a few of her biscuits.

I like working here. I know what it's like to be a tourist, visiting the village. That's why I'm suited to the job. I'm not from here myself, not originally.

Mum said we could be at the seaside every day, if we moved here. Dad tried to take us to the beach once, me and Bobby, only it was at night. I imagined ice creams and sandcastles. Arcades. We were squeezed into the front, and Bobby and me were bounced about as the hired van sped down the road. We got on each other's nerves for a while, but Bobby was soon asleep. Not long after we set off, there was a thunderstorm. Proper horror movie stuff, which only made our destination more exciting. That's how I remember it.

Dad had mentioned changes at work. He didn't say much else. Perhaps he'd been promoted. It was confidential business, I realised, being as he worked for the council. Things were going to be great.

It seemed like we were driving in the dark for hours and hours, and all the time the windscreen wipers were going like mad. Mum would have been having the time of her life I suppose, in peace and quiet, with the house to herself. Then Dad woke us up looking wild-eyed and tearful, looming over us, and shouting that the van had broken down, and he was going to have to walk up the road to find somewhere that had a phone.

I was so disappointed, not going to the beach. I don't think I ever forgave him.

Sunday, 11ᵗʰ August

Kirk knew all these places. He said we weren't to go to our shelter, in case people found out about it. He drove us in a brown estate car that had a carrier bag in the back full of dirty magazines.

'I didn't know you had a car,' I said.

'I don't,' he said, all mysterious. 'You daft fucker,' he continued.

Kirk's pimples had flared up across his forehead. He'd bleached the top of his hair, which in Whittard made him almost a criminal. I didn't comment. He parked badly, up a muddy slope across the back of the old primary school that had closed, I suppose because there weren't enough kids.

He set off and I followed him, sort of like I was a dog myself or he was my dad. He was cradling the body like a baby and his eyes were red and weepy. I wanted to ask where we were going, but silence felt better, more apt. I felt a few fat spots of rain. I knew Kirk wanted to bury the body, and I supposed we would talk about it then. And after that we would never talk about it again.

I watched his broad back and stooping gait. We could be friends. We had to be. The skull daubed on his jacket made him like some cult priest. What did that make me?

I could smell the animal now, all putrid, and I thought about where we could bury it. In the sand on the beach maybe, but Kirk said no – what sort of a stupid fucker would suggest that. It would admittedly be hard to dig a grave in sand, I realised. Though if we waited long enough, a chunk of cliff would surely come storming down and bury it. If we waited a week or two maybe.

We couldn't risk that.

I trudged beside Kirk, past the old school fields, his breath heavy. We followed a long, craggy incline, the wind gathering strength as we crested the hill. There was a kind of stone hut up ahead. Kirk nodded towards it and glanced at me. Beast's head lay at a strange angle over Kirk's shoulder, its eyes half open.

'Army pillbox,' Kirk said, solemnly. His jaw, in profile, was like a Roman statue.

It began to rain hard as we came closer. Some kind of summer. I was glad I'd brought my poncho, although I struggled to get it on in the wind.

We crouched in the dim light that slanted in through the opening at the back. I couldn't see much. I wished I'd thought of a torch. Kirk placed Beast on the ground inside, knelt, laid a hand on its flank for a while as if expecting it to come alive again, then sat against the curved wall, pinching his temples.

He took a flat bottle of something from his coat, drank deeply, and offered it across to me.

It didn't seem well. It didn't seem happy with its situation.

I honestly wasn't sure if you could feed a dog Fruit and Nut bars, or if so how many. They are mainly fruit and nuts, it says so on the adverts. And I'm sure I've seen Jim Hammond give it chocolate treats, outside the chippy. I don't know if those might not have been real chocolate.

It was almost the end of my lunch break and I would have to be getting back. Not that I had much to do at work. I stroked its neck and head while it ate, inside the shed. It seemed to like it at first, staying for more and panting. I guess it was pretty hungry anyway. I wondered what breed it was, or if it was one of those mongrels. If I had a dog, I'd go for something big, with a hide like Mum's suede boots. Not this kind of yappy fur-ball.

There was only a bit of puke, at first.

I gave it a bowl of water, watched it sniff the bowl, and locked the door.

'Wipe that smirk off your face, Newtown,' Kirk hissed through his teeth, shoving me against the wall at the back of the betting shop.

He never called me Frank.

He had my collar in his fist. He was just being friendly.

He dropped me and said we should go and check on the Beast.

It was my day off. I wanted to go exploring on the beach, by myself.

'All right,' I said. 'Yeah.'

'Give us a ciggie. Let's go to the lake first.'

I never knew about the artificial lake, until I went there with Kirk.

I liked the sounds of birds, and insects, and leaves rustling in the wind. I'd never heard anything like it before.

We watched some red-beaked sea birds that had landed on a floating log. They kept landing there and flying off again. Kirk said they were terns. It was high up on the cliffs – what they called the Whittard Nature Reserve. Hardly anyone else was ever there. All you could see behind it was sky. If you flew over the lake and kept going, you'd be soaring above the cliffs and the beach, heading out to sea.

'There's a poster up,' I said. 'In the window at the chippy. Missing dog.'

'Uh-huh,' Kirk said. 'Any reward?'

'I don't think so.'

Kirk chucked a bit of bread into the lake, for the birds.

'Tight fuckers.'

Kirk said he wanted to bring Beast here. For a run around. Then he asked if I could take Beast home with me.

There was no way that would happen, with Lawrence being such a maniac about dirt. And I didn't want Mum getting into trouble.

'I don't think so,' I said. 'I'll ask though.'

We finished the cheese sandwich Mum had made me – I'd given Kirk half of mine – and followed the path around the lake, cutting through to the slip road that led down to the back of the petrol station on the dual carriageway. There was a fair bit of traffic and I had to wait to follow Kirk, who had sprinted over like a lunatic, with a lorry blasting its horn at him.

The shed stood in a concrete yard, behind a hedge on the abandoned farm. Kirk spent forever trying to undo the combination padlock. It was more like an aircraft hangar, for keeping tractors and stuff in, with gaps around the top of the high, steel walls. We could hear Beast yapping from inside, while Kirk turned the wheels on the lock with his stubby thumbs. I wondered if he was applying a trial-and-error method, in which case we would be there for a while.

'Here's the numbers,' he said, showing me his wrist where he had written them in biro. 'I can't get them to work. You try.'

Beast sprang at Kirk as he swung the iron door open, letting the light flood inside. There was a foul smell of dogshit and stale piss. Beast whined and yapped. His fur was all mangy. We could take it back, I thought. Leave it tied up outside the chippy.

We fed Beast some dog biscuits Kirk had shoplifted from the Co-op. It took a couple, but mostly nudged them with its snout and whined. Kirk threw the chew ball but it didn't run for it.

'Daft little shit,' Kirk said, kneeling and fussing over it. 'What's the matter with you?'

I went home via the library and found a book on caring for dogs. Kirk and I could both learn something in that department.

Friday, 26th July

I wanted to ask Kirk what St. Stephen's was like. If I had to start there, after the summer, if Mum and I moved in with Lawrence, moved here for good. What would it be like? I didn't want to mention Lawrence though, him being Deputy Head, and such a chronic berk.

It was late. Mum would be annoyed.

Beast, forelegs quivering, eyed Kirk with wary expectation as the last of the Winalot plopped into the bowl. The dog whined, nosing at the food without eating.

'Daft bugger,' Kirk said, cupping its reluctant head. He had massive hands.

'What do you think, then?' he said, not looking at me. 'Cute bastard isn't he.'

I thought: that dog's name isn't Beast. And it's no stray. It's Jim Hammond's dog that's always tied up outside the chippy. Jim Hammond lives with his gran and isn't right in the head, people say. I didn't know its actual name.

Kirk lit his camping light, bathing the interior of the hideout in a deep, frightening red. Why had I helped him? I'd tried not to. Beast whimpered and lay down, its muzzle on Kirk's lap. Stockholm

Syndrome they call it, don't they?

'Yeah,' I said. 'Sweet.'

I took a fragile rollie from my tin and got it lit. Kirk took one and stuffed it in his pocket. Lawrence had told me about Kirk. Dangerously antisocial, he said. He was scared of Kirk, I reckoned. I'd seen those St. Stephen's boys, chucking cans across the street at each other.

'Anyway mate,' I said, getting the rollie going strong. 'What's Stevo's really like?'

Saturday, 13th July

Every Saturday morning, I see the boy leave his house just before eight o'clock. I hardly catch sight of him apart from that. Sometimes he says something over his shoulder to someone in the house. His mum, I would guess. She goes with him sometimes, but usually not. I've never seen a man going in or out.

His leather jacket has a white skull painted on the back. I wonder if he painted it himself. It's good. Artistic.

He stops on the corner, gets a packet of ciggies and some matches out of his jacket, and lights up with what looks like a practised flourish. He leans back on a wall, one foot pressed against it behind him, looking up and down the street. He doesn't check his watch. I don't know if he has one. I'm guessing he times himself by how long it takes to smoke his cig. He takes a couple of last, deep drags, looks at the end of it, flicks it onto the street and heads off. There was one time he must have overslept. He stopped for his fag, same as always, but the bus rolled by him at the T-junction and he absolutely legged it.

It's the bus that goes into town before trailing along the coast, and I need to get into work early and make a good impression. I put a few extra rollies in my tin and take two Cokes from the fridge.

Nothing has ever happened here.

Welcome to Whittard on Sea. The town can trace it's history back to [Frank – find something to put in here. We need something at least as old as what Whitby's got.] Enjoy the many amenities such as it's beach [can we get an award], penny arcades, and the remains of our famous pier.

If you ask me, the best thing we can advertise, as a tourist office, is for people to come and watch bits fall off the cliffs. It'd be like the northern lights.

Whittard has enjoyed many visitors. [Many visitor's have enjoyed…?] Examples being Margaret Thatcher, and Hollywood actor Yul Brynner. [Frank – has e.g. Cliff Richard ever been in Whittard?]

[Sponsors text here – tbc. Looking like the funeral place will be our best bet. Please think how to mention them!]

It wasn't too hard. They'd had no other applicants. I'm officially the only breadwinner in the family now. Not including Lawrence, but he isn't family.

The tourist office is the most modern thing in all of Whittard. Built with lottery cash, although Lawrence, who doesn't like tourists, says that half the things it was supposed to be spent on never materialised, and he's checked the details in the Council records. As holiday jobs go, it could be worse. Sheila leaves me to get on with things. By her own admission, she's best off in the stock room or doing the admin. She's best with numbers.

The spare room at Lawrence's has a mattress on the floor for me and Bobby, and a shelf full of books on subjects like erosion. I might put up one of Dad's paintings. I wouldn't mind moving here, although I don't know anyone. There's a boy at the end of the road who looks about my age, maybe older. Their house is divided into flats, and the front wall's smashed.

Mum says the sea air would keep me out of trouble. I can't imagine what she means. I wasn't doing the bullying. I miss Newtown when we're here. I don't like staying at Lawrence's. He always thinks I'm up to something, and he can't tolerate dirt. It's enough to drive you insane, and I don't like the way he shouts at Bobby. He won't even have a TV and there's no way he'll ever allow video games. Mum told me the kids at school call him Machine, which evolved from 'Mr Keane, the Dog Breath Machine', as he'd confided to her in a tearful interlude. Mum said I wasn't to let on that I knew, because Lawrence was sensitive - although she giggled. She was speaking so softly, watchful, like a bird building a scrappy nest out of the smallest, feathery twigs. Out of whatever she could find.

Lawrence, sensitive..?

There's no point looking back, Mum says. Bobby loves the sea, the beach, the cliffs.

He does.

He'll forget all about Dad, and Newtown. He's got Mum, and they've got me.

I can keep myself out of trouble.

Who Stole Our Fish?
Harry Turnbull

The day I saw my dad cry was the worst of my life. I was eleven years, three months, and twenty-two days old. It was even worse than when Afua wrote 'loser' on my *My Little Pony* t-shirt with felt pen. Actually, I didn't even know dads could cry.

Why was he crying? I thought it must have been granny, as she had been very poorly. Or maybe one of his favourite teams Liverpool or Senegal had been beaten in the football cup. He has a big green shirt and a big red one and on the back of each it says 'Mane', the name of the best player in the universe - or that's what he says. I don't really like football but my brother Bongani loves it and he and dad play all the time.

But it wasn't any of those things. It was the day he had feared would come. It was the day that for the first time ever in the history of fishing in Senegal he returned home with an empty basket. There was nothing. Not a crab, not even a little tiddler. And so he cried.

I rubbed his back and said: 'Don't worry, there is always tomorrow. We still have some bread.'

'There are no tomorrows, my dear. The fish have gone.' Another tear trickled down his bristly cheek.

Later in bed I thought about what he said. The fish have gone. Where? How could fish disappear? Had they all swum off? I always wondered why they stayed, just to be caught and then sold or eaten by us. Maybe they thought, 'enough is enough.'

This would require some more thinking time. Perhaps I could ask my teacher Mr Cissoko, he knew everything in the world.

The next day at school I did just that. I put my hand up while he was talking about how many stars there were in the universe. He said there were more stars in our little bit of the universe than all the grain of sands in the great Sahara Desert. I thought he must have made a mistake, but I didn't say so.

'What is it Olivia?'

'Well, my dad went fishing yesterday and came back with nothing.'

'That is bad news but what has it to do with the universe?'

'Oh, nothing, I just thought you might know why.'

'Tell you what. On Friday I will explain about all the greedy people stealing our fish, OK?'

Hmm. So, the fish were being stolen. Did that mean kidnapped? Were they being held hostage somewhere? Perhaps there was an underwater cage in the Gambia River. It was still all very strange. I wondered if police were looking for the missing fish. I knew Mr Cissoko would provide some answers on Friday.

That night at home there were a lot of people. Some of them were fishing friends of dad's. Bongani and I were told to stay in the back and not interrupt the adults. I asked my brother, who was fourteen, if he knew where the fish had gone. 'Foreign people have got them,' he said very mysteriously.

'Like the French you mean? Why do they want our fish?'

'No, not the French. They are our friends, Well, that is what they tell us. It is people from a long way away.'

'Oh, like the Eskimos?'

He burst out laughing. And wouldn't talk any more.

That night in bed I decided to pray. Hard. Maybe Lord Jesus could help find the fish or maybe he could produce five thousand for the whole village. I prayed but Jesus didn't come.

Instead I had a strange dream. A mermaid came to me and began speaking. She had long black hair and a long fishy tale.

'I thought you were supposed to have golden hair' I asked.

She laughed. 'Oh no, we are all different.'

'But you have black skin like me, mermaids are white.'

'Only in the imagination of white people my child.'

'Why are you here?'

'Well, you have been praying. Very hard.'

'Yes, but to our Lord Jesus.'

'I know. But he has many messengers.'

'I thought they were angels.'

'Ah but this different.'

'Why?'

'Well, it needs a very good swimmer and wings would get in the way.'

She laughed again and started to disappear but ended saying: 'Meet me at the beach when it gets dark tomorrow.'

The next day I had a breakfast of fruit and checked my long purple braids before setting off on the walk to school. I sat next to Afua. She offered me a fruit gum but I said no because they stick in your teeth. She pinched my leg and I yelped. I decided to tell her about the dream. She made fun of me and began singing 'Livy's seen a mermaid, Livy's seen a mermaid.'

Mr Cissoko came into class. He peered over his spectacles that somehow made him look older and he was already ancient at thirty: 'Quiet, everybody. Now today I will tell you a story. For many years, hundreds of years, the people in our villages had lots of fish, in fact so much bonga and sardinella they were able to sell it to other towns and villages. You remember, Olivia?'

Oh yes, I remembered some big catches, but they became smaller and smaller.

'My father and his father and his father, for a long time, our family have been fishermen. But now they have all gone away.'

Mr Cissoko said, 'It is not a case of the fish disappearing. They have been stolen!'

Of course, I already knew this.

'You see, our people have small boats and baskets and so when they catch fish there is always enough to go around. But in faraway places they have big boats, very big. Did you know one big boat can steal a thousand baskets of fish a day and our little boats can only fill ten?'

Afua's hand shot up: 'Why do they come here to our sea?'

The teacher looked sad. He said, 'It is very bad. Our government gave big ships permission to steal our fish in return for money.'

The shock was like seeing a poisonous snake hiding under your pillow.

So now I knew, the government was stealing our fish, or at least selling them.

Mr Cissoko continued. 'But when the people saw Mr President riding around in a Rolls Royce car paid by stolen fish they started to get very angry. Do you know what they say when new people come into the government? They say, 'it's our time to eat'. That means the president and his friends and family get all the nice jobs and sometimes take our money. So, the people got angry and got a new president and he said no more foreign ships would be allowed to steal our fish.'

A cheer went up from the class.

I was still puzzled.

'So, who is taking away all the fishes now?' I asked.

'Ah, my dear, now the big ships come in secret at night with no permission and cast their nets. Do you know some are a mile long?'

Goodness. A mile long. That was as far as our house to aunty Miriam's.

'And not only that. These nets don't just steal our little fishes, they trap other big creatures like sharks and turtles so they cannot breathe and die. But I will tell you more about this next time.'

On the way home I thought about all I had learnt. Then I remembered I had to sneak out at sundown to meet the mermaid. I was nervous but excited.

We had rice for tea and then I said I was tired and went to bed. When it began to get dark my brother was still playing football, so I put a pillow in my bed, to show it was me asleep. I crept out of the backdoor and ran down to the beach.

It was only a few minutes away but in the fading light all was silent. The mermaid didn't say exactly where she would be. I waited by the trees overlooking the great Atlantic Ocean.

Suddenly, there was a plop noise and the mermaid appeared at the water's edge. Her tail glittered in the dark like the fireflies that sometimes dance around the bushes at the back of our compound.

'Come with me', she said.

'Where are we going?'

'Far out to sea.'

'I'm not sure I'm allowed. Also, I did not bring my costume.'

'Don't worry, you won't get wet.'

'Will I be safe?'

'Of course. You remember that time granny was ill and everyone prayed for three days and nights?'

'Yes, how did you know?'

'Our Father sees everything. You trust Him, don't you? Here, climb on my shoulders.'

I did as she said and we were off, skimming through the water like one of those eels you sometimes see in the river. We crossed the surface until some lights came into view and there rising high above us was one of the big ships. It had many lights and was enormous. From the back it pulled a gigantic net.

'Can you hold your breath,' said the mermaid.

I told her my record was forty-two seconds.

'That's good, but you won't need that long'.

Then we were diving, fast and deep, while I held my breath. The big net was full of little fishes but also some sharks, a small whale, and a ray. The mermaid flashed her tail, its end like a super-cutting knife slicing through the netting and freeing the creatures. Countless times she slashed at the net until every single creature escaped.

We rose to the surface and I breathed deeply and felt very happy. There was shouting on the boat and lights searching the water.

'What will happen now,' I asked.

The mermaid allowed herself to be caught in the glare of the lights. We heard the men shouting with fear.

'Now, my child, they will tell of the water-spirit that visited them and freed all the fish. They will never come back to this place and they will tell everyone they meet it is cursed. But of course, it is now blessed.'

As we bobbed up and down on the silver dark waves more boats came into view including a government vessel with guns. The mermaid said it was time to go and we skimmed our way back to shore.

We returned back to the beach and she was right; I didn't get wet, in fact I was completely dry. She smiled and then disappeared into the water. I sneaked back to bed exhausted. We had saved the fishes! But would anyone believe me?

At school the next day, Afua made fun of me when I told her I had met the mermaid and saved the fishes. Everyone laughed and called me crazy girl.

Mr Cissoko came into class while this was happening.

'What is this, what is so funny?'

Afua at once told him: 'Olivia has had another dream about a mermaid and claims she has saved the fish.'

'It wasn't a dream,' I said angrily.

'Olivia, tell me what happened,' said Mr Cissoko.

I recounted the story about meeting the mermaid, saving the fish and scaring off the big boat.

'Hmm,' said Mr Cissoko. 'That's very interesting. Did you know what happened last night at the coastal villages by the lagoon?'

We didn't.

'Well, the government has joined up with Greenpeace. Do you know who they are?' We did not.

'Greenpeace is an organisation that likes to protect the world and all the animals and of course, all the fishes. They have boats that patrol the ocean and last night they took the government soldiers to chase away the big ships who have no permission to be here.' A big cheer went up around the class.

'So now the big ships will be told to stay away, the fish will return, and your father, Olivia, will be able to catch them again. Now to your dream, well, I should say, your experience. Many things happen in dreams that can seem true. Did you know special people hear the word of God in dreams? Now you all know the story of Jesus and the five thousand fishes he produced for hungry people. The fish is a symbol of our prosperity and our faith. When they are taken away it is a sign of wickedness and evil. But now they will return.

I believe you are one of the special people. Olivia, you prophesised our salvation thanks to our Lord. You are a prophetess!'

At this, everyone in class cheered again and started singing my name. So, I was just like mum. She often saw things in dreams.

I went home walking on air. Dad came in with a few fishes in the basket.

'Will it get better now father,' I asked.

'With God's will, Olivia, yes.'

Then father's face broke into a huge, wide smile and the tears were gone.

Abrasion
Simon Flower

They'd have to change the curtains, the estate agent said. Curtains and the wallpaper. Those are always the big ones in these situations. He said *situations* with a weird inflection, like it was a question or something. You don't want to go too modern with it though, he stressed. Not round here. Definitely not too modern.

David thumbed the lace. The curtain was a thin, ratty old thing – fading, like much of the house. Across the street, mirror images of the same house stared back. Squat bungalows, light beige brick, with driveways just big enough to squeeze a car onto, and plants wilting under the front windows. The coast curved away about a quarter mile south these days, and the sea breeze pushed hard to announce itself. Over a fence at the end of the cul-de-sac, the wheat stalks tore at their roots, swinging wild. Some distant turbines hummed a soft blur. There was another buy sign on a lawn a few houses down, rattling in its posthole. How long had that been up? He tried to remember if he'd seen it last time, but then, he'd probably been focused on other things.

'How much do you think it might go for?' Becca was saying.

The man managed to make a show of not really giving an answer. The phrase *this climate* was thrown about a lot. She nodded and did that thing with her eyes where she shows you she's really listening.

'Would you say there's renting potential?'

The man hummed and hawed before saying he would have to ask his colleague. Maybe not round here, but you never know, do you. David suppressed a snort. The man clearly didn't know anything. In fact, he looked barely done with school. Chubby cheeked and drowning in a squeaky suit.

He came away from the window. 'How long would you

want to rent for anyway? Considering.'

'It was just a question, David.'

'It's a bit of a drive, isn't it? If there's a problem or something.'

'Well, not if …' she shook her head. Her hands drifted to her belly. 'It was just a question.'

They all agreed a cup of tea would be the thing, so David went away to the kitchen while the other two discussed whether a bathroom refitting would get the profit up at all, do you think, or is it just a wash in the end.

There was a row of seashells on the kitchen windowsill and he picked one up as he waited for the boil. There was a lot of junk in this house he'd always seen but never really noticed. Knick knacks and the like. China figurines, tatty sea trinkets, fridge magnets. Stuff you accumulate as time ticks. None of it really meant anything to him, Becca neither, but he expected she would want some of it anyway.

He ran his fingers over the shell. Amber, with black ripples. He couldn't tell if it was real or not. It felt too smooth. But then, water could do that. That was the thing. He listened to their voices drifting down the hall. Fancy talking about renting. It would be all they could do to sell the place before the taxes and the bills gobbled everything up. Supposedly the council had plans for it all. Some barriers that were going to fix everything. Hulking piles of rocks along the shore to take the brunt. Aunty had been confident it would all be fine. Clearly. He poured the kettle and steeped the water, pressing the bags against the sides and watching it all rush brown.

He'd seen this coming, of course. It's something that becomes obvious after you've moved away. Gone inland. Everything seems smaller when you come back. Shameful somehow. But maybe you didn't notice it living so close. Bit by bit. Day by day. Particularly after he'd met Becca, that was when it had really started getting to him. Because then it was an occasion, to come back. A display of sorts. It always rubbed him the wrong way, being forced to do all the touristy things with her. Getting fish and chips as if you can't anywhere else. Playing the slots. Dipping your toes and freezing just because it's there to do. Can't wait 'til we bring our kids here, she always used to say, and he'd squeeze her hand and smile because that's what you do when your girlfriend says that kind of thing. And it was nice really, to be confident about the future like that. It's not the kind of thing you should get mad about.

It had been a good thing that she liked it here. Really. It had certainly made things easier. After they'd married and the future became something not so far off. After the return visits became more of a responsibility. A duty of care.

Now this.

He watched her sizing up the living room as he brought the drinks out. She already knew how it would look when she was done, he could tell. She might even trick someone into buying it.

She caught his eye as he handed her the mug. 'What?'

He realised he hadn't said much to the estate agent yet, so he inquired about how soon they could get a proper valuation, and was there any way to speed things up at all.

After, they went to the same greasy spoon they'd always used . to. It had tablecloths so it made you feel like it was a bit classier than the others around the way. Becca was pleased it was still the same old lady in charge, but, of course, he'd known it would be. The woman looked a bit surprised to see Becca, but she switched to her usual chit-chat quick enough. She sat them at the good table, near the back and up the bit with the couple of stairs. He helped Becca sit down and the wicker chair groaned a little, which was understandable, but so did his even though he'd finally been exercising. They both had haddock, chips, and gravy, and Becca got mushy peas, which she normally despised but today she mashed into every bite.

They planned next moves as they ate. Lawyers. Decorators. Was a second opinion worth a look or are they all the bloody same anyway?

David chewed around a small bone in his fish. 'He was a bit useless, that guy. Wasn't he?'

She rolled her eyes.

'Well he was. Umming and ahhing all day.'

'I thought he was sweet.'

'Should make them finish school first.' He shook his head. 'Still, doubt we'll find better anyway, round here. All the smart ones will have packed up if they know what's good.'

She let out a very long sigh, then reached for his hand and gave it a squeeze. 'It's all doom and gloom, isn't it?'

'I'm just saying.'

She hit him with a look, like the one she would give their kitchen sink when it needed fixing. 'Have you been doing okay with it?'

He pulled his hand away. 'Bit late for that now, isn't it?'

She pursed her lips. 'That's really not fair, David.'

'Sorry, I'm just...' He waved a hand. 'It was a long time coming.'

'Still sudden.'

He watched a couple with a young child walk in, all wrapped in puffy coats for the wind, despite the season. The little girl's zipper got stuck and the mum had to help her. 'We shouldn't have left her out here alone. All cut off from everyone.'

'Where'd you have had her? Your little flat?' Becca shovelled peas onto her fork. 'She'd have kicked and screamed if you'd tried to take her out of that house.'

'Maybe.'

'She liked it here. You can't hold that against her.' She shook her head, smiling. 'Look, in the end she lived on her own terms, and you can't say fairer than that.' She said this with a kind of finality, like it was a presentation or something. Like she'd practiced it in the mirror. Her grin faded. 'Don't start,' she said.

'I'm not.'

She frowned at him.

'Thanks for coming today,' he said. 'You're much better at this stuff than I am.'

She was looking at the family. 'Can you help me up? I need the bathroom again.'

It was freezing up on the bluffs. The wind screamed, thick and wet with the stench of brine. Becca had left her clip thing she always used somewhere, and her hair whipped around her face. She clung tight to a box of leftovers, the grease dripping through the cardboard and on her hands. It hadn't been spoken, coming here, they'd just walked after leaving the café and before they knew it, they were halfway up. There had been a bench at the top once, but it must have gone now. They'd never used it anyway. They lowered themselves to the sea-damp earth and felt it bite through their trousers.

David looked out across the water, to the grey blur where the clouds misted and spilled. It wasn't right, the way everyone was just carrying on. Like it was all the same. Like everything would just stay in place if no one moved or reacted. Clinging, like all the coins in the penny pushers. Down on the shore, a man was walking his dog. The stupid thing kept leaping at the waves, baiting them.

'How long are we sitting here?' he said.

'Don't be a grump.'

'It's just water, you know.'

'It's nice.'

'It's water. You don't stop and gaze at your tap.'

'I just want to see it, is all.'

He checked his watch. Then down. Then again. 'Well how

long does it bloody take?'

'Can I just look at the fucking sea please? You can go back if you like.'

He stayed where he was, made a show of it even. This had always been Becca's way. I've decided, and if you don't like it, I'll do it without you. And god knows she would. She'd proven that. He traced a line in the dirt with his finger – smooth and concave. 'No one in their right mind is going to buy that house.'

'Not with you selling it.'

'What, and that toddling estate agent?'

She sighed. 'We couldn't just have two minutes.'

'Well for Christ's sake, Bex! Do you remember where we were? How much more there was? Even a few years ago. What it looked like? At this rate. Well.' He could see that she didn't want to hear it, that he should stop now, but he couldn't. He was off. All the science of it. Everything he'd been reading. Abrasion. Shore drift. Formulas. The lot. He could feel himself going red and after a while he could tell she'd stopped listening. And without a real point or destination in mind, he gradually ran out of steam and puttered out. Suddenly, it was hard to look at her.

She waited until he was well and truly done, then shook her head, slowly, like a teacher after a long day. 'You know, something I'll never understand is, I thought you'd have loved an extra person to make miserable.'

He let her look at the sea.

The tide was getting up and the waves rolled closer up the shore. There was a hole someone had dug in the sand down near the boardwalk and the water rushed in, foaming. A bright orange spade – the kiddie, sandcastling kind – spilled up onto the sand, landing just out of reach of the waves, for now. The man and his dog came upon it as they left. The dog tried to grab the spade between its teeth, but the man pulled on the leash and they kept walking.

Becca was tucking into the box of leftovers. She pulled out

a chip, ate it, then licked the gravy off her fingers. She extended the box. He didn't want any, but he felt that declining was secretly the wrong answer. He declined anyway.

'Do you think she forgot?' she eventually said.

David chewed his lip. 'I've been here a few times this year. I don't see how she could have.'

'Not us. The will, I meant. To take me out.'

'No,' he said. 'No. I think she took your side, to be honest. She'd probably have scratched my name out if she had to pick.'

She ate another chip. 'I've missed coming here. If I had the money, I'd buy your half.'

He let that go. They sat for a while longer. She rubbed her stomach, but stopped when she noticed him watching. When the beach had all but gone, he helped her to her feet. And as they walked back to their cars, a rock, the size of a tennis ball or grapefruit or something, broke from the cliffs and tumbled to the waves below.

David felt his pockets for keys. There was an arcade on their right and Becca's face shone in the bright lights. She seemed so close, then. Maybe it was worth a stop at Ikea on the way back, see what curtains they had. Did they do paint there too? Becca would know. They could go together, even. Do it all properly. The whole house. Spend the next few weeks out here, before she was due. Before her new life took her away. It was worth a shot.

The sea roared and crashed. It rang in his ears, like white noise. Swirling. Foaming. Static. He approached the parking meter. But then, it was getting dark. It might just be too late in the day for all that.

Fairbourne
Jane Smith

It's a difficult thing to describe a place you love - one small patch of the huge, round, swirling, vulnerable Earth. What *I* love about a place might be so different to what *you* might love about it – or you might not even like the place at all. I could tell you about the quality of the light at Fairbourne beach, so distinct to this coast of North Wales; or the way the lights of Barmouth town and its funfair twinkle in the distance; or how the miniature steam train winds its way through the sandy expanses almost unnoticed, where the Mawddach estuary quietly melts into the sea. But how we feel about places is also about what we feel when we're there – what those places inspire, or perhaps what's happening in our own lives while we're there. And what I remember most about Fairbourne is the feeling of being *alive* there.

For me, Fairbourne is about the salt on my lips and the wind in my hair. The wet sand between my cold toes and blown spittle from the sea landing on blanched driftwood. It's about my old dog Buster, so invigorated by the sea air and the space and the freedom that he becomes a puppy again, sprinting figures of eight, frolicking in the waves and taking himself off to swim in the sea in a steady, stately loop. And if I'm really honest, Fairbourne is the place that springs to mind if I think about living in the moment, enjoying a deep personal connection with another being, and both of us communing with our shared environment.

One evening five or six years ago I went for a walk along the beach with Buster. I remember the soft touch of the light, with the beige of the sand and the slate grey of the sea so gentle on my eyes. A mild breeze was skimming foam off the waves and onto the beach; some of it landed on Buster's nose and he looked at me as he tried to shake it off. I couldn't find any decent sticks for him to play with, so I threw seaweed clusters into the waves, him retrieving them and dropping the heavy strings of black-green sea pearls onto my feet: 'Again! Again!'

Most of all, I remember walking up the beach towards the cliffs by the Tywyn road, watching Buster trotting ahead with his once black but now greying fur blowing in the wind, my boot prints following his paw prints in the wet sand. I wished the moment would last forever.

All along the sea front at Fairbourne, just further out than the defensive sea wall, is a long row of concrete posts used as fortifications during the Second World War. Flat-topped, they're now used mainly for impromptu pebble-stacking games. Many times, I've arrived at the beach to be greeted by an unlikely line of Zen-type sculptures silently willing me to photograph them with the omnipresent horizon of the Irish Sea as their backdrop. Fairbourne, now I think about it, has always carried a vibe of distilling a moment in time.

For several years I had the idea of coming to live in the hills above the estuary just inland from Fairbourne. My fantasy was to bring my family up into the foothills of Snowdonia, to live off-grid in a little cottage with foot-thick walls and low ceilings. I used to think we could somehow dodge the worst of climate change, myself and my children, by living high in the hills, feeding ourselves with our own food, drinking from our own well and generally living far away from major roads in a relatively inaccessible place. Though dressed up inside a rural idyll, my Snowdonia project was basically the product of a bunker mentality. If our civilization is facing collapse through environmental degradation, can any of us really escape it? Slowly I came to understand that the answer was no. There was no escape, even here.

What I didn't know at the time was that Fairbourne, with its 850 human inhabitants, was about to become the first community in the UK to be 'de-commissioned' due to climate change. Sea levels are expected to rise so sharply there, and the cost of maintaining the sea defences so significant, that the entire village is being slowly evacuated and then demolished through a 'managed retreat', leaving the area to return to salt marsh. *From salt were ye made, and salt ye shall be.* This will take years, of course, but it's a real-life situation, as of now, with council decisions having already been made about the de-commissioning.

Ironically, my off-grid Snowdonia fantasy would have put us bang in the eye of the storm as far as the realities of rising sea levels are concerned. But in reality, of course, the storm is everywhere - and what's more, it's coming for all of us. It was while I was walking along the shingle beach at Fairbourne that the truth settled on me like the brown froth blown in from the sea – I can't forsake the place where I'm from and run to another place. Everywhere shares the same ecosystem, and I'd still be a human being in a human society. I'd only be taking my huge anxieties about the future of the world to what only *felt* like a much smaller place.

Once, I'd seen a typhoon shelter on Cheung Chau Island in the South China Sea. Nestled in a cove, with a strikingly narrow opening for access, a breakwater had been built so that the little fishing boats could shelter safely from the wind and waves. Over the years, entire communities had sprung up in such shelters, with impoverished fishing families spending their entire lives there and 'floating schools' serving the communities who even developed their own distinct wedding and food rituals. These communities had made their lives among disaster preparation infrastructure.

Looking back, my own plan of moving to the mountains of Snowdonia behind the sea wall at Fairbourne was just privileged and idle disaster preparation disguised as a white-washed daydream.

There's no escaping – literally – the fact that climate breakdown will affect everyone everywhere, and there's no surprise that many peoples of the global South, and of the circumpolar North, are first in the firing line. In the cities of North America and northern Europe, rising sea levels will affect poorer communities first. They will be destitute or displaced or drowned while other people elsewhere, richer and higher and more mobile, will look on and wring their hands.

I no longer cling on to my own selfish escape plan. But how can we prepare? What are we to do? Where do our responsibilities begin and end? With our own defences made as redundant as Fairbourne's sea wall, what do we need to be doing as this great tide of climate emergency rolls in?

Although there's no meaningful compensation as such for the local people having to move out of Fairbourne forever, and although the wholesale evacuation of any community is tragic, we can assume the Fairbourners will at least be able to settle somewhere else. How many low-lying coastal communities and even cities in other parts of the world, much poorer and in countries without social security nets, are going to be subjected to emergency evacuation in the coming decades as the sea levels rise, but with nowhere to go and with zero help? The harsh reality of Earth 2.0 is that while climate breakdown is going to affect us all, it will come first for the poorest and most disenfranchised.

My dog Buster died this year, aged nearly thirteen.

A couple of weeks after he died, the vets rang me to say his ashes were ready for picking up. The mundane shoe-sized box contained a pretty card from the cremation company and a surprisingly large amount of sand-grey ashes. I kept some aside for my children, put some into a silver pendant I'd bought myself, and decided to scatter the rest over Buster's favourite places, along with some forget-me-nots from his favourite part of the garden where he used to lie in the sun with his eyes closed, only opening them lazily if a bumble bee droned by.

Fairbourne had certainly been one of his favourite places, where he was at his most relaxed. But knowing that Fairbourne would be completely inaccessible within a few years, once the sea wall was no longer maintained and the village was decommissioned, I thought twice about scattering his ashes there. In a way, taking them to a spot which itself would soon be returned to its original state made sense – but I wanted to be able to visit places where his ashes had been scattered, and Fairbourne would soon be off-limits forever. So, I chose another beach seventy miles away, his second favourite.

Being thrown into a state of personal mourning made me think, too, about the other, wider sorrow in my life which has characterized the past decade – environmental grief. Softer but longer, its hue was different, but it certainly shared the unspoken persistence. I used to think climate grief was easier to bear because we could do something to change the outcomes. Nowadays, I think it's more a question of how we face the inevitable, how we move towards and perhaps through its stages. When a great sorrow of our own collective making descends on us, I now think that what matters is how we walk towards catastrophe together, how we take responsibility, and what we bequeath to those who will outlive us.

Yesterday I drove to Fairbourne for a walk along the beach, on my own for the first time. In many ways nothing had changed – the watery grey horizon, the sea spittle in the air, the crunch of seaweed underfoot, the lights of Barmouth town and its funfair two miles up the coast. It's easy to be in a place when you know it so well, an old friend appreciating your visit. Although Fairbourne didn't seem to change at all, *I* must have changed over the years, my hair going from all brown to brown-and-grey, my skin becoming drier and my eyes less sharp, and my young dog, who became my old dog, no longer with me.

As we ourselves age against backdrops of familiar landscapes, it's less easy to imagine that the places themselves grow old. Beaches and coastlines usually seem not to. But it's even harder to imagine that where you're now walking will, soon enough, be returned to the sea.

I've walked many times on the whale-backed hills of the Peak District where tiny fossilized shells in the rocks reminded me that the landscape all around was once under the sea. Fairbourne is the reverse of that.

I looked out at the sea for a while, wondering whether there was an impatience there to reclaim the land after millennia of water touching the beach and the more recent decades of waves hitting the sea wall. I couldn't feel any hurry, but I sensed an inevitability. I was here but one day I wouldn't be, just like Buster. Fairbourne was here but one day soon it wouldn't be. Although the thought should perhaps have been frightening, it was strangely calming.

Turning around, I glanced at the pebble columns made by children on top of the sea wall. Perhaps there is only the present, in any place - even when it carries the soft kiss of the past and the dark seed of what is to come.

The Tightrope
Harry Wilding

Thursday

The month of Valentine, 2019: I sat across from the wonderfully attractive Victoria against the big window of the ornamentally-decorated former music hall Malt Cross. We had matched on Tinder earlier in the week and I felt uncharacteristically shy as I tried to keep the fresh ladder in my tights from her view. Her nose ring, smattering of tattoos, sense of humour, and super cute laugh meant that after one pint I was worried that my face basically looked like that emoji with heart eyes.

Despite the good start, it inevitably came up.

Victoria asked if my second beer was 'vegan, then?' as she placed it in front of me. Some of hers spilled over onto the table as she sat down with it. Buttocks clenched, I braced myself for the conversation ahead.

'The German lagers are yeah, because of some, like, purity law from the 1500s which means they can't add any shit to it.' I raised the glass and took a sip, before joking: 'Love a good accidently vegan product!' Ugh, what a dweeb.

'Interesting,' she claimed. I briefly focused on a rose tattoo peeking out from the low collar of her top. Strangely enough, it was in the kind of style I draw in. I wondered how big it was, where it extended down to. She broke my focus to tell me 'you don't look like a vegan, Robin.'

Oh no.

'What does a vegan look like?' I asked, slowly, with a nervous laugh. I noticed some of her spilt beer had started snaking towards me on the wonky table.

'Oh, I d'know,' she cute-laughed. 'I'm being silly.'

Yes.

I desperately tried to think of something else to talk about before we were overtaken by an awkward silence or, worse, more vegan chat. I failed.

'I could *never* be vegan,' she stated.

Some sudden feedback from the stage across the other side of the pub made me jump slightly. A guy began saying '1, 2, 1, 2' into a mic.

If I behaved 'badly' here, my actions would mean that I would be tarring every other vegan with the same brush. Plus, it would scupper any chances of a shag. Any hint of pretentiousness or aggression will risk the logic of the argument becoming lost, seemingly forever. Talking about veganism to a non-vegan is like trying to walk a tightrope that the other person can change the tightness of at any point, simply because they might feel bad if you made it to the other side unscathed.

'Why?' I asked, with immediate regret. Victoria's spilt beer had met mine.

'I'd miss bacon cobs too much, I think,' she said, with a completely serious face.

It wasn't anger that I felt building up in me, exactly; it was more a crushingly overwhelming sense of disappointment. The guy on stage was now testing out his guitar with sudden and incomplete riffs. It seemed louder than necessary. I realigned myself on the loosening tightrope.

'But, like, your Tinder bio said you're an animal lover and, earlier, you were talking about the cute piglets at White Post Farm and how your nephew loved them and stuff. How do you couple that with eating bacon?' I was smiling and had an upbeat tone, but this was precarious. Carefully does it, Robin.

'Things can be cute *and* tasty,' she shrugged, smiling.

Jesus.

'Okay, but, like, animal cruelty and death aside' — *abandon tightrope, Robin, abandon tightrope!* — 'what about the, like... environmental impact? We were moaning about climate change denial earlier, so you're obviously concerned about that.'

'Sure,' she nodded.

'Well, meat and dairy agriculture is a massive contributor to the problem.'

'But cheese, Robin!' she exclaimed, cute-laughing.

I outwardly smiled and I inwardly screamed.

'These arguments of yours are incredibly compelling, Victoria,' I said sarcastically, in a jolly sort of way. I took another drink. My hand was slightly damp from the spilt beer, as it absorbed into my pores.

We were distracted, perhaps saved, by some screaming from outside, disorienting as it mixed with the continuing soundcheck. Two young women had spilled out of The Roebuck opposite and were (just about) prevented from killing each other by a total of five struggling men. Their level of anger and frustration probably best summed up by the fact that they were eventually compelled to lob their mobile phones at each other.

I walked home alone, along the canal towpath, the chorus to 'Victoria' by The Kinks looping in my head. The path ahead of me gave an alcohol-induced sway as a group of leaves scurried across it. They looked like tiny people, happily dancing into the polluted canal ahead of them.

I liked so much about Victoria. To be honest, everything except her attitude to veganism. Has this really become a deal-breaker for me now? Though, to be honest, perhaps there were more issues – such as buying an iPhone every time a new version was released and driving to an office that's a twenty-minute walk from her house – that may well not be compatible in the long term. I wasn't sure anyone else would be suitable ever again with these standards I couldn't help applying. Such a great arse, though.

I had turned off the towpath, feeling slightly safer on the better-lit streets, as I headed for the Beefeater car park. The boatyard was beside me, attached to the marina. The idea of living on a narrowboat kept crossing my mind. I wondered if it was as cool as it seemed.

Victoria and I had hugged when saying farewell for the evening, without giving any assurances about whether we would see each other again. It might be worth another go. If she was willing, of course.

Once inside my flat, happy with the relative warmth, I headed straight for the kitchen and, more specifically, the kettle.

I looked at my phone as the water boiled. I had three Tinder messages from Jenny (29) who I'd matched with earlier that day and was yet to chat with.

Hahaha youre a vegan i just realised
No can do
I can put you in touch with my pal you can have convos about being vegan. She going vegan camp too
Fuck sake.

I should have left it but I couldn't resist replying:
Vegan camp sounds great! But if we must stay segregated, your pal sounds lovely

By the time I had poured the tea, Jenny had replied and, to be fair, her awfulness was comedy gold:
I find vegans pointless we could argue but theres no point. My mates lovely
Shes 38
No kids
Rides a bike

I stared at the last message, turning the three words over in my mind – *Rides a bike*. It was worded as if that would be the thing that would definitely convince me that her pal could be 'the one'. I was tempted to keep the conversation going, simply for comedy purposes, however, I decided it was safer to just unmatch her and thus scupper my chances with a childless vegan cyclist forever.

I sat on the floor next to Kerry and Willow (my friend and her four-year-old daughter). We all had a bongo drum in front of us, like the twenty other kids and parents, ready for some noisy fun in the community centre.

'So, hello all!' the teacher said, giving her drum a couple of rhythmical whacks. She looked exactly like what I presume Victoria thought vegans looked like – white, dreadlocks, baggy colourful clothing and so on. She held her drum up and told us that it was an authentic African bongo drum, just like all the others in the room (cool, as long as there was no exploitation of the makers) and that the top was made of the skin of an animal (oh…) and could anyone guess which animal (*Jesus*, really?). I looked around and no-one else seemed to be showing any sign that this was a really weird question to put to children. To put to *anyone* with such enthusiasm, to be honest. I resisted shouting out 'human', as Willow enthusiastically guessed 'platypus'.

After half an hour of enthusiastically banging on flayed goat skin, Kerry and I sat on a playground bench watching Willow play in the sandpit.

I had been friends with Kerry since secondary school, at a time when there were no peers who seemed to be anything like me. It wasn't until I went to college that I realised people could actually have decent music taste and think outside the box a bit. I love Kerry, don't get me wrong, but we would never have become friends if we had met post-school. I wondered if she would agree.

'How's your love life?' she asked, eyes on Willow. She took a drink of her coffee from a disposable cup. I quickly pushed down the pang of annoyance I felt because I had bought her a bamboo re-usable one for Christmas.

I took a swig of my bamboo-enclosed coffee in what felt

like a small act of defiance.

'I'm on the Tinder train again,' I answered.

'You're on and off there more than the conductor is on and off an actual train.'

I laughed. 'Yep, always tempted back.'

'Any luck on it this time round?'

I thought about Victoria. I had messaged her before leaving the flat for bongo drumming, asking if she wanted a second date. She was yet to reply.

'No, not really,' I told Kerry.

We sat in silence for a minute or so, watching Willow making mounds out of the sand. I was glad when she finally started making a third one because they were reminding me too much of breasts. I felt a brief moment of melancholy about being so horny that two crudely, and completely innocently, made sand domes had turned my thoughts to pure filth.

'You should come on holiday with me, Steve, and Willow in the summer,' Kerry suggested, dissolving the image of a topless Victoria that had formed in my mind. 'We'll be staying at the villa in Spain for a couple of weeks in August.'

'I don't want to feel like a third wheel-'

'You'd be a fourth wheel,' Kerry reasoned, smiling. 'Perfect!'

'Maybe.'

'It'd be so cool if you could! It's really nice round there, not far from Valencia and stuff. We could leave Willow and Steve at the villa and go for a night out there or something.' She did a weird, but thoroughly endearing, little dance in her seated position, before she gave me a suggestive elbow to my side. 'And we can find you a sexy *señorita*.'

I laughed and shook my head in mock offence.

'We'll see,' I said, thinking of my recent reluctance to take flights anymore. Stupid carbon footprint. Stupid conscience.

I watched the man in disbelief.

I noticed him standing in front of the onions, as I grabbed a couple of sweet potatoes. He had a small plastic bag and proceeded to put a grand total of one (yes, one) onion into it before tying the bag and popping it in his basket with his four carrots in a plastic bag, two courgettes in a plastic bag, and plastic-wrapped broccoli. I had to commend him for his healthy diet, at least, but for fuck sake.

I had recently started cutting single-use plastic from my life – a task much easier than I thought it would be once I'd simply accepted I'd have to a) sacrifice a few things and b) spend a little extra money. The state of other people's trolleys now seemed grossly obscene.

I crouched by the communal door of my flat block and placed the spoon of sugar water by the lethargic bee.

'Come on, mate.' The bee gave a quick, somewhat uninspired, buzz in reply, but didn't seem to be turning towards the water. Maybe I should help it with a nudge? My phone alerted me to a message. It was my friend Jo.

No Facebook and now no WhatsApp? I know that you're always no more than 3 miles away from me at any given time but somehow impossible to contact! I replied that there was normal messaging as well as Signal, adding a rolling eye emoji for good measure. Deleting Amazon and Facebook stuff from my life had made things more difficult, no doubt, but one of the biggest struggles was being so alone in these actions. I hadn't even made an attempt with Google – that was going to be the biggest challenge yet.

The bee had made it to the spoon and seemed to be getting more animated. Excellent. I was looking forward to getting some of my new birthday card designs finished. I was particularly happy with my 'Happy birthday, duck' one; that should sell well locally.

I heard the door open behind me. I turned to see my middle-aged neighbour, Dan, his arm round his partner's shoulders. I hoped our interaction would be limited to a friendly hello as they went on their way.

'Bit warmer today, ain't it,' he said enthusiastically.

Dear God. The weather.

'Yeah,' I smiled.

'What you up to down there?'

'Just helping this bee with some sugar water.'

'Aw, that's sweet,' his partner smiled.

'Literally!' I joked, standing up. They laughed, much more than the joke deserved.

'You off out tonight, then?' Dan asked.

'Yeah, I think so. Waiting on confirmation about plans and stuff.'

'Young pretty gal like you should be partying,' he stated. He turned to his partner: 'Ain't that right, Ann?'

'Yeah, I was always out at your age,' she told me, laughing. 'Still am!'

I forced a laugh.

'Where you off to?' I asked them, not caring. Why didn't I care? Perhaps I should.

'Meeting some mates at the pub to watch the boxing.'

Boxing. Christ.

'It's got more popular with ladies now, it has,' he continued. Ann nodded enthusiastically.

I found it frustrating when women wasted their rising equality to make the same awful choices as men have previously done, becoming boxers, ruthless CEOs, working class-hating Prime Ministers, etcetera.

'It's just not my thing really.' You know, because it is a sport in which the participants can legally win by *knocking another human being unconscious.*

I stood in front of the street art, somewhere between pissed off and amused. I'd helped my mate spray this modern *Guernica* onto the wall a few months back – minus the recently added cocks and balls.

I turned to walk towards the pub, accepting the fleeting nature of graffiti.

I'd received a message from Victoria just before leaving home. She'd apparently had a 'great time' and had 'enjoyed our chats' but didn't feel 'the chemistry was there' and we 'should just be friends'. I wonder how she'd react if I genuinely took up her presumably empty promise of friendship. Anyway. I saw this coming, and it's probably for the best, to be honest.

Despite being a little blue, I actually enjoyed the night out, moaning with friends about Brexit and Theresa May – subjects I was in the same echo chamber with them on. I was even with my Corbyn-liking friends, a man disliked by a surprising amount of people who share all his opinions and values.

It was getting on for 1a.m. when I decided to give in and start my walk home. I swayed down Exchange Walk, towards the glaring artificial lights of the McDonalds. My eyes were drawn to the many people contained within, chomping down on various fast-food delicacies and, as my heart skipped a beat, I focused on a familiar wonderfully attractive face.

Victoria.

I didn't hang around to stare at her, I kept my wobbly pace going uninterrupted, but I saw enough for my good mood to be destroyed for the rest of my walk home.

She was sitting with an equally wonderfully attractive woman, laughing and very close. Close in a way that suggested they were definitely going home together tonight after they had eaten their fries and cow flesh cobs. Good for them, the understanding and logical part of my mind kept saying, as it was drowned out by the alcohol-soaked, dramatic section of my brain devastated that I was missing out on hot sex just because I didn't think a meat and dairy based diet was an ethically sound idea. I knew that, in the long term, Victoria was not for me really, but I wanted her to be – just with a couple of tweaks, a couple of well-intentioned pointers, we'd be giggling away together before walking home to the same bed. But where would we be giggling together? There were no vegan fast-food places open at 1a.m. around here.

The back and forth in my mind had continued for much of my walk home. The innocent quacking of the ducks along the canal sounded like mocking laughter, adding to the familiar underlying anxiety of walking home alone after sunset. The increasing downpour accompanied me through the dark and deserted supermarket car park, not far from the shelter of my flat.

The bright lights of another McDonalds caught my eye. An overwhelming urge to just give in and grab myself a Big Mac rose and fell in an instant.

I turned away from the domineering double arches, twisting my ankle awkwardly as I avoided stepping on a snail. I stopped walking for a second, to fully concentrate on shouting obscenities in my head, before limping on.

I felt a crunch under my foot.

I looked down as I moved my foot away to see a snail, crushed violently under the drunkenly-guided vegan Docs of a horny loser.

I closed my eyes and took a moment to try and compose myself. However, instead, I found myself crossing the road and bursting into the McDonalds. I limp-marched towards the counter, where a man stood ready to take my order.

'Big Mac!' I exclaimed, over-dramatically. The guy actually flinched, fear lingering in his eyes for our entire interaction.

'Any, er, fries with that?' he asked.

'Go on then!' Was I crying? I couldn't tell, having been rained on for the past fifteen minutes. I widened my smile to hide the possibility that I was.

'Would you like a milkshake or-'

'Yeah, why not!'

Three minutes later – fast, indeed! – I was sitting on a table with my food and drink laid out before me. It actually smelled good. I was hungry. I stuffed several fries into my mouth. I wondered how much of the content was salt – 80% perhaps? Apparently that is what people liked, so I *had to adapt accordingly*.

Next: chocolate milkshake. The taste of cow's milk had become disgusting after only a few months of coming off it. My Grandma had kept making me milky teas, she just couldn't quite grasp it, and it was as if I could taste how ill-suited it really was for human consumption. Straw primed between my lips, I sucked on the plastic and the sweet liquid sprayed into my mouth. Yep. Disgusting. No. *No.* Had to be more positive. I endured another sip, trying to focus on the chocolate, before turning to the burger.

I was at the point of no return now, of course. It'd actually have been worse if I hadn't eaten it. Right? 'You killed me, cut my body into pieces, burned my flesh, and then you just chucked me in the bin?' the wise young cow ghost would say, in horror.

I picked the burger up carefully. The steam flowed upwards, into my nostrils, making me think of those old cartoons. It somehow smelled bad and good at the same time, as if my nostrils had competing opinions on the matter. It looked like a cartoon burger, too. The bun, the square melted cheese slice, the meat patties seemed so uniform. An imitation of a burger. I closed my eyes and bit into it. It wasn't bad. Certainly the tastiest thing I had consumed in the last five minutes. It was kind of like cardboard, cut to shape and injected with flavourings. It was perfectly edible. Of course. Yet so unnecessary in its current meaty form. I had expected some kind of unique and irreplaceable taste sensation, even if I didn't like it. The fact that the meat could be easily replaced by a vegan alternative without any consumer *even noticing* was so sad and horrific that hysterical laughter was the only way I could process my despair.

I walked out into the rain (imagining a collective sigh of relief from behind me) and skipped up the steps. In jumping from the penultimate step towards street level, I bumped into a passing man holding a bunch of individual roses. One fell to the ground.

'Oh shit, sorry!' I crouched down and picked up the rose, avoiding the thorns climbing the stem. It was delicate and flawed, all the more beautiful for being fleeting, its energy to be gradually transferred elsewhere upon its death. A fake one would look okay at a glance, but would remain unchanged, stubborn and unmoving, slow to become part of something greater than itself.

'It's all right,' he said, with a comforting chuckle, in a way that seemed about more than bumping into him.

I held the flower out to him.

'Why don't you keep it,' he smiled.

I brought it to my chest.

'Thanks.'

With a reassuring nod, he turned and continued his walk down the glistening street. I watched him for a few seconds, before looking at the rose in my hands and feeling hope sweep over me. Just for a second.

I turned and started towards home. A cold wind cut across my exposed face and drew my attention to a flag caught up in a tree, violently flapping. The tree was full of green a few months back but the old branches now clung onto the Union Jack, proudly displaying its torn and twisted shape.

I looked back down at the rose. A petal had been torn off with the wind, lost to the storm. I continued on, shielding it from the elements, noticing a spray-painted logo on a fence, a kind of hourglass in a circle, as I avoided crushing any other living creatures underfoot.

Mermaids Moved into the Village
Ale Malick

I wasn't opposed to it. I wasn't one of *them*. You know the type, don't like the sea, believe the hype, easily led. No, I liked the idea. I thought it could be good for everyone, to get a bit of culture. Well, someone else's culture. I'm not saying the village doesn't have any. We have dances monthly, competitive bingo, darts and Ping-Pong for the young ones. We get the cinema screen set up occasionally and one time we even had a theatre company come down from the big city. Right good laugh that was. Don't know why they never came again. Then there's the sea shanty lot, but you know that's not happening anymore, obviously.

No, I wasn't opposed to it, per se, as they say. I wasn't going into the streets to protest, although no one else was either. Not then. But I heard grumbles, and comments, and little snide jibes. Unnecessary, I thought. Bit callous. Bit narrow minded. 'There by the grace of God,' and all that I'd think, but I didn't say. I know I should have said something, but honestly, I'm not as tough as I look, I'm a bit of a conflict avoider. Conflict resolution is great, but conflict avoidance is a close second in my book and my book always opens at that page.

No, I wasn't opposed to it, but the but! I know, there's always a but isn't there? This is where you really think bad of me and say I'm just like the rest and all that stuff. That I'm hiding behind my liberal ideas of freedom for all but when it comes to my backyard, then it's 'no, no, no'. But that's just it. It really was my backyard. Literally. Well, the thing is, the thing you won't like, is that frankly we were too small for all those Mermaids to turn up and take over.

There I've said it. I might as well have gone ahead and called it an invasion, a takeover, an annexation, 'overrun we were!', because I know what you'll be thinking; 'where's his heart, where's his compassion, what would happen if the fin was on the other foot?' I know. I know all of it. I've thought it myself, about myself, more than once, these last few months, but in the end, I've got to say I'm sticking with it, sort of, however it makes me look. I just have to be honest with you. It was all too much, that many mermaids in the village.

They arrived late spring, though we'd been expecting them for some time. The coast, which had been a stone's throw away (we had, after all, been a fishing village once) had started receding at an alarming rate. I blame climate change. Some deny that and say the government just wanted to rearrange the coastline to give other villages a chance to be by the sea. I didn't believe the government were that powerful, but it's true old friend, you who lives in the 'middle' of the country, was a hundred miles from the beach but now you can cycle there in twenty minutes. That really true? You seem happy at this turn of events! And it is certainly true that looking at a map of the country now is like looking at one of those moving pictures in *Harry Potter* films. It keeps changing, with every wave it seems.

So yes, it was all pretty bad for anything in the sea. Some fish, the few fish that were left, we guessed there were probably some, but we never saw any these days, must have gone out deeper, or swam round to your side of the country, but some can't do that. They need to be near the shore as the temperature just ain't right further out. Some creatures of the deep, or of the shallows anyway, need a bit of a certain kind of coastline to stick with. We lost the birds, the ones that nested on our cliffs. There were no cliffs now. Not sea cliffs I mean. City folks come in from, well, cities I guess, to climb on them, now they can reach them from solid, dry land and no longer risk getting swept out. I couldn't see the sea anymore, not even from my attic window, just this dry, barren waste land.

We knew where the Mermaids roosted or nested or sat on rocks, I'm not clear about the terminology, and I was always a bit too in awe, or scared is probably the more appropriate word, to ask them these kinds of things straight out. Their place, their home I suppose I should call it, was far out on a bunch of sticking up rocks that were not quite an island but not a place you could sail through safely either. We knew about them of course because our grandfathers had all stayed well clear of it when they had been out shopping for fish. I mean fishing for fish, though I have only ever shopped for them, when I could afford them that is. Anyway, that array of rocks, well, they went and turned into quite the sizeable little island a year ago, and then a tidal island and then an outcrop and eventually a peninsula. By that time it was all up for the Mermaids and they started arriving in the village, their home was no more than a dry little hill.

It was OK to begin with, they weren't the first Mermaids we'd ever seen. The oldest in the village, the ones who'd been fisherman, they knew them in their natural habitat, when they'd got close, but for us youngsters, well it was only 'cause of ol' Joe Fadden that we had any experience of Mermaids at all. He only liked Mermaids he said, not humans. They kept better company than the rest of us, he said, and he loved their singing more than the drone of the church organ or the squeal of the sea shanty fiddle player. His words not mine. But it was true, if the truth be known. They could sing! All the Mermaids he had at his cottage on the hill could sing, we heard it drifting down the valley, you remember from when we was kids? Old Joe seemed to have a different Mermaid with him every month but each of them had a unique but always brilliant set of songs and voices. You remember we tried to copy them? And it was as awful as a baby crying! It was probably one of the reasons they came to us, rather than the other villages, so many had been there before.

Joe was always marrying Mermaids. We knew he was a thief by trade and so he was an ace at creeping up on an unsuspecting lady of the sea and whipping away a comb or a mirror they'd innocently left on a rock beside them. Then you see, as legend has it, they have to marry the thief and go and live with him! It's all rather different to our ways of courting I know but, never having had much luck with dates, it does have its appeal to me. You did alright though, didn't you! That picture you sent, your fiancée is lovely. But as good as Joe was at winning over the ladies, in the way you win over these ones, he wasn't very good at keeping them. For years, all the Mermaids had to do was to say, 'Joe, do you have a comb I could borrow, I want to fix my long, beautiful hair.' And Joe, he would jump up and rush to the hiding place he'd made for keeping their possession secret and give them back their comb, grinning happily that he could be so helpful to such a beautiful woman. If the Mermaid was smiling, that smile would fall away, and they'd not look back the moment it was in their hands. They'd be out of the door and back on the rocks before Joe could hardly comprehend his mistake. Poor Joe, everyone used to say. 'Poor Joe, he'll never make a Mermaid happy, you can't make a Mermaid happy, no one will ever stay with him. Get yourself a human girl, Joe.'

He didn't give up though. He got wise to that simple trick and didn't rush to bring them their mirrors, or whatever, when they asked for them. But by then the other Mermaids, half of whom seem to have married ol' Joe at some point or another, had told the others where his hiding places were. So, moment he went out the house they'd grab the thing he'd stolen and slope on back to their home on the rocks. Undaunted, Joe would be back there the next day, looking for a new wife. It went on for years and we heard a lot of singing in that time. But all that new wife business stopped by the time you left. He hasn't had a new one since.

He's had the same Merwife for twenty years now. The story is that although his hiding places got better and better, they were never good enough to fool a clever Mermaid. No, they weren't taken in by a fake bottomed chest, a freshly dug flower bed, or a suspicious walled off alcove. No, they knew alright, even his current wife knows. She told one of the ladies, who told her friend, who told my cousin, who told me, that she knows her belt is in the teapot. He never drinks tea, and it rattles when she moves it, but she said she loved Joe, he was kind and funny. She didn't want to go back, she was happy in the village, and so she doesn't find it, because if she did, she'd have to go home. That's how tradition works, you see. Harsh.

That's why it didn't work, them coming to us like that, not in ones and twos but by the dozen, by the score, much more than a hundred I'd say. They turned up on the 1st of June, in trucks, full of water, ferried there by what the villagers called 'the do gooders, doing bad and getting out quick brigade' or TDGDBAGOQBers which you'd have thought they'd have shortened but instead they turned it onto a word you could actually say: The Gabacoques. Well, barely say. I stuck with 'do-gooders' when talking to Mermaid sceptics and their official title, Marine Legends Saving Team, or MLSTs, when talking to people in the village who had some empathy towards the poor, hopeless sea creatures. There weren't many of us like that to be sure, and less after a few weeks. Joe of course threw his weight behind the pro-Mermaid lobby, even if he was constantly bumping into ex-wives as he walked around the village. The hostility they encountered pretty much confirmed his way of thinking about the other villagers, that they were a bunch of haters, without a clue to rub together. None of us went up in his estimation around that time, even when we made the effort like I did.

I had five Mermaids in my pond, I even dug it out a bit deeper and wider, bringing in some rocks that Gabacoques were providing as 'refugee relief' they said. Which was kind, but my dahlias and great patches of my lawn don't thank me for the relandscaping. I had one come into the house, 'temporary', to sit on my loo by the filled bath. I've a downstairs loo and shower as well, so I could cope, but it was never temporary. The Gabacoques never came back to fix any other accommodation up. I'd not had a bath in years but suddenly I longed for one. You know how it is.

Joe was not diplomatic about his feelings towards us all either. At the town meetings he'd yap on that we were a bunch of heathens, and I'd tell him I'd done my fair share, and he'd say showing off about it just showed I was virtue signalling and not serious at all. (For an oldy he knew all the young people words better than me. Maybe it was the Mermaids told him them.) Soon as I showed off about it, I lost all my credibility he said, and made it clear I wasn't doing it for the right reasons and that it must be horrible being a Mermaid living with me. I don't think it was. I think they were as happy as homeless legends can be. But it seemed his hatred for those doing the right thing was greater than for those who didn't take any Mermaids in, and were actively trying to get rid of them! No one ever understood ol' Joe, except perhaps his Mermaid wife Miranda. Maybe she got him. We never could.

The final straw came a day after the Major had made his announcement about the swimming pool. This year's spare cash was to go into building a swimming pool he said, to a stormy reaction in the hall. The Gabacoques had told him it would be a way to bring the two parts of the village together, help to build bridges, he said. Well, the 'Mums for the Village' group had wanted a better play area for their kids, the 'Villagers for the Village' bunch had demanded better lighting, because they didn't think the village was safe anymore. The old folk had clubbed together to agree a fully equipped day centre for them was the only sensible way to spend the spare cash. I wasn't in any of these groups and had enjoyed swimming once, when the sea was close enough to walk to comfortably, when we were kids, so I thought it was a good idea. I was nearly the only one though. It was voted down and nothing was agreed except that a swimming pool was a stupid idea and that we were sucking up to these outsiders like those Gabacoques and of course the 'maddening mushrooming of multiple marauding Mermaids' that were ruining the village. So much so, people had now started calling the village a town, in a sarcastic way, to show it had become far too big, and far too multicultural. Like those big nasty, stinking places: towns. Like where you live perhaps, old friend! No offence!

Joe wasn't there to shout for the 'good guys' as he'd have seen them. I was surprised, but no one else seemed to notice his absence in the scramble to shout down the Major. Or the 'Mermajor' as he was dubbed, before being voted out of office in an emergency loss of confidence motion.

Joe was gone you see. Left that evening, with Miranda, while we were all fighting in the Village – no, sorry – *Town* Hall. I heard later she'd just had a batch of children, I think that's what you call them, a batch, more than a couple anyway, and then, well, I got it. This place was no place to bring up children anymore.

The sea shanty crew left the next evening. That was the big final straw, see. They were out-sung again by the siren sounds coming from across the street, where the Mermaids met at the little pond, to share some community time. They huffed and puffed their way off the stage, cursing the Mermaids, and shouting, 'You'll miss us when we're gone.' Despite all the bile and loathing we collectively had for the finned ones, we rather did enjoy their music more than the sea shanty crew. But no one said that. It was just obvious when it went quiet between songs in the bar, when we could hear that the Mermaids were singing beautifully, and sighed when the fiddle was taken up again and drowned them out.

After that… I hardly like to describe after that… After that it was horrible. You'd have hated it. I hated it. Be glad you weren't here. After that it wasn't only Miranda leaving. Yes, without the sea shanty band interrupting our enjoyment of the Mermaids song, that was better, you'd have thought, but even so, people didn't like losing them folk singers. They blamed the Mermaids for that, they blamed them for everything. Two weeks later they were gone. The Gabacoques had come in with some kind of emergency team and airlifted the last of the stranded Mermaids to safety, because it was getting unsafe for them. I don't like to say why. Ugly.

I watched the last helicopter go and I looked around at a

village sighing a collective relief.

I couldn't take it though. The quiet, the last link with our sea history gone, the cruelties we'd witnessed, encouraged, or taken part in. I even missed Joe and Miranda because now the village was always quiet. No one left to sing at all.

That's why I wrote to you, my friend. That's what I wanted to explain. That's why I want to come and see what your place is like, on the other side of the country. The sea will get all the way to you soon. It's a magic place you know. Look after it.

Go Tell it to the Dolphins
JB Polk

The trip from Rio in the twin-engine Cessna Skylight was exhausting. The small plane shook like a half-empty box of matches every time it hit a warm jet stream and the fasten-the-seat-belt sign had remained on for the duration of the flight.

With nothing else to do, Irene checked and rechecked her briefcase, browsed through the ancient courtesy in-flight magazines promoting the Sugar Loaf, and sipped the lukewarm whiskey in which quickly dissolving ice-cubes clinked against the glass. For the second time since she'd boarded, she went through the dossier the newspaper had compiled on Inacio Oliveira, the mayor of Manaus.

Aged forty-five, a hard-core capitalist and take-over tycoon, Oliveira had been elected two years before on the strength of the slogan '*Mayor of people, not of animals and the jungle*'. Progressive Brazilian newspapers accused him of nepotism, bribery, and keeping his pre-electoral pledge of civilizing the Amazon and bringing wealth back to Manaus, the impoverished capital of the 19th century rubber boom. At all costs. Whatever it meant, even if it included destroying the native flora and fauna.

Following complaints from tourists that large sums of money had been paid to clear Manaus of all types of troublemakers - ecologists, wildlife watchers, and resisting natives - international organisations began to keep a watchful eye on Oliveira. But as long as no blatant attempts against foreigners were made, consulates and embassies were powerless.

It was a different story with the local mestizos and the indigenous population. Mutilated bodies had been found on the banks of the Amazon, their tongues cut off as if to indicate that their protests would get no further. They had been silenced for opposing the construction of the new dam and the power plant upstream from Manaus, a project staunchly supported by Oliveira and funded by his cronies. The construction meant that thousands of hectares would be flooded, and people forced to move further inland, away from their ancestral home and worse, away from the city where they had access to education and healthcare services. No-one dared to accuse the mayor openly, but below-the-surface whispers pointed to him as the person behind the murders. Or, at least, the man who bankrolled them.

The story had been dumped on Irene. Not exactly Pulitzer Prize material, but better than the assignments she'd been given lately; the predictable fluctuations of the Dow Jones index; the childish pranks of ageing Hollywood stars; the thrilling reports of how silicone implants might affect post-menopausal women. In fact, she was grateful for any story at all.

When she had first started, a young journalist of twenty-five with hardly any experience, she was overjoyed thinking that her critical thinking and her background in environmental studies would add to the editorial line of the rather conservative newspaper. But she'd been wrong. Her progressive views were ignored and instead, she was constantly questioned.

Trying to preserve some dignity, she wrote pieces on the viability of sustainable cities and questioned the real impact of global warming. Seeking balance, she interviewed scientists and environmental experts but also climate change deniers. She spent hours talking to readers and gathered their views, even if they contradicted her own. But her efforts were valued little, and the editor returned her articles slashed by irate comments and exclamation marks. Consequently, she struggled against wave after wave of self-doubt knowing she only had two options - remain at the newspaper and accept the constant bashing of her ego, or give up the ineffectual efforts and become jobless. For the moment, there was nothing she could do. Nothing but hope that an unexpected event would relieve her from the responsibility of having to decide, or that would galvanise her into action. Whatever the outcome.

So, when she'd been offered the trip to Brazil, she considered it an opportunity to get back into her editor's good graces. She was determined to write an article that was well-researched and unbiased. One that would earn her kudos both from her colleagues and her readers.

As the Cessna descended, the Manaus airport, an impressionist painting of spontaneous and bold brushstrokes, greeted her with rain so intense that it blurred the contours of buildings and the tarmac resembled Degas' 'Rainy Day in Paris'.

As soon as she collected her luggage, a taxi took her to the Tropicana, an old five-storey hotel with a flashing yellow-and-green neon sign shaped like a giant pineapple.

The receptionist, a morose teenager with pupils so black that they seemed to melt into the whites, gave her a clumsy looking key and directed her to the third floor. The room was small but equipped with a double bed, an ample shower cubicle, a sixpack of beer cooling in the minibar, and the Gideon Bible for the consolation of the soul in the drawer of the bedside table.

She decided to relax for the rest of the evening. After all, there was no rush. She was glad to have got away from the bedlam Washington had turned into during the past few months, the battle of conflicting political egos tearing deep into its flesh. The nation had never been divided more than now, and the supporters of the candidates from both sides repeatedly posted disinformation and fake news on their Facebook and Twitter accounts.

Election years are always the worst, she thought. *And now, with the accusations of fraud, even before anything has actually happened, the tension is becoming unbearable.*

She showered to wash off the clammy sensation one gets in the tropics and settled in front of the TV with a can of Caxias do Sul to watch a Brazilian soap opera. It reminded her of the old version of *Dallas*: two women dressed to the nines, with puffed-up hair, heavy makeup, and beringed fingers, screaming at each other about a betrayal and an inheritance.

Outside, dusk was beginning to thicken. Scatters of laughter filtered through the wall from the room next door. Her eyelids struggled to remain open when a knock brought her back from the precipice of sleep.

'Miss Almeida?'

'Yes?'

'Someone to see you.'

She switched off the TV. The young receptionist's face showing in the crack of the door reflected a mixture of admiration and fear and his black pupils seemed dilated with foreboding.

'Two gentlemen,' he whispered. 'They want to see you...'

Somehow, she didn't like the sound of the word 'gentlemen'.

'Irene Almeida?' one of the visitors asked. He was tall and gangly, his dark pock-marked face and slightly slanting eyes betraying more than a drop of indigenous blood.

'Yes. What can I do for you?'

'You could start by inviting us in.'

Reluctantly, she let them pass. They entered with the confidence of owning not only the hotel, but the whole of Manaus, then sat on the bed taking inventory of the room, scrutinising her in the process. She had the impression they liked what they saw.

'I didn't get your names,' she said to break the silence.

'No need for names. It's better to remain nameless. Besides – what is a name? Just a handful of sounds,' the man with the pock-marked face chuckled.

Although her grandparents on her father's side were Portuguese, Irene found it hard to understand the Brazilian version of the language.

'I guess I'll have to remain at a disadvantage,' she muttered.

The man smirked. 'I guess you will.'

Something in their bearing made her wary and prevented her from turning her back to them. She felt safer standing against the window, keeping a permanent eye contact.

'Did you have a good trip? Those Cessna planes can be a bit bumpy,' the other man asked. He was squat like a coal scuttle, and his cheap, synthetic suit looked even cheaper and more synthetic on his bulky frame.

'Not bad,' she lied.

'Let's talk about what brought you here,' the squat one said.

'Let's not. I guess you'll have to remain at a disadvantage here.'

He chopped off her protest with the wave of his hand, his eyebrows rose, and he made a clucking sound with his tongue.

'It's bad to start an acquaintance with a disagreement, Miss Almeida. Bad. Very bad. Senor Oliveira hoped you'd see things his way. Because... that is what you've come here for, isn't it? To write an article about Senor Oliveira.'

Manaus suddenly seemed small. And Oliveira in charge.

'You seem to be very well-informed,' she said.

He smiled indulgently as one might at an underachieving child who needs an explanation of even the most basics facts.

'We know what's to be known. Senor Oliveira makes it his business to be well-informed.'

'His business is multifaceted, then. Mayor, politician, trade expert, private eye. Have I missed something?'

'No need to be sarcastic.'

'No need for names... No need to be sarcastic... So, what is there a need for?' she asked.

'The mayor would like to know what it is exactly that you are planning to write,' he gave her a long, speculative gaze as if assessing her breaking point. She had the impression again that he liked what he saw.

'First of all, it's none of his business. Or yours. But if Senor Oliveira were really all that well-informed, he should know it already,' the words left her mouth harsh and rude.

'Maybe he does. Maybe he knows and he doesn't like it too much... Maybe all he needs is a confirmation. A confirmation that you've come to snoop about the power plant.'

'I'm not confirming anything! Not for the mayor and not for the pope!' she was getting fired up.

The squat one sighed with an exaggerated sadness.

'Irene – you don't mind me calling you that, do you?' then without waiting for her reply went on.

'Let us get things straight. As you so perceptively noticed, the mayor knows a lot of things. He knows that you are with The Gazette, a diligent journalist although your boss thinks you might be getting too involved in all that bullshit about climate change and similar crap. He fears, and I have it straight from the horse's mouth,' he winked at her, 'that your feelings towards some radical environmental groups are, how should I put it… too warm, no pun intended. And because of that, your professional judgment could be somewhat clouded. Shall I go on?'

The bitter tang of anger, or maybe it was fear, was beginning to fill her mouth.

'Senor Oliveira is eager to help. He's the answer to your prayers, if you believe in God, like I do. I believe in God, and I believe in Senor Oliveira. Both have proven to be infallible. And generous. But they can also be quite vengeful. You know what they say: if you can't beat them and so on and so on. Join Senor Oliveira's winning band. He'll pay well for a good story. Along his lines,' he babbled in gun-fire rapid Portuguese she was finding increasingly hard to follow.

'It was nice talking to you, but now I'd appreciate if you got out of my room,' she looked at them with more resolve than she felt. 'You've overstayed your welcome. By a full ten minutes.'

A nasty laugh gurgled out of the squat man's mouth now twisted into a sneer. 'I still think you don't get it, Irene. Let's put it bluntly, then. *You* are the mayor's guest. The Tropicana belongs to him.'

She cursed the damned newspaper. There were dozens of hotels in Manaus, and they had selected this one. But then it dawned on her. It was no coincidence. She'd been set up as another way of testing her loyalty to The Gazette. Oliveira's arms reached far. And her editor's.

The man took an envelope out of his jacket pocket.

'Ten thousand crispy green American dollars. It should pay for a couple of weeks of fun in the sun. Rio, perhaps? Or would you prefer Miami? They say the restaurants there are spectacular for *huevos rancheros* and *tequila margaritas*. And the beaches. Just a few strokes of a pen, or is it a computer you journalists use nowadays? As easy as that. I wish I could write.'

Sweat broke out on her forehead. 'What's my other option?'

The tall man chortled and got up.

'Try to answer it yourself. You have the whole night.'

The squat man put away the envelope, approached her and grasped her hand in his sweaty palms.

'Until tomorrow, then,' he said and blew her a noisy kiss.

When the door closed behind them, she began to shake. She needed a drink badly. She opened another Caxias do Sul. It frothed over the edge and spilt on her trembling fingers. Despite the numbing effect of the alcohol, the bitter taste in her mouth remained.

Ten thousand dollars. Rio sounded fabulous. And she'd never been to Miami, not even on her college spring break. Her old Toyota Corolla was long due an overhaul. Her student loan could also do with a helping hand... And her job would be safe. That's what they wanted her to do, wasn't it? To conform, to show her loyalty. Worse things had been done for less. Who gave a damn about the Amazon, anyway? And perhaps the things they said about the mutilated bodies were not true either. The powerplant also seemed like a good idea. Cheap electricity for the locals. And jobs.

Through the open window she could see that the rain was debating whether to become a drizzle or a downpour. She left the room and walked past the receptionist who bent his head and pretended she was just a waft of wind blown in through the open door.

Manaus was deserted and the rain finally decided to cease completely. Pools of water steamed on the sidewalks. Somewhere in the descending night frogs croaked a throaty concerto.

She walked toward the spilt ink of the river drawn by the whispers of waves licking the banks. The obsidian sheet of the Amazon reflected a woolly balloon of the moon. It was the same river that was soon to flood hundreds of hectares of land and submerge everything under it surface.

She stood in the semi-silence watching. It was like a stage set for a Wagnerian spectacle - gaudy and unreal. *The Nibelungs* maybe. Or *The Lohengrin*. Any moment, a huge plaster swan would emerge, the orchestra blare at full blast, lights chase away the darkness and a black-clad singer would intone the *'Grail Aria'*.

'Uncanny, isn't it?' a voice behind startled her out of her reverie.

She turned around. It belonged to a small woman whose white triangular face peered out of a moist sleeker.

'On a night like this, dolphins come near the banks. I've always wondered what tells them that they are safe, that there's no-one to harm them.'

'Dolphins? I thought they were marine creatures,' Irene answered.

'The Amazon is full of pink dolphins, small and swift. You know what the legend says? After the rain, they leave their bodies to turn into humans. Many children born out of wedlock are said to have been fathered by them.'

Irene's heart was making a terrible din. A tingling sensation rose up from her toes as if she were standing barefoot on ice. But it wasn't fear anymore. It was the woman's physical presence that made her nervous —round piercing eyes as though she could see right through her, into her, could touch the heart that was cantering wildly against her ribs.

'Do you come here often?' she asked finally.

'Like the dolphins, only after the rain,' the woman laughed.

She added after a pause, 'Is there something worrying you? A problem?'

'Not really, it's just...' Irene stammered.

An urge to tell her everything, to unburden herself, to get rid of the strangling sensation of guilt rushed over her.

'Yes, there's something. A problem... you see...'

'There! There they come!' the woman interrupted.

'The dolphins!'

The river rippled. A pointed nose emerged. More and more of them disturbed the black surface, their gay chatter joining the frogs' guttural song.

'You know why I come here?' the woman asked then continued without wating for an answer. 'To talk to them, to know I'm not alone. If there's anybody who understands, it's them.'

Her raincoat rustled as she moved closer.

'Maybe that's what you should do. Tell it to the dolphins.'

Irene looked at her with surprise. The woman's eyes lit up and shone like two bright coals on a bed of ashes.

'It helps, you know, to tell someone. Anyone. They can't answer, but they listen. And it's you who will make the final decision.'

Her hand descended on Irene's shoulder and propelled her lightly towards the Amazon.

'Go on, tell it to the dolphins.'

Irene felt compelled to take a few steps forward. Part of her said it was ridiculous. She was a no-nonsense journalist, a fact finder. Her world was not inhabited by dolphin children. But part of her wanted to believe in castles in the air. Or in the water.

Around her everything was black, only the stars like tins of condensed light blinked in the now cloudless sky and in the river.

The dolphins chattered, poked their noses through the surface then sank again amidst a whirlpool of bubbles.

And all at once, she understood. Everything crystallised. No matter what, no matter how much Oliveira and others like him tried, there were things that could not, would not be influenced by the action of man - they'd stay sculpted in the bark of trees, marked on the firmament by comets that happened to pass every hundred years, signs engraved in every leaf and every blade of grass along the banks of the Amazon. Or scribbled on the water by dolphins.

And she also understood that she could not continue along the same path she'd trod for the past few years. She had to relinquish the powerful God who wore Armani suits, smelt of Issey Miyake and whose name was sometimes money and sometimes the betrayal of principles. She saw his feet clearly now - they were made of clay.

Irene turned around to thank the woman, but she was gone. She could hear the murmur of her raincoat in the mist but maybe it was just the last raindrops falling from the trees.

She started back. It was nearly midnight, but she was impatient to begin. At once, before it all blew up in her face. Before she could be seduced into conformity again. She was glad she had told it all to the dolphins. She knew what kind of article she was going to write. And she knew that her editor wouldn't like it.

A Modest Proposal
Rae Toon

For preventing the poor and old people of the UK from being a burden on the Earth's natural resources and for making them beneficial to the state.

Decades ago the sensible among them thought the Referendum was a forgone conclusion: let them have their vote, we all know it will never actually happen, they told each other. And plenty of politicians felt the same way. Just look how that turned out.

Who knew in the years running up to the vote what a wedge it would drive between the two sides. 33.5 million people with so much in common were persuaded to regard each other as sworn enemies. At that point it all changed. Because we knew we could wield that power to convince them of almost anything. Almost.

I mean, just look at 'Shop a Santa'. A few naughty St Nic's plastered across the tabloids was all it took to convince law abiding, tax paying parents that this jolly old fellow was an outdated custom we no longer needed (much like Captain Pugwash, Ronald McDonald, and Jimmy Savile). Anyone with a white beard had to shave it off or else go into hiding for the duration as the public conducted their own Santa Trials over the socials. Of course the Republicans were up in arms, and who could blame them? Because if the press got behind the #BanishAndrew campaign the whole house of Windsor could have come toppling down. Better to sacrifice one seasonal saint than throw an entire clan of year-round news worthy sinners to the hacks. Besides, those hacks know which side their bread's buttered.

If I'd suggested #FidoOrFelix when I first got the idea, I would have been laughed out of every think tank in Christendom, let alone the One Grand Parent Policy. Back then, my job title was a mere germ of an idea, planted with the assistance of copious Cognacs at an exclusive Carlton Club gathering I blagged my way into. I'm not sure what our greatest achievement was: getting the opposition to agree to the Department of Divide and Comply (full title: Manage Division and Facilitate Compliance, but let's not quibble over semantics, the two verbs are interchangeable) or getting them to vote for the Pasture Fed Alternatives clause to be written into the Agriculture Act. That was a landmark piece of legislation, because beforehand, Brits had always considered dobbin well and truly off the menu. It was something the French did; so barbaric. After all, it's part of our cultural identity, isn't it? Being a nation of 'animal lovers'. We're also a nation of meat eaters; how do you reconcile these two conflicting values? The first pandemic restrictions had set a precedent for this phenomenon: on the one hand the fundamental idea of democracy was being eroded and on the other the institutions of family and health care were being put at risk. When it comes to abstract belief systems versus flesh and blood bonds, we now know which side the rabble will pick. It's always easy enough, in any argument, to find some total nutter amongst your opponents who will serve as the perfect illustration that you are in the right. Enter Lord Jab-Me-Not and his anti-vac disciples; we didn't need to construct an actual debate at all. Anyone who didn't wish to be regarded as insane by their friends, family and work colleagues, would take any anti-vac sympathies to their grave.

As with any radical agenda, a baby steps strategy was the way to adjust thinking – a sort of feeding conversion by increments. For the introduction of nag to the meat aisle, we just had to find a way to turn the masses against the stinking rich *and* the gypsies. Because horse ownership is quite remarkable in its polarised nature. We did dabble with warmbloods versus common cobs: let the poshies and plebs fight it out at the polls. But that would have ruled out an awful lot of chow; obviously the warmbloods would have been spared, surely the tenderer, more appetising option. Who really wants to dine on something that's spent its life grazing in a mud patch on the end of a chain? As with all carnivorous options we need choices: stewing steak might suffice for the proles, but Food Insecurity Crisis or no, some of us will settle for nothing less than sirloin.

In the end it came down to a simple choice: gradual rationing with all meats phased out entirely over a two-year period, or dropping any sentimental pretentions for the noble steed. Of course, anything with papers would be spared in the name of sport. Managing the climate crisis has always been a fine balancing act with protecting the economy and this was the only way we could keep the Royals on board. Any worries about a Roma uprising were soon dispelled; the didicoys applied in their droves for the fast-track Butchery Scheme and soon turned the whole situation to their own advantage. Previously they had to work at finding buyers for the horses they bred; now they had a guaranteed source of income. Sales were slow to begin with, but once the new butchers on the block started to undercut the high street and even supermarkets, things picked up. As with any new product, so much is in the marketing: a cow is a cow when grazing in a field, but once it enters the food chain, it's beef. No grocer worth his salt would try and sell sheep meat or pig meat. Horse meat is loaded with unappetising connotations, from the glue factory to the dog's dinner; we needed a palatable table term for the fodder and herd hit the mark. It took away the individual character of any single beast and reduced the entire species to their practical function. The 'Have You Heard About Herd?' campaign was a stroke of genius; actually convincing consumers they were missing out if they hadn't tried it. This was followed up with 'Herd's The Word', 'You Herd It Here First' and 'Follow The Herd'; the possibilities are endless.

Once this adjustment was made, it paved the way for other domesticated pets to be considered. But kitties and pooches: was it a step too far? Conjures up images of cowering creatures in rusty cages down the dark alley of a back street market someplace south of Russia. The thing was, by this point we'd drummed up a fair bit of resentment towards our favourite four legged friends, based on the unsustainability of their own dietary needs. The pet food industry emits more greenhouse gasses per year than Mozambique; we share the Earth with 471 million dogs and 373 million cats and it takes an area twice the size of this green and pleasant land to produce their dry food supplies for one year; our furry friends consume one fifth of the world's meat and fish.

The One-Pet Policy was, in principle, the fairest way to share food sources among humans and non-humans. It had the additional benefit of producing a surplus meat source (in the excess pets taken for culling). At first this was offered as an alternative to the insect-based pet foods that were by this point starting to compete with traditional varieties. And of course, this was another highly effective means of leverage because none but the very most extreme of the Insulate Insane brigade could stomach a diet of grubs for themselves (watching has-been celebs forced to eat creepy crawlies might make an entertaining feast for the eyes, but few would contemplate it as a civilised dietary selection). The main grounds of resistance to mutts and moggies was disease, of course. After the first two pandemics, there was still relatively little data on transmission through pets. Opinion was divided between those who believed eating contaminated meat would actually strengthen their immunity (since no animal that died of any natural causes was allowed to be sold as meat, it followed that these animals, if infected, had fought it off; thus their meat was imbued with Super-Anti-Bodies) while others were convinced it would kill them (citing the BSE crisis of the nineties and a certain fast food chain's boycott of British beef after burger sales plummeted). No amount of Public Health messaging could combat these theories; yet more proof that the Department of Divide and Comply was functioning effectively on at least half its obligations.

We were more than happy to let the electorate manage their own risk on this one. We didn't need to convert everyone. Eventually a three-tier feeding system naturally established itself: with the very poorest forced to eat Grade C 'unlabelled' (the meat that dare not speak its name); Grade B, Herd, proving a firm favourite with the hoi polloi; and only the most well off able to afford Grade A 'Bone Fide' cuts and joints, bringing a whole new meaning to the term Kosher.

From the start records were collected on infection rates among the three food groups, after all, at some point we might all need to de-carnivorise. It was always a win-win situation because if the underclass were slowly being poisoned en mass, well that would go some way towards reducing the surplus population; if they thrived, well we would have a tested alternative to Herd to offer the JAM's.

As I write this, the scientists are still scrutinising the granular data; no conclusions can yet be drawn, but things look hopeful. I cannot pretend though that this entire process has been plain sailing. Recently a clash has broken out between the panivores (or 'new Neanderthals', who believe anything is fair game: if you can hunt and kill it – it's dinner) and the Plantvangelists. Pressure is mounting for the fox hunting ban to be reversed as the food hypocrisy argument gains support. But it wouldn't end there, would it? Decriminalisation is a slippery slope. The Lynx was only reintroduced five years ago; the population is growing slowly, but we're hardly over run. Yet the poachers have it firmly in the sights of their pellet guns. Encroaching on wildlife is what got us into this mess in the first place; if anything the laws need to be tightened.

My next proposal speaks to this very issue: The One-Grandparent Policy. We've been skirting around it for too long, focusing on greener ways to sustain ourselves, when the real problem is the ageing population. They were my masterplan from the beginning, but folk are so very precious about OAPs aren't they? In the nation's imagination their beatific fragility is surpassed only by their dignified resolve. The fact is they are a burden we can ill-afford to lavish limited resources on.

What's that? Life is sacred? Maybe – depending on geography. The lives of the Kiribatians were of little concern to the Western world when their island became the first casualty of rising sea levels; proving that one man's disaster is another man's bucket list. There was the minor inconvenience of bluewashing the region from maps, but it barely made the evening news, other than to demonstrate our magnanimity – we ensured the £40 million given in aid was broadcast. What wasn't reported were the strings attached to this gift: we insisted a large chunk of the money went into eco-tourism. The challenge? To create a Drowned Island Divers' Paradise along the lines of Atlantis, where scuba fanatics and travel vloggers could really get their money's worth out of the latest waterproof digital devices (we managed to negotiate a nice deal with GoPro into the bargain). All this with a view to building a Britlantis once the rising tide swallows up our beatific isle.

I seem to have allowed myself to be washed away further into the future than I had intended. Forgive me. While we may have been willing to benefit from the experiments of a benign Mexican outpost, we were less inclined to learn from Asian micro-biologists. Lab grown meat should have been the answer to all our prayers, but the anti-commie narrative bit us on the behind there. If only we could have swallowed our pride and just said, 'Yes, they're onto something with this.' But the endless jabs really shut down this option: vaccine fatigue led to a more suspicious attitude to cloned nuggets and a dogged insistence on knowing what was passing the lips.

As for Earth 2.0, that most elusive of billionaire playgrounds; if a superhabitable planet is out there, I can assure you that even for the super-rich, this is a race they just can't win because the last runner crossed the line hours ago, the course has been dismantled and the marshals have all gone home.

No, I'm afraid if we hope to sustain ourselves there really is only one option and it is as ancient a concept as the Ouroboros and as modern as pop will eat itself. Those who missed the opportunity to die for Great Britain the first two times around can have their chance now. They can be heroes. And that's what we'll call it – this tough as old boots meat! Hero Steak. And why stop there? I am also calling for the immediate enacting of The Assisted Dying Bill. And not just for the terminally ill. If some poor wretch wants out and they need a bit of a push to get the job done – let's not deny them their dying wish. I can see the slogan now, '*their* sacrifice on *your* plate.' What could be more patriotic than that?

Consumption
JP Seabright

This is the story of the last journey I will ever take. I am writing it down because I want there to be something left of me after I'm gone. Some remains that sum up the weight of me, the accumulation of time and thought and pain.

When I put it like this, I realise how pointless it's all been, all these years. Life's purpose seems to be purely to consume and then be consumed. Where is the beauty in that? The joy? The glory? Where is the justification in all that consumption? I am bloated with the world's greed and selfishness. I am constipated with humanity's relentless urge to burn everything in its path for that brief hit of the blaze - the flame of consumerism and capitalism - its degeneracy. How we have been fooled into thinking more is better.

Not all of us. There are some cultures, clearly more advanced than the so-called developed West, who are not hoodwinked by the ephemeracy of shiny glittery things, the transience of all this fucking *stuff*, who are not infected with obsessive consumption disorder. I suffered from it too once. I know how it feels. I was caught in that trap - consume or be consumed. My foot on the accelerator. My heart in the garbage. But now I must take my leave.

I walk to the bathroom. This is the last time I will brush my teeth. I better make it a good one, clean them properly. A full two minutes. Thirty seconds each. My molars aren't in bad shape, only a few fillings, not too bad for a forty-something. I pick at my top left canine. I always felt mine looked particularly wolf-like and unattractive. But that won't matter anymore.

Two minutes doesn't sound long but it's long enough. Long enough for lots of things. As it turns out I don't even need thirty seconds. I twist and pull and wrench out the tooth with pliers in only seventeen. It hurts. It hurts like hell and there's a lot of blood, more than I was expecting. I hold the canine aloft in front of the bathroom mirror, baring my bloody new lopsided smile. I should extract its twin on the other side too, but it's really fucking painful and I have other things I need to do today.

I wipe down the sink to remove the globules of blood and throw my toothbrush away, then retire to the lounge. Clearly this phrase is an invention made up by people who watched too many Merchant & Ivory films in the 1980s, but I've always liked the sound of it and wanted to write it down. I sit on the sofa for a few minutes, pause for thought. I know exactly what I should do next, I've been planning this for over a year. My last day on Earth.

I head into the kitchen and open the fridge. It is pleasantly empty. I have been gradually working through my food supplies over the last few weeks in preparation for this day. Finishing off the fresh items, leftovers, and emergency processed goods at the bottom of the freezer, then tins and packets from the back of the cupboard. I've enjoyed planning my food shop so much more whilst working out the minimum number of items I could buy to have *just* enough food to last me through the week. It's been quite a challenge. I have found the minimalism, the extreme avoidance of waste, most satisfying. It's had an impact on my waist too. I'm noticeably leaner, tighter, emptier, and this has immeasurably improved my mood. I've found the increasing light-headedness has its own meditative quality.

My jaw is throbbing. Pain washes in and out of my mouth in waves. It's a welcome change, something intensely tangible to focus on for a while. I consider pulling more teeth. I'd rather like to empty my head in the same way I've gradually emptied my stomach, but the kitchen clock reminds me that I don't have time. The last thing I want is to feel rushed today.

I take out the half-empty yoghurt pot from the fridge and eat it standing with the door still open. It reminds me of previous years when I would bathe in the illicit and alluring glow from the open fridge door in the middle of the night, searching for snacks, looking for comfort, turning to food to fill me when everything was empty inside. I note with satisfaction how much I have evolved since then. How I am now emptier than ever, truly so, having purged myself of so much unnecessary consumption. As a result, I have never felt better.

The yoghurt is cool and soothes the raw bloody gap between my lateral incisor and first premolar, the one that contains my first ever filling. Perhaps I should have removed that one, I wonder, to rid myself of all impurities? But it's too late now, and it doesn't really matter. I drop the empty yoghurt pot into the bin and wash the spoon under the tap before placing it back in the drawer. I close the fridge door out of instinct, then open it again, forgetting myself. It is now completely empty. I switch the fridge off, leaving the door ajar to avoid mustiness and take out the rubbish from the kitchen bin.

The morning air is cold, but not unpleasant. The bitter chill of winter has done its worst, spring will soon be on its way. I wonder, briefly, if I should not have stayed around to see it. But no, it's better this way, no need to get one's hopes up. The stripped back astringency of winter suits me better than summer's overblown excess.

I'm ready; everything else has been sold, donated, or recycled. There is nothing more for me to cleanse, purge, or excrete. Except myself.

I close and lock the front door. Then think better of it and unlock it again. No need to lock it anymore. No point. It would be silly and wasteful if anyone in the coming days or weeks should have to break the door down. I lift the bolt from the inside, put it on the latch, then close the door softly again. It's sufficiently stiff, a good tight fit, so it's unlikely to swing open unless in a strong gale. I walk to the front gate, open it, then close it behind me, leaving the modest perimeter of my property for the last time.

I walk at a comfortable pace, but one with purpose and

anticipation, towards the Metro station. Somewhere above me, on one of the few remaining trees on the street, a blackbird chatters to itself. The sun weakly, almost apologetically, appears from behind a cloud, as if it had been doing something out of sight it shouldn't have been, and knows it's a little late for its appointment. I, on the other hand, am perfectly on time for mine. It is shaping up to be a good day.

Except the yoghurt pot bothers me. Why did I put it in the general rubbish bag and not wash it out and add to the recycling as usual? This is most uncharacteristic. I was clearly not thinking, not in my right mind. Am I in my right mind now? Am I nervous about my appointment, or excited? Either way, distracted. Perhaps it was the jarring pain inside my jaw, the missing tooth causing an absence of thought. I consider for a moment going back to fish it out of the rubbish, cleaning it and putting it in the recycling instead. But the recycling bins were taken by the council yesterday morning. They always arrive just before 6a.m., waking me without fail. I took it to be a good sign that the recycling was due for collection the day before. It pleased me greatly that the last detritus of my existence wouldn't remain on my property after I'd left. But the empty yoghurt pot preys on my mind. I didn't even wash it.

People don't realise that most of their recycling is never actually recycled. It all has to be clean, you see. Emptied of any remnants of food or dirt, any non-recyclable material removed, and then washed. Properly washed. Otherwise it's treated like any other item of rubbish. I was shocked when I discovered this, having made efforts to be environmentally conscious and to always place items in the correct recycling bins my entire adult life. But this is the big Eco-con. I have been religiously deconstructing items and washing them ever since.

I haven't travelled on the Metro now for a few months. I avoid it whenever possible, but for my last job it was unavoidable for the commute into the office. Since I left, I've had no need to travel across the city, or even into the centre. What is of interest there? Just more shops, more restaurants, yet more places of endless consumption and waste. Wasteful consumption. Utterly pointless. Consumption simply for the sake of consuming something, for people to fill up their empty lives. Not for me anymore.

Since I left my job - I resigned *before* I was sacked, it was no longer tenable to stay in those circumstances - I've been happy to live a quiet life and remain in the small periphery of my local community. I had my house and garden. I could buy what food I needed from the local farmers' market. If it hadn't been winter, I might have tried to grow my own in the back, convert the rhododendron bushes into a small vegetable patch. For a few weeks I wondered if it might be worth staying around a little longer in order to try this experiment. To live as cleanly and lightly as possible, to avoid placing my footprint upon the earth. But it's already too late, I know that. I've already consumed far more than I ever needed. Than I ever deserved. Than I can ever repay.

It's dirty and noisy in my Metro carriage, and the sheer intensity of the noise, the fluorescent lights and unavoidable proximity and unpleasantness of other people is almost more than I can bear. I have to force myself not to disembark when the doors next open. I remind myself that this is the last time I will ever have to ride this train, to interact with other people. It will be worth it in the end.

A young man joins my carriage. He may technically still be a boy, it's hard to tell. His limbs are long and gangling as if the rest of his body hasn't caught up yet. None of this is a concern to me, but he opens a large greasy bag of chips and the smell of fat fills the air. This is a concern. It's nauseating. I fear I'm going to throw up. To avoid this potential social mishap I hurl myself off the train as soon as its doors open at the next station.

I'm only two stops from my destination and the gaps are shorter as we near the centre. I reckon I can walk it from here. I check my watch. I've got time. I'm running ahead of schedule so I would otherwise be early. I need some fresh air, to get away from the stench of that greased-up food, tainting the inside of my mouth, still throbbing and raw, and coating it with fat. Even the thought of someone else consuming such fattening waste makes me gag.

I ache to be empty. I wish to be purged. Instead, I'm still full to bursting, in belly and in brain. For, despite myself, over the years, I have spent hours, days filling myself up, again and again. But no longer, no more. Today is the day of the Great Cleansing.

I thought I would enjoy the walk, the 'fresh air', although it is no longer fresh in this sad and stultifying city. I thought I would enjoy the exercise, and the chance to see life and buildings and people and history and... But I don't see any of those things. Just excess, waste, overconsumption, and flagrant greed. It brings up the bile that I had swallowed down earlier in the Metro, and now wish I hadn't. I wish I had let it all come up, vomiting out whatever is left in there, and dumping it onto the dirty grey tiles where it belongs. I arrive at my destination with only seven minutes to spare. But it's enough time to get settled, to prepare, relax. I'm having an enema, or rather a colonic irrigation; there's a difference you see. I didn't know this previously, but I've had time to look into it. An enema involves a one-off infusion of water into the colon. A tube up the bum, basically. This can be useful as a quick fix, a bit more than a good wipe, to clear out the lower colon. In contrast, a colonic irrigation is a thorough cleansing. Multiple infusions, a veritable baptism of the bowel, to sluice away any last remains of sinful consumption.

I'm not a religious person, but I do see this as something of a spiritual experience. A rebirth. Being born anew. If only for a few hours.

I haven't written any details about the colonic. I don't think it's likely to be of interest to anyone who might read this diary after I've gone. But I will say that afterwards I had the most beatific moment of utter peace. More than that - of grace. With such utter emptiness, this cleansing - a purification no less - I felt blessed. Forgiven. I'm not ashamed to say that I shed a few tears. The lady with the hose, as it were, said that people often respond in this way and it's nothing to be concerned about. She prattled on. I wanted her to be quiet, to leave me in this state of gentle awakening. I felt weightless, floating, transcendent. It was, I hope, only a glimpse of what is to come.

Unfortunately, this state of bliss was broken when I noticed the practitioner, or 'cleaning lady' as she jokingly described herself to me, throw her mask, plastic gloves, and gown in the bin after the procedure was finished. I asked if they could be recycled, and she almost laughed, 'Oh no dear, they get incinerated. No one would want to use them again!' I tried to explain that the recycling process would render them entirely new in that respect. The plastic and materials used would be melted down, re-moulded and thoroughly disinfected, so there would be no danger of any cross-contamination. She shook her head at me, as if I was crazy imagining that anyone would ever want to reuse them.

This lack of understanding, peoples' unrepenting refusal to even try to understand the process and benefits of recycling has driven me to despair over the last few years. I became an environmental evangelist. Not quite an activist, that seemed to require too much proactive interaction with other people - social engagement has never been my strong point. But I vowed never to let the opportunity go when it presented itself, to educate those who had yet to see the light, on what capitalism and consumerism had done to them. Has done to us all. We are literally eating ourselves and this planet alive.

My last job was a stopgap, something to tide me over whilst I looked for something more convenient, easier to get to, perhaps with better benefits and holiday entitlement too. It wasn't a bad role, Senior Sales Manager, but the agency hadn't been entirely truthful about the product I would be selling and the end user in the supply chain. The 'product' being our waste. Yours, mine, the entire output of recyclable waste in the United Kingdom. Or so we are led to believe. Since this waste isn't recycled, it's shipped. All 300 tonnes of it. That's 300 tonnes a *day*, well over 100,000 tonnes each year. Loaded onto vast container ships and sailed thousands of miles across the globe and dumped, literally, in Indonesia, Malaysia, and the Philippines.

Some of it used to get tipped into landfill, back in the optimistic days of Reduce-Reuse-Recycle, and there are various sites still scattered around the UK, mainly in so-called 'undesirable' areas. The sort of places that are prime real estate for nuclear power stations. But there's just too much of it and we've run out of space. And like nuclear waste, it's a ticking time bomb. There's just too much waste for us to bury or burn safely in this country. So we ship it somewhere else, to a country we don't give a shit about, and where it doesn't matter (to us) whether it's safe or not. I was shocked when I discovered this. No, more than shocked. I felt I had been lied to, cheated, that everything I thought I knew was wrong. The morning after this painful realisation, when a colleague finally explained to me the 'products' that we were shipping across the world, I woke as if from a dream, as if the scales had been lifted from my eyes. I was finally seeing the world as it really is, not how our politicians and media want us to believe. It was unbearable. A sudden psychic shock to my system. I had seen the future, and it hurt.

I left the clinic feeling physically lighter and mentally cleansed, but with the nagging splinter of the lady's words reminding me of the sordid waste-heap of humanity I have been forced to live in. It brought back to mind my yoghurt pot, sitting unwashed, and therefore unrecyclable. I feel I have failed that yoghurt pot, but I cannot return home now, there isn't enough time. I will pay for it at least, one way or another.

The nurse at the colonic clinic wouldn't let me leave the room without drinking half a pint of water, in order to rehydrate myself. I don't mind the water consumption but, being such an empty vessel, I feel it sloshing around uncomfortably inside me. I want to be empty, completely empty. Purged. Tabula rasa.

And now, here we are. At the end.
A different clinic, but not so far away. I was able to walk again, this time by the river, avoiding people as much as possible. I am here early for my late afternoon appointment as there's a lengthy check-in process and I'd like to see the sunset one last time.
I feel serene. Calm. Composed. The yoghurt pot is no longer a burden. I have forgiven myself in advance of my forthcoming rebirth. I do not wish to be concerned with material things any longer.

I am asked if I wish to phone anyone or have a last meal, but I am confused by the concept of the first option and disgusted by the latter. It raises a sudden fire in me, a frustration. Why would I want another meal, why would I wish to consume anything? Have they really not understood? But I calm myself quickly, reminding myself that the person asking is merely a nurse assisting the process. No doubt he hasn't read my file; he doesn't understand my reasons for being here.

I ask instead to have a few moments to finish writing my diary. There's no need to document my final moments or movements any longer, but I wish there to be an accurate record of why I am doing this. My last consultation with the doctor went well. She asked all her questions. I answered them, presumably to her satisfaction. I signed the consent forms, the insurance waivers, the legal rights of any potential beneficiaries to make a claim. You can choose, if you wish, for certain items to be stored for a length of time – I believe fifty, seventy or a hundred years are the options – depending on the age of the client. But, other than these written notes, I do not wish for anything of my existence to be kept. Why would I? The whole point is to burn my existence and the last forty-five years of its unnecessary gross consumption off the face of this Earth.

A year ago, when my application was provisionally accepted, I was asked to keep a detailed diary for the last six months to prove that I am of 'sound mind'. Apparently, a lot of people change their mind about the procedure as a result of noting their thoughts and actions in the months and weeks leading up to it. If it hadn't been for these rules, I would have done it ages ago, but I understand there's the risk of legal action from estranged relatives that the clinic itself needs to avoid, as well as ensuring there's an appropriate paper trail to satisfy the ethics board when you help people to end their life.

I check the electronic clock positioned high up on the wall. It is nearly time. Any minute now the last shipment that I was responsible for, before I left my job, will be coming into dock. At Harwich they'll be expecting it empty. Hundreds of vast containers that were loaded with the effluence of our consumption, returning for a refill, the contents having been dumped in Jenjarom and Klang for small children to pick through the rubbish-rubble mountains searching for something they can clean and sell, or take back to their family to use themselves. Plastic bags and yoghurt pots.

But the container ship won't be empty. I changed the instructions to logistics at the last moment. It will be full, full to bursting with the detritus of our lives. And then the containers will be delivered outside Parliament and dumped. It wasn't easy to arrange. It cost me. I re-mortgaged the house, but it will be worth it. There is an underworld of waste-management in much the same way there are drug-traffickers and an underground slave-trade. Just because it's under the surface doesn't mean it's not there. Where there's demand, there's always supply.

The doctor returns with my morphine injection. I didn't ask for it, but it's compulsory. Since euthanasia was legalized in this country, clients have been able to choose the method of dispatch, but pain control is still mandatory. There are several options for death. There was a menu. It came with the glossy acceptance pack that also contained advertising for coffins and funerals. I found the thick paged glossiness of the package unnecessary and distasteful. I recycled it as soon as I had chosen. For me there was no real option. I have to be consumed as I have consumed.

She has administered the injection and I'm left alone in the Peace Zone, as they call it. But I will not find peace until it's finally happening, until I am no longer a stain on this once-beautiful Earth. No longer able to defile it with my waste. As lightly as I have stepped these last few months, even that has been too much. I've felt it. It pains me. Even my breath is sordid, tainted, a further burden on the slagheap of humanity. In a few minutes she will return and take my notebook away, lock it in the storage box bearing my number for the minimum fifty years. No point keeping it longer than that. I expect the police will come looking, but they won't find anything in there. I've not tried to hide anything. It will be apparent very soon, and once the flame is lit, it will be too late. So what happens next? A sublime beautiful nothing. Utter emptiness and weightlessness. I can't wait to feel that for the first time in my life, even if the experience will be fractionally brief. I will soon be led to 'The Exit', as I overheard a nurse calling it earlier. The room in which my body, emptied of everything I have consumed, will itself be consumed. To the flames.

And then I will disappear. Into thin air.

The Whether Man
Teo Eve

Whether or not it was going to rain or cloud was entirely down to him. Cupping his hands like imagined judiciary scales swinging from the pendulum of his chest he weighed up the pros and cons. One hand was bucketed by rain and fell to his waist; the other swirled with sunshine and sent the first bouncing up to the sky. If only there was a way to get them to even out like a spirit level! But soon the phone would ring and he'd have to make up his mind. There were arguments to be made for both sides. Sun meant summer, meant long days on the beach, meant sunburn and skin cancer and drought. Rain meant a bountiful harvest, meant nature's beautiful music playing against the rooftop, meant flooding and frostbite and thunder.

What would the public want? At least there was a way to find out. Surely that would be the just thing. He wouldn't even have to send out poll cards and make arrangements in libraries and schools; he could just text the nation and get a solid 70% turnout in five minutes. He loved his job, but sometimes he even had to wonder whether he had too much power. To think he now had the chance to change the weather! Just five years ago, that would have seemed unimaginable. He didn't even understand the science behind it, though admittedly he never gave understanding a fair shot. Academic reports were never really his thing. He was just happy to press the buttons and rack up his cash, though – admittedly – he usually had more nuanced options than this. Sunshine or rain? He'd send out the text to everyone in England, then consult with The Party and decide whether to pass the motion. Then he'd press the button that had the most votes, the rest be damned.

The results came flooding in with a Biblical speed. They had always known it was going to be a slim margin, but no one could predict just how tight it would be. How could so many people wish for rain? It seemed entirely counterintuitive. Of course, he could just overturn the vote; after all, there was only a discrepancy of two or so per cent. Maybe some people had voted for rain by mistake; surely, a number were misinformed. In recent months, advertisements about the benefit of rain had reached fever-pitch; those in charge of the pro-sunshine movement seemed to have stopped trying. Why would they bother anyway, when the rain group blatantly ignored the budget without any consequence?

The Whether Man lay back in his chair, tapped his fingers against the desk. The phone would ring any second now. Surely there'd be outrage if he turned his back on the vote. It was only informative, but it would be bad form to go against his decision after already extending an olive branch to them. The people wanted rain. So, why not give them rain?

His hand hovered over the big red button. He could press it now, get it over and done with, just deliver rain and move on. But he should wait, would wait, for the call. Then at least he could air his concerns; if the people on the other end of the line told him to give the people sunshine, he could at least say he was following orders. But following orders from whom? Surely everyone saw him as the one in charge.

After all, giving people sunshine would not solve all their problems. The people - just over 50% of the just over 70% of those who could vote and did vote - were sick of sunshine. There had been sunshine for too long, the reign of sunshine was bound to come to an end. Once there was a time the same sorts of people loved the sunshine, when it never set on the British Empire, but now there was so little of it all, a slender ray passing over the island for a few measly hours a day, that they had developed a sort of resentment for it; a nostalgic hangover that reminded them the sun did not shine the way it used to. The same people said there was too much sunshine, and we had to worry about droughts and the limited amount of supplies our country could produce. They scoffed at the idea of trade deals; international travel would just speed up the accelerating sun.

Those who were pro-sunshine, who dreamt of Mediterranean beaches and exotic holidays, warned about the floods that would come with the rain, that rising sea levels would kill the crops at a faster pace. They cited their sacrosanct research, which in the rainers' religion was considered blasphemous. The sunshiners struck fear in the hearts of the people, told bitter lies to get their way.

It was too much, too complicated, too black and white and greyscale. Never before had he waited so desperately for the phone to ring. He picked it up, smooth and paperthin, and turned it over in his hands. He sighed. Soon he'd retire, and would no longer have to deal with this. He thought about stepping down, calling it quits right after bringing the rain and flying off himself to a sunnier place. Maybe Malta: English enough to be understood, Italian enough to feel like being somewhere else. The Arabic and African influence were but a hazy memory, an ancient overhang.

Yes, Malta would do the trick. A country small enough for every decision to be made by text. When the sun would rise, when it would set; maybe they could even get an instant consensus on how much rain there should be every day, how much cloud and how much thunder. There had to be balance somewhere, achievable in the distant country of cyberspace. Very soon, every decision would be made by algorithms, complicated apolitical formulae that would render democracy unnecessary. The Party just had to hold out until then. God, he couldn't wait. To be able to push the buttons without having to think!

Whose cruel joke was it anyway, to give him only two options today? Why couldn't they just stick to the regular schedule? Clearly some decisions were being taken he had not been made privy to. Serious steps were being taken by those up above, determined to assert The Party's sovereignty. Sovereignty - he always thought of it as an ugly, ancient word. What does it mean, to be sovereign to/of/in our own destinies, when humanity is no more than an interlacing web? One strand always shakes the other. If he were ever to set his thoughts to paper -

The phone rang. The metallic screen lit up. A bright green symbol of a phone - or, a 2D model of what phones used to look like before the word meant something different entirely, before its definition had changed forever and its original usage had not yet slipped from collective memory - took up the entire screen. He wondered when people would forget what this strange, curved symbol, a horseshoe bracket with two bricks bolted on to either end, had meant, when it would become an undecipherable hieroglyph which would still mean 'answer', though nobody would understand why.

He did not answer. He stared at the phone, tried to ignore the screech of the unbearable ringtone (government-issued; he had never figured out how to change it) until the last moment. He counted down the seconds. These things never lasted more than ten. Seven, eight, nine…

He picked up the phone.

'So?' The voice cackled on the other end of the line.

The Whether Man cleared his throat.

'What will it be? Rain or shine?'

'I decided to ask the people,' the Whether Man said, squinting in anticipation of the inevitable roar.

The voice on the other end sighed. The Whether Man could hear the voice's eyes rolling in his sockets. 'And what did they decide?'

To rain or shine. To be or not to be. There was no way they would ever know. Voting results had stopped being public knowledge decades ago. But he had been a supporter of democracy, once, in an idealistic youth he tried too hard to forget until it made a permanent imprint on his mind. There will always be one version of ourselves that will never forgive our actions.

'To rain,' he said, the words practically forcing themselves out of his gritted teeth.

'To rain,' the voice repeated. 'To rain.' It chuckled, then laughed, then burst into hysterics. The Whether Man couldn't figure out what was funny about it.

'Oh, Dave,' the voice said. 'You never fail to surprise me.'

The phone clicked and the voice was gone.

The Whether Man laid the phone on his desk slowly, his hand trembling. The room seemed bigger than it had before. He became minutely aware of the cold metal touch of the phone, the desk, the chair, the processed air flooding in through the ventilator.

Before he even touched the button, thunder started to roar. Zeus had been woken from his long slumber. Oceans of rain slammed onto the roof like a hail of bullets. The Whether Man ducked underneath his desk for cover, and listened for the first shard of ice to pierce the console above him and crunch the metal, the first inch of water to lap at his feet.

He shut his eyes, and counted to ten.

When the World Froze
Tina Sang

The following text is a transcript of interviews featured in the documentary "When the World Froze" originally aired April 22, 2025.

What was that line people used to say? "The only thing constant is change." That was *one* truth I used to live by – as people, I knew we had to continually adjust, adapt, and assimilate, if we wanted to be happy. But then, that changed too. No one noticed it at first. Clocks kept ticking, electricity kept running, planes didn't fall out of the sky – everything that was man-made, part of our society, kept on going, oblivious to what had occurred. It was everything natural that froze. People gawked at all the pigeons frozen in midair, like some crazy art installation. Rain droplets suspended across London. Rays of sunlight. Fog. Even falling leaves that didn't quite make it to the ground. It didn't affect us, not really. Except that half of the world was suddenly dark forever and the other half wasn't. We still went on keeping track of time, living our usual way. In the city, we didn't even notice the difference at first, because we were so far-removed from the natural world. Not much changed, at least not for us normal folks. Scientists were the only ones in a frenzy to figure out the cause of all of this. Everyone else was told to stay at home until further information was found. We sat in trepidation, feet-tapping, coffee-sipping as the days dragged on. When all the news reports finally came through, it was a flood of differing opinions. No one could agree with one another. It was almost reassuring, if not deeply troubling: there was debate, there was disagreement, and the world remained divided into factions – that much stayed the same.

Celeste Dong – University College London Student

The authorities in Oxford have spent countless hours discussing all the possibilities behind what is currently occurring. Theories include our solar system is approaching the event horizon of the black hole, and as a result, the orbital rotation is rapidly slowing. Or, the Sun's electromagnetic radiation is decelerating the general rate of growth of life on earth. At present, we lack any plausible theories. Our colleagues in Philosophy have attempted to derive some universal truth from what is happening. Perhaps as humans, we were always meant to evolve to a position of independence from nature. Personally, I think it's complete nonsense. But, believe what you will.

John Gulliver – Tutor of Physics at University of Oxford

Perpetually frozen at the twilight hour of 2a.m., in China people have built artificial sunrooms for waking hours. In Singapore, they have successfully created synthetic meat, lab-grown from cells and entirely non-reliant on nature. Certain places have become sought-after tourist destinations: Flight tickets to Europe and parts of Africa have now increased to an astounding ten-thousand pounds, thanks to its luck as the one time zone that remains standing in sunset...

Madeline Smith – BBC One Reporter

At the center of all the baffling occurrences that have befallen the human race is this persisting question: Why are we still unfrozen? Scientists have made the recent discovery that we aren't as untouched as we originally believed; we aren't aging. At first glance, it seemed like a good thing. Eternal youth is all we have ever dreamed of. However, the euphoria may be short-lived. We have been robbed the experience to grow up, settle down, and grow old. And if things stay the way they are, are we still maturing, without aging? Will we soon have a twenty-year-old inside a ten-year-old's body? Should all the age-laws still be respected, with regards to drinking, driving, and voting? This entire freeze hasn't only affected nature; the entire legal system has been thrown into utter chaos.

Peggy Winters – Lawyer

Ever wanted to live in paradise forever? Algeria has all you will ever need. Come take a glimpse at what promises to be the most beautiful sunset in the world, forever captured in time. You never need to worry about missing it! Come traverse the exotic Saharan Desert, sit on camels, swim with crocodiles, pet a cobra, all without any fear of danger! Algeria is a natural wonder, captured for your enjoyment. A full holiday package is now priced at 20,000,000 dinar, including unlimited food and drink, and a choice between sunset watching from our VIP beachfront, a hot air balloon trip, or atop the great endangered African elephant. Book fast, tickets are disappearing!

Omar Saidi – Tour Guide at Discover Algeria

In this difficult time, we send our prayers to everyone. It is a terrifying time, but the Christian community must stay stronger than ever before. We must aid each other, be kind and helpful to our brothers and sisters. It may seem as if God has abandoned us, exiling us from Eden. On the news, all the scientists are claiming Man must truly fend for himself. However, I believe this is Him giving us the golden opportunity to prove our love, once and for all. We have arrived at the Trials of Judgement, and if you have been good, you have nothing to worry about. Let us reassure one another and remind ourselves to stay true and just. God be with you all.

Michael White – Pastor at St. John's Church

Running out of natural resources, they used to complain. Well now, look at how plentiful everything is! We don't have to worry about deforestation any longer. Tear down the bamboo forests, I say! The pandas? Who cares about the frozen stuffed animals clinging to those poles? Put them in a museum or sell them as statues for all I care! In fact, that'd be a great product, wouldn't it: Buy an authentic frozen panda, best living room centerpiece ever. What happens when they wake up, you ask? Try *if*. We're in a new age now, darling, and we must move on from the past. All is not what it was before, and that means adaptation! That's what humans are best at, isn't it? Everyone needs to grow up and quit griping. So many new doors have been opened, and yet all you lot care about are the broken windows. Let's be realistic - we stopped caring about nature long ago. We stopped caring when we mass-produced plastics, when we burned fossil fuels. We don't really care about the consequences, as long as we reap the benefits.

Jeffrey Banks – CEO of Valdivian Inc.

The situation grows more dire by the day. Summer and sunset countries are becoming overpacked, to the point where countries like France, Switzerland, Sweden, Algeria, Libya, and Chad have invented a lottery system to admit people. The queues allegedly stretch five years into the future. These systems are not without corrupting, with many of the rich bribing the officials, which is creating a huge rich-poor divine, with the poor left stranded in places of perpetual darkness and winter. With garbage no longer decomposing, landfills cover a staggering 20% of the earth. Scientists are currently working on an ocean deposit system, where garbage will be buried deep in an excavated pit in the Pacific. It is uncertain whether we still live on a habitable Earth. With the natural climate and ecosystem unchanging, it seems hopeful we may be able to sustain ourselves for a remarkably long time. However, that does not mean there will not be dire consequences to face as well.

Madeline Smith – BBC One Reporter

As a scientist, I often turn to hard facts in my darkest hours. However, on this unprecedented occasion, I must fall back on my intuition. Perhaps it is not that we have risen above nature, but we have caused nature to abandon us. I imagine we have been exiled to in an insulated pocket of time to self-destruct, far away from everything else. We've railed against climate change for so long, taking our miniscule steps towards a more sustainable lifestyle. We have learned our lesson far too late: The goal is not to learn how to use nature, but to learn how to co-exist with it. Nature isn't simply there for us to exploit it. We are not gods, but merely insignificant organisms sharing a planet. Our world serves a larger function than providing mere resources for greedy human beings to devour. It appears we are too late. Ladies and gentlemen, welcome to Purgatory.

John Gulliver – Tutor of Physics at University of Oxford

Microbial
Claire Dalkin

Water laps against the hillside, barely visible through the haze. Even half-way up, residents have to build their dwellings on stilts. Since the floods, millions of homes have been lost. New wetlands form, new reefs; and the wildlife that comes with them causes the last humans to retreat into tight little urban pockets. They build vertically: stacks of flats, farms and offices, like heavenly in-trays for the Almighty.

Down on the promenade, which is now doing a good job as a seabed, ancient hire bikes float just above their tethering stations. All along the skywalks, in spite of the poor air quality, people are milling about, a moving mosaic of colourful robes and gas masks. At the edge of the crowd, head bowed, hood up, a woman makes her way. Dressed in earth brown, with gumboots, she looks like an autumn leaf amongst summer blooms.

Celeste takes the Sky-train to her 'office'. Apparently, the world once looked like a blue marble. She shakes her head. She remembers when her mother told her about how work was all sharp suits and stiletto heels that caused GBH to the wearer and she half-smiles, observing her muddy boots. Her mother also described sunbathing, beaches and breathing unaided. The Sky-train slides into the port, depositing Celeste upon a springy, sedum-cloaked platform, to face the unblinking eye of Security. Every day this causes such discomfort that she makes as little eye contact as possible, by allowing her gaze to shift diagonally to the floor. Every day Security forces her to wait, until she raises her head, no matter how briefly. Once admitted, she pads along the corridor to emerge into a vast, transparent dome.

Above the haze, sunlight hits glittering panes of tinted graphene. The Domes are stuffed with life: supported by vines, forests, meadows, pools and waterfalls. At the entrance, she removes her head dress and overcoat with its cumbersome oxygen mask. Next, her clothes are placed into a cleansing basket and a fine mist sprays over her, killing harmful pathogens, begetting good bacteria. Celeste closes her eyes against the soft spray, breathing deeply, thankfully, allowing billions of tiny lives to thrive on and in her bodily city, while the water soothes tiny welts and scratches on her skin.

You had ice cream and kitten heels, mum, but could you wear nothing at work and have no one bat an eyelid?

Now she is immersing herself in temperate rainforest. Other humans work in the Domes, but they keep mostly to themselves and Celeste can work for weeks without seeing anyone. Birds and small mammals whistle, chuckle and screech, snug in the greenery. Slivers of insects glisten around her, curious, hungry; some come for a sip of her blood, others, like the butterflies, come to drink the beads of sweat that form on her upper lip: forming a psychedelic, tickly moustache. She fills the hanging bird-feeders. A nightingale sings its thanks from the edge of a nearby bench and soon, bees are fussing around her while she prepares their energy snacks.

As she works, she sings, or hums along with them. The bees drink, buzz their approval and move on. She has just turned her attention to the seedlings when out of the corner of her eye she notices what appears to be a crow, thirty metres away. She turns sharply; no, it is a cyberpriest, hunkered dark and thrumming against the green, with various symbols etched in gold across its body. A high-pitched wail floats down through the air. She looks up at the platform by the Dome's entrance, where mourners, weeping, in multi-coloured fabrics, bear a shrouded body. Many of the cemeteries around the coast are now flooded, so other arrangements have to be made...

Slowly, the platform is lowered towards the earth where the 'priest' hovers at the head of a long, shallow bamboo box. This is piled high with sticks. The relatives sing as the deceased is lifted onto the pile, a few words are spoken while foliage and dark grains are scattered over the body, layer upon layer until it is covered. The singing dies away and the mourners stand in silence, holding one another. Five minutes more and they are rising back up to the Dome entrance. Celeste turns back to her work, but her brow is furrowed. She does not watch as gardeners arrive to pour fast-acting fertiliser over the mound and starts when something lightly touches her arm. It is the cyberpriest.

'Celeste?' it buzzes, gently. She nods, eyes widening.

'Do not be afraid,' it intones. 'You are an invaluable resource, and now you can always be with us.'

The bot turns towards the mound. 'When is it you retire?'

Celeste is trembling violently, but she manages to whisper, 'Friday.'

'I will collect you,' says the cyberpriest, 'and you may bring a companion to comfort you in your last hour.'

It rises and accelerates away. 'Enjoy your last days, dear Celeste!'

She feels her legs give way. Two other gardeners have been watching and they make their way over to her, gently helping her up. One of them hands her a hot drink.

'I don't need to *retire*,' she splutters. 'I'm not sick, I'm strong; I work hard!'

The workers nod sympathetically, but neither of them can be more than eighteen.

'There just aren't enough jobs, or places to live any more', says one, apologetically.

'You're amazing,' she adds. 'None of this would have happened without you."

'Yeah,' says the other. 'You've worked so hard to help build this place and you never complained about anything. We learned everything from you.'

Celeste manages a small, tight smile.

'We'll always remember you,' he adds, patting her arm

awkwardly. They back slowly away.

As the humans retreat, fear and grief advance. Celeste misses her mother every day and the feeling is still raw. The world she lives in now is one where old friends have disappeared, or moved hundreds of miles because of the new safety rules. It was her mother who helped her navigate life, kept her safe when she could not manage to look after herself. It was only once the Domes had accepted her that she found her place. Celeste lives for nature, revels in it, believing these animals and insects to be her true family, her tribe.

But now......

Who will save me?

The bees?

The birds?

She looks down; her cup is empty.

Outside, the mist turns to rain, clearing some of the yellowing smog from the lower slopes and the sea swells thick and dark. The humans clock off work for the day and head for their shelters. Celeste stands motionless beneath the green canopy, picturing her body petrifying into stone; the solid image helps to slow her heart.

Perhaps I'll stop now.

She moves deeper into the foliage and, leaning into thick creepers, closes her eyes. Mosquitos head in for their evening meal and, although the bites are uncomfortable, Celeste smiles.

I'm still useful.

Apart from her own bed, Celeste has never stayed anywhere overnight. Her heart thumps joyfully in the darkness, as sky turns to cloud, turns to stars, turns to cloud... The moon peeps through and sends split beams through the Dome. One lights up Celeste's left foot and she gasps as though someone has touched her.

The following morning, Celeste is back at work, checking her vegetables, feeding her bees, chattering to the birds. The weather is changing outside: the winds are rising, while deepening banks of cloud sail, ever faster over the Domes. Soon, rain hurls itself, as though enraged against the panes. She looks over to the forest area and misty waterfalls but sees no-one. Not even a shadow is moving. For the first time in many years, she feels lonely, but then, a hospitality bot leads two new recruits past her plot and she can see that they are no more than eighteen. Shining eyes and glowing limbs momentarily turn her way. She grimaces.

Saplings. Enjoy the next forty years.

It is her penultimate day at work. As she clocks off, for the first time ever Celeste slowly raises her chin to stare hard into the onyx eye of Security, waiting for something - a word of thanks, or explanation maybe. It remains silent and then, to her astonishment, lowers its gaze diagonally to the floor. Celeste feels her mouth stretch itself into a smile.

Well, I'll be off then.

Watching her city through the Sky-train windows, as it hurtles her through various levels of living quarters, she racks her brain for options.

I just won't go back. I'll lock myself in. I'll get up extra early tomorrow and move on. No - it's my apartment, I can stay there, I just won't go in anymore - I've got some savings...

The Sky-train is slowing down for her stop; second from lowest level, where her block looms, grey and dead-eyed. If buildings could be psychopathic, this would be one of them.

Celeste and her mother once lived together here, in an optimistically labelled 'garden flat'. This means a drab bedsit with enough room for a bunk bed, one cooking ring and a fridge big enough to put a jar of pickle in. The bathroom is shared with ten other inhabitants and is rarely clean, the electricity is equally dirty, flickering constantly, and the one window looks out onto a mouldy yard, housing one dead tree. The tenements here are tightly packed, so sunlight is rationed. On bad days, killer smog steals into the space just outside her window, when it remains tightly shut. Beneath the bunk bed, an oxygen cylinder lies in the shadows, just in case.

From the top mattress, Celeste looks at her life and wonders how she might spend retirement.

I'll try out new recipes. I'll listen to music. I'll read a book. I'll grow an indoor garden. I'll-

Every ten minutes a train rattles above, causing the room to shudder. Her phone never has any signal here and she struggles to read much of her mail, while the outside world passes her by. The block has been designed so that people rarely see each other, just muddy footprints that appear here and there, or a new stain on the lino in the hallway.

I can run away. Go travelling…

She laughs out loud. She had been inseparable from her mother; her only living relative and close friend. The people who run away are fugitives, or thirty years her junior; itinerants following work. The streets and hills are humming with drones, pursuing anyone who leaves their natural daily course. She has never really thought about the future; her retirement plan was left to her mother, and Celeste never had the confidence or foresight to ever ask what it was. Since her mother's death, she spends longer and longer at work each day, submerging her loss in the abundant life around her.

Celeste sits up. It is past midnight but the trains are still running. Pulling on her overcoat, mask, and boots, she runs from the building and doesn't look back.

The Sky-train takes her above the gloom to an indigo firmament, draped in swathes of stars, with the moon shining its spotlight on her as she pulls up to the Domes platform. She flings off her coat and kicks off the boots. Running along the corridor, Celeste drops her mask onto the sedum floor to stand tall before Security; the computer blinks its eye once, opens the doors and as the moonbeam follows her down into her domain, she feels like a queen.

All her birds and bees are asleep.

Celeste drinks from a flask of water and pours the remainder over a patch of loam. Next, she buries her hands within the mud and begins to smear it over her body, washing her hands as though with soap, rubbing it in her hair, everywhere she can reach, using her toes to wiggle her feet firmly into the earth.

Now I'm home.

Tall and wide as the mountain in her imagination, she waits for morning.

Sunrise. Celeste walks. She breathes in the perfumes of nearby flowers, brushes against long, feathery meadow grasses, strokes the furry backs of bumble bees and once, a velvet pipistrelle bat that has fallen asleep before it has reached its roost. Its little heart quickens at her touch and she moves away. Reaching the waterfall Celeste stands beneath and feels shriven as the water pummels the mud away. Her hair is matted but she doesn't care.

She has a sudden desire to wear something as colourful as the blooms around her, knowing her mother would have approved. Slowly, she wanders back towards her plot, where the birdsong seems to be the loudest. It is too early for the first shift, but she picks up her watering can to drench the sunflowers. The slightest of breezes alerts her to the approaching cyberpriest.

'Good morning, dear Celeste! Are you ready?'

She nods and wordlessly follows the small, shining orb through the grasses and flowerbeds to the lift, where they rise up to the higher platform.

'There will be company, unless you really wish to be alone,' says the priest.

They are in front of a metal door.

Celeste tries to calm her thudding heart as the door slides open.

'If you would like a sedative…' begins the bot but she shakes her head and steps through.

The room is bathed in soft, warm light, as though the sun is setting. Three multi-coloured forms float before her.

'Celeste!' they speak as one. 'We are here to help you transition. There is no pain; only love.'

Before she has time to say anything, they are encircling her with flower-bright gauze, the priest is thanking her for her selfless work and repeats that she will always be part of life in the Domes. He gestures to a tiny wafer and vial on a tray.

'Eat and drink of these, in order to become one with the body of the Domes.'

The last physical sensation of Celeste is a taste of dark cherries.

The figures flow around her, moving faster and faster until she and they become a rainbow blur.

As the room disappears, Celeste knows her feet have left the floor. She seems to be growing, spreading, dispersing. From far off, a crowd is cheering, clapping in the distance and she hears the priest.

'…to mark the passing of a selfless woman, who served the planet in life and death. All creatures and bacteria rejoice, for through her other worlds are born….'

As all around her fades, she senses, rather than sees her mother.

If you ever visit the Domes, or work there, you will meet Celeste. She is in the air, in the plants, in the tiny worms as they forge their way through the warm earth. She will look at you through the eyes of birds, she will call from their throats and dance through the waterfall as you pass by; she shivers with delight through the flowers and just listen to the bees, they are humming along with Celeste as she sings.

History Lesson
Paul K Joyce

'Good morning, Year Two. Okay everyone; sit up straight and pay attention, please. You can turn on your screens now. Main app. Can you see the module? Swaraa, you know perfectly well why there aren't enough screens to go round. Just make sure you can see. Module One, please. The one at the top. History. What was that, Joseph? Yes, it's history today. Now, there's no need to make that face. We can learn a lot from the past. Yes, Helen? We'll do butterflies another time. Isobel Jones, are you chewing something? Teresa Czechowski—sit down, please.

If you can all look this way. Ignore that sound, they're just testing the system in case of a rise. Don't worry, I'll tell you if it's the real thing. No, Alesha, of course that won't happen. It is June after all. Where did you hear that? Well, maybe they just made a mistake. I'm not sure that feed is reliable. Yes, we all want it to stop raining. No, I don't know exactly how many weeks. Maybe six, maybe seven. Yes, Jamal. It's very good for the trees. And the grass. Thank you, Amanda.

Alright everyone. If I can have your attention. I don't want to have to raise my voice. We're looking at Module One. History. We'll start with the title. It's made up of two words. Who can tell me what the first word means? Yes, Mohamed? No, not quite. Break it down into smaller pieces. Amy—good. It does sound like *climb*. And the second part? Yes, Antoine—ate. That's right, but it's not about food. You can tell me what you had for breakfast later. Can anyone put the two pieces together? Very good. Climate. Can we say it together? Excellent. What lovely voices you all have. Rafic, what does the word mean to you? Did you hear that, class? Stand up, Rafic. I can hear whispering at the back. Stacey and Iris, we're listening to Rafic. Thank you. He said climate happens in the sea and in the sky. Can you think about that for a moment? That's right. It's about the weather. What was that, Andrea? I can't hear you. Stacey and Iris. I won't tell you again. If you want to say something, put your hand up like the others; and I'm Miss Phillips—please don't use my first name. Thank you, Andrea. Well, the word is warming, not warning, but well done anyway.

Climate. It means we're talking about something that is very important and affects all our lives. Yes, Alana, that includes Barney. Pets are very much part of our lives. Declan, I'm sorry your puppy has a sore paw. Okay. So, we know the first word is climate. And the second word? *Ch* is for chief, yes. But this is a different word. Someone other than Mohamed. Nearly. You're thinking of what you need for your car. It's very similar to charge. Change. Put the two words together and we have...? Exactly. Class, that's very good. Settle down now. So what do we know about Climate Change? Natalya? When things got hot. Good. But what else? The rains. Yes. We're used to them now, but there was a time not so long ago when there was more land in this country. Before you were born. Before the floods.

Who can tell me what it was like before? That's correct. We didn't need boats to get around. The river wasn't so wide. What else? There was more chocolate? I'm sure that's right, Ian, but it's not quite what I was after. The main thing, children, is that many people who lived here in London had to leave and move to other parts of the country. It's alright Jacob; speak up so we can all hear you. Your aunty used to live in Stratford? I'm sorry to hear that. That's Olympic Lake, now. Why? Because the Olympic Games were held there in 2012. No, not on the water. There used to be houses and a big stadium there before the flood. Yes, they're all still there under the water. It's great that your daddy lets you steer the boat. No, Mia. Hammersmith wasn't always an island. Maybe one day it will look like the photos again. All right now, class. Keep it down, please. If you all talk at once, then no one is heard. Mia is saying something really interesting. Don't worry, Olivia, the boat won't go back without you. Carry on, Mia. Yes, but the word is overwhelmed. I'm sure your mummy is right. It's just that when they built the Thames Barrier, no one expected anything that big.

So, who can tell me what the big events were that changed everything? No, not Star Wars, Daniel. We're talking about Climate Change. What other really important thing happened? Yes, the storms of 2025. Well done. Ibrahim is saying that there were fires as well, during the summer. Like the title of our module, we had to change. It's alright, Ian. Don't cry. We're all here, aren't we? Doing our best? That's a good boy. Here, dry your eyes and give your nose a good blow.

So, what do we learn from history? That's right, Mustapha. It tells us what we should do now. And what *do* we do now? How do we help stop Climate Change? How do we make a better world and help the environment? Anyone?

Yes, Felicity. That's one way. We are nearly all electric, anyway.

Don't waste anything. An excellent point.

Repair things that are broken.

Put on another layer of clothes. We need to conserve energy, don't we?

That's a good point, but not everyone can afford a wind turbine.

Simon says that his mums would like to go somewhere warm for the holidays—somewhere where it isn't raining. But what does that take? What do we need to power aeroplanes and boats? That's right. Petrol and oil.

Who knows what a fossil fuel is? Don't laugh, class. No, Valerie, it's not made with dinosaur bones. Fossil fuels are brought up from below the ground and it's burning them that's bad for the environment. So what else can we do to help?

Yes, very good, Ishmael. It is better if we use our bicycles, and try to walk to more places. And is what we eat important, children? Yes, that's right. We did used to eat a lot more meat, and moving to plant-based foods has helped combat Climate Change. We'll be learning about nutrition next week.

Well done, Year Two. I think we've covered most of the major points. Now, before first break, shall we sing our song? It's the one where we do the actions. Here's the first note.

Row, row, row your boat
Gently down the stream
Merrily, merrily, merrily, merrily
Life is but a dream

Row, row—

Hold on a moment. Yes, Matteo. That is the warning sound. Children, we should head to the boats just in case. Quick as you can.

Don't forget your coats.'

What's in a Name?
Craig Smith

*In memory of Stokely Carmichael (Kwame Ture), Medgar Evers,
and Emmett Till.*

Stokely stood in front of his old house. Or rather, what was
left of it. He was nineteen years old when it was ripped from
its concrete pilings and disappeared into the rank waters of the
bayou, along with his family. That was eight years ago. He now
lived in a sacrificial trailer home, made from reclaimed materials,
which sat on the house's old concrete footings. Stokely lived in
Morris Park, a predominantly Black neighbourhood, which lay 25
miles southwest of the rich elite who resided within New Orleans
city limits. The city was protected by a colossal government
levee scheme, while he was left to face the brunt of numerous
destructive hurricanes, flash flooding, and severe winter storms,
with little to no protection.

A bright smile lit up Stokely's face as his friend, Medgar,
drove up in his battered fuel cell truck. They were both second-
year dropouts from an unscrupulous football scholarship at
Lafayette University and had remained inseparably close friends
ever since. Unlike Stokely, who was a native of the Seventh Ward,
Medgar was originally from Decatur, Mississippi. He was a well-
built man, covered in silver tattoos, which were slowly becoming
camouflaged against his own dark brown skin. People often
commented that they looked like brothers.

'You finally got the old girl running then,' Stokely said, as he
opened the passenger door and climbed in. The truck had been
giving Medgar some problems, which was no surprise given its age
and condition.

'Hey, there isn't nothin' I can't get started. You know that.'
Medgar patted the side of the rusty door, lovingly. 'Unlike you,
who couldn't even start a fight.' His deep, contrabass laugh

boomed around the cab.

'So, what was wrong with her?' Stokely asked.

Medgar rolled his eyes. 'The fuel cell membranes were shot. All the platinum had clumped together like ships in the doldrums.'

'Sounds expensive. Where did you get the money to replace them?'

Medgar smiled knowingly. 'Let's just say that I found a donor vehicle and leave it at that.'

Stokely shook his head in despair. 'You're a bad man, Medgar.'

'Jus' put the radio on and keep your thoughts to yourself. My clandestine activities get your sorry ass to work every day, right?'

Stokely could not deny that. Like most people who lived in Morris Park, he was not able to afford a vehicle himself. They both shared the cost of the hydrogen fuel, which was not getting any cheaper. Energy prices were continuing to skyrocket against a backdrop of diminishing raw materials, heatwaves, and hurricanes.

'Do you think we'll be able to work today?' Stokely frowned, as he looked out at the steaming swamp. He was already sweating profusely, and it was only 6.30a.m.

Medgar looked concerned. 'We betta. I can't afford to keep hidin' out in a public coolin' shelter.'

The southern states now faced the longest number of days where working outside was impossible. In Louisiana, they both sacrificed nearly $9,000 in wages each year because of lost work time. Frighteningly, this figure was growing every year as global temperatures continued to climb.

'We should migrate, like them nomadic rich folks, and live in the New North,' Stokely said with a grin.

'Yeah, get a big boat house on Lake Superior. Put your feet up and enjoy Armageddon.' Medgar laughed. 'Like that's ever goin' to happen.'

The Great Lakes were still desirable habitats, despite getting warmer, wetter, and wilder. The eight states that border them had aggressively closed their state lines to climate refugees years ago.

Now only the rich and famous could afford a State Transit Visa, to roam around the country as they wished.

Stokely and Medgar were part of the 'Trapped Black Populations', referring to people who were trapped in environmentally high-risk areas due to economic restraints. They thought this was a travesty, as their people were already burdened by poverty and oppression due to the colour of their skin. They now had to suffer the harsh consequences of climate change when they had contributed the least to its decline.

'Where are we going today?' Stokely asked, as he curled his nose up at the unpleasant smell of bacteria, which emanated from the foul waters hugging the dirt track road.

'They said on the radio that there's day-work out at Laplace. The government is strippin' out the old solar arrays.' Medgar sighed. 'Yes, I know it's lousy work, but I couldn't find anythin' else.'

'Did I say a word? I love separating glass and aluminium in a heatwave,' Stokely said, sarcastically.

'Hey, don't knock it. Ducks have been reported in that area. We could get lucky and shoot dinner while we're workin',' Medgar said optimistically.

Stokely shook his head. 'I don't believe that. There have been no shorebirds around for years. Plus, I'm not eating anything that can't walk or hold its head up.' He had not seen any healthy birds for as long as he could remember. They were all full of botulism toxins since the wetlands had warmed and stagnated.

'You've always been too fussy.' Medgar laughed. 'You get that little bird roasted nicely and you'll never know the difference.'

'Maybe not with your iron gut, Med, but I'm not chancing it.'

They both sang along to a Chuck Berry classic on the radio as they cruised into Laplace. The road into town was flanked with piles of crumbling rubble, which had been used to try and abate the contaminated floodwaters. Despite the town's best efforts, the surrounding river basin had eventually filled up and drowned out most of the local inhabitants. But there are always some brave souls who refuse to be moved on; not that the government provided much in the way of climate relocation funding anymore.

Medgar slowed the truck down to a roll. 'Do you see how high the water level is behind that barrier?'

Stokely whistled to himself. 'Yeah, this town won't survive another storm season. It's history, man.'

The downtown area was a ghostly line of empty stores, deserted sidewalks, a struggling diner, and a few abandoned warehouses. The only shop that looked open was a water store.

'Hey, how many water vouchers do you have with you?' Medgar asked as he looked around the cab for his 5-gallon plastic container.

Stokely fished around in his skinny wallet. 'Five gallons worth. How about you?'

'I've got a five-gallon voucher left too. I gave the rest to my sister for the kids.' Medgar flipped down his sun visor and retrieved it.

Rationing was now a permanent situation. Without a voucher, no one would risk a custodial sentence to sell you treated water. They pulled up in front of UNCLE JO'S H2O. It looked like something from an apocalypse movie.

Medgar passed his friend the battered container. 'Fill us up. Here's the money.'

Stokely jumped out of the truck and rang the shop's buzzer. The windows were heavily fortified with steel-plate and warning signs, designed to deter anyone stupid enough to try and rob it. You were likely to be facing the muzzle of an Uzi submachine gun, bolted under the serving counter, as water was now more precious than gold to the severely dehydrated.

After ten minutes Stokely climbed back into the truck, shaking his head. 'You were short, Med. It was $16.00 for five gallons of 3-Star.'

'For 3-Star quality water? No way!' Medgar exclaimed. 'That's way too expensive.'

Stokely nodded in agreement. 'That's what I told him.'

'What did he say?'

'He said that everything's expensive. It's expensive to build a water re-use facility, and it's expensive to protect it from people like us.' Stokely cringed as Medgar's shovel-like hands quickly formed into tightly clenched fists. He was not known for his patience when it came to racial abuse.

'Easy tiger!' said Stokely. 'He's just some sun crazed local with a grudge.'

Medgar curled his lip. 'The more we keep turning the other cheek, the more these fools seem to keep pushing their luck.'

'Hey, it isn't worth doin' time for, Med.'

Medgar looked him in the eye. 'I remember a time when it didn't take much to ruffle your fur. Like that kid in the diner who you found havin' sugar rubbed in his eyes and ketchup smeared around his head.'

Stokely smiled thinly. 'I was just exercising my self-defence skills in the aid of a minor.'

Medgar's booming laugh resonated around the cab. 'Is that a gentle euphemism for hospitalizing three white bigots who deserved it?'

'Just drive the truck, smartass.' Stokely reached in the glovebox for a water test kit.

'If that test comes up positive, I'm goin' back for that Cajun conman,' Medgar rumbled.

3-Star was supposedly sourced from rain and pond water, which was then sediment filtered and sterilized with ultraviolet light. It was a far better option than 4-Star, which carried no safety guarantees at all. 1-Star was now reserved for society's elite and could only be found in wealthy neighbourhood stores.

Stokely dripped a sample of the water into a plastic vial, replaced the cap, and shook it vigorously. After 20 seconds it turned purple; a negative result for coliform bacteria. This was the only test they could afford. Unfortunately, it did not provide a result for all the other nasties that might be present. The poor had to take their chances drinking water that contained chemicals, metals, and radiological contaminants.

Medgar glanced down at the purple vial. 'He's one lucky swamp rat, that's for sure.'

As they drove towards the defunct solar farm, the wetlands looked like a tattered remnant of what they used to be. Hampered by levees, the strangled rivers had reduced the amount of sediment, nutrients, and freshwater that washed into the marshes, causing a sharp increase in salinity as the oceans continued to rise. This led to vastly fewer fish and shellfish, which in turn decimated commercial and recreational fishing.

They both stared silently at a pile of derelict crab traps, lying next to a sun-bleached pelican skull at the side of the road. Like humanity, they would soon lose their identity as their physical forms slowly eroded into the drowning landscape.

'Do you remember when they used to harvest blue crabs year-round?' Stokely had a slight longing in his voice.

'Do I ever. Sittin' in the Blue Crab Café with some salt crackers, a cold beer, and half a dozen fresh Jimmies in a newspaper. That was the life,' Medgar lamented. 'I even carried my own one-piece knife for peelin' 'em, remember?'

'Yeah, now all you can get is a fried worm po-boy, sold to you as an upmarket, delicious sandwich. Who cares if it's high-quality protein when it tastes like insects,' Stokely replied.

Medgar glanced at him through the corner of his eye. 'Hey, we were all too selfish to forgo immediate pleasures for what we considered distant benefits. Now we're in the outer circle of Hell, it's easy to forget that we're all responsible for how we're livin'.'

'So, what would you do differently if you could go back in time?' Stokely asked.

'I'd go to the Blue Crab and order two dozen crabs, a keg of beer, and a large bathtub of iced spring water on the side.' Medgar laughed his deep, hearty laugh. 'Hey, I'm only human.'

Stokely shook his head. 'That's never been a good excuse, and you know it.'

'What about you?' Medgar asked.

Stokely suddenly had a look of self-determination on his face. 'I'd start an all-Black revolutionary party. Finally taste the political and economic power that we never experienced growing up.'

'Admirable.' Medgar nodded and pushed out his bottom lip. 'Would it have an ideology of nonviolence?'

Stokely laughed. 'That all depends on how we're received. I'd teach self-defence and firearms training to all our community. Stop the beatings and murders I witnessed as a child.'

Medgar was not so sure. 'Sounds like a great world, Stoke. I'm sure that racial healin' will follow their sincere contrition, right up to the point where you are gunned down by trigger happy U.S. Marshals.'

'So, what would you suggest?'

Medgar shrugged. 'With hindsight, I think it would be better to burn all the flags and emblems from that old world and start to think of ourselves as just one race: *humanity*. It's too late for social and political reform. What does colour have to do with anythin' when we're all bound for Hell?'

There was no speculation about global warming being a reality anymore. The bitter evidence was waiting outside your front door every day. Earth was rapidly becoming unliveable for everyone, irrespective of race, colour, or wealth.

The sight of a long line of dishevelled workers, dressed in dirty jeans and ragged T-shirts, silenced their debate. It looked like a summer queue for the hottest attraction at a theme park, slowly snaking its way along the water's edge. Stokely's heart sank.

'This is looking bad, Med. Some of these people could have been waiting since 4a.m. We'll never get picked.'

'Don't be so sure. The government doesn't care about first

come, first served. They're just lookin' for strong backs.' Like all manual workers, Medgar had himself been prey for the so-called recruiters who managed work sites, seeking dubious fees and kickbacks from the desperate souls who waited to earn a day's pay.

They cruised up to the front of the line and found a spot to park the truck. An officious-looking man in a Hi-Viz waistcoat, carrying a clipboard, was reviewing the potential workforce. He acted like he was judging a 1970s beauty pageant, carefully looking the hopeful contestants up and down with a critical eye. He didn't appear to be very happy with the specimens that he had to choose from.

Medgar and Stokely walked confidently towards him. 'Excuse me, sir,' Medgar said respectfully. 'We were sent here by the Temporary Agricultural Workers Agency in Baton Rouge. I was told to ask for Mr. Tomball.'

The government official looked confused. 'I don't know a Mr. Tomball. What division is he with?'

'That I don't know, sir. We were both solar farm installers before we started to work for the agency. They said that we should drop our existing contract and come over here today. Mr. Tomball is supposed to provide us with day permits to work.'

The official looked them both up and down and smiled. They were by far the best physical specimens he had seen that morning. 'Well, I'm sure he will be along later. The day rate is $7.50 per hour. Go along and get signed in.'

Medgar nodded and smiled, ignoring the torrent of abuse that came from the other men standing in line.

'Mr. Tomball?' Stokely whispered as they walked through the armed security gate. 'Where did you drag that name up from?'

Medgar shrugged his heavy shoulders. 'It's a small town outside Houston that just came to me.'

'Someday we'll be those stick-thin, infirm deadbeats that don't get picked. You know that, right?' Stokely was racked with a strong sense of guilt.

Medgar smiled. 'That's right, so just be glad that it's not today.'

The site foreman provided them with the proper permits and explained their task. He was a brute of a man, called Mo, who looked like he had felt the burden of hard physical work every day of his life. His T-shirt slogan said it all: *a mullet isn't a hairstyle, it's a way of life.*

'Take down the wind deflectors first, then the mounts, then wiring and any other metals, and place them in the skips provided. Panels need to be stacked at around 20-per-pallet. You got that?'

Medgar and Stokely nodded their agreement.

'You better watch out for gators. I know these waters are too briny for them these days, but you never know, the noise might attract a rogue female.'

'Do we get to keep it if we kill it?' Medgar asked, thinking of his stomach.

'I'll take half a tail and a rack of ribs. You can keep the rest.' The foreman laughed, as he wiped the sweat from the back of his neck with a soiled handkerchief. 'It's been years since I had any swamp chicken. Perfection with a citrus marinade.'

Global warming ensured that all new gator hatchlings were female. This provided an effective extinction of the species. The wetlands and the Cajun locals suffered greatly from their absence.

Mo made them sign for a battered toolbox, which was attached to an old crab trap float, just in case it fell off the duckboards into the murky waters. Any loss of tools was deducted from your pay. They were each issued with a pair of nearly worn through glazing gloves and half a gallon of water. The water was fine to clean your hands and body with, but the tell-tale brownish tinge made it look unappetizing for drinking.

They trudged onto the floating platforms and started their day's toil in the endless sweltering heat. Their only desire was to stay as cool as possible as they humped the redundant equipment into the recycling skips at a steady pace. After a back-breaking morning, the lunchtime whistle blew, and they wandered back to the truck for lunch.

'How you are you holding up, Med?' Stokely was exhausted. His mouth, lips, and eyes felt dry, despite the sweat dripping from his body.

'Better than you, by the looks of it.' Medgar handed him the water from the cooler. Not that it was much of a cooler without ice. They had already consumed over a gallon and a half of water between them, which did not feel like enough.

'Thanks, man.' Stokely swallowed down the lukewarm fluid, while the fan in the truck bathed him in warm air.

'Is that any better?' Medgar asked.

'I'll be fine. I just feel a bit lightheaded, that's all.'

Medgar raised an eyebrow in concern. 'How does it feel to be working on the water again after all these years?'

Stokely shrugged. 'I still feel like one of my family will lurch up from the depths at any moment. But I'll probably feel like that forever.'

Medgar nodded in sympathy. 'You did all you could. It's a miracle that you survived that storm.'

Stokely had witnessed his family drown when hurricane Valarie made landfall. He was finally rescued from a rooftop by a Navy helicopter and taken to the New Orleans Superdome, which became a last-minute shelter space. Despite knowing their fate, he spent every waking hour scouring the message boards that were filled with photos and notices from people looking for lost family. The scene was madness. Reports of rape, looting, and gun violence were rife as food and safe water were exhausted in the disaster zone. Stokely's life would be forever shaded by the tragedy.

'What scares me, Med, is that they are forecasting the likelihood of another category 5 this season.'

Medgar gulped down some water. 'It's inevitable if the Gulf continues to boil. How we'll live through that level of devastation again, I don't know.'

Stokely agreed. The prediction of storms was no mystery anymore. 'I heard some scientist on the radio talking about sending up an enormous sail into space to act as a sunscreen. It sounded ambitious, but probably the sanest option they've considered.'

Medgar let out a deep, scornful laugh. 'My belief in human ingenuity is not in doubt. But the scientist's ability to restrain themselves is. If we're not careful, we'll accelerate our own demise.'

They both unpacked their French bread po-boys in silence. The finger rolls were filled with roasted crickets, which were a regular favourite. But when people will shove just about anything that moves into their mouths, this was no recommendation. They both instinctively closed their eyes before they ate.

'The legs are weird. I never get used to them.' Stokely cringed as he chewed.

Medgar nodded in agreement. 'The free-range ones are definitely tastier. Farmed always carry a strange aftertaste.'

'These are supposed to be tomato and oregano flavoured,' Stokely added.

'I don't taste that. In fact, they don't taste of much at all. We should've gone for the chili buffalo worms.' Medgar would eat anything except pinkies; small pupae harvested from green bottle flies. He regularly joked that he would eat people before maggots. Stokely was in full agreement. He did not believe the marketing messages that said they were, 'rather tasty'.

The end of lunchtime whistle shrilled through the buzzing marshes. They finished their meal and sprayed themselves liberally with jungle strength mosquito repellent, before wandering back to start their afternoon of toil. The thermometer in the truck read 42°C, with a relative humidity reading of 75.0%. Just being outside felt like a physical burden.

Mo came and found them at 2.30p.m., as they had decided to close the site for the day. Most of the workers were reporting symptoms of heat-related illness as the temperatures continued to soar above the thresholds considered safe for heavy labour. They were both given an option to return the following day, which they readily accepted. Their pay came to a meagre $35.50 each, after union deductions.

As they drove back towards Morris Park, Stokely and Medgar enjoyed the sensation of the hot wind blowing through the truck's open windows. Anything was preferable to the stifling stillness of the marshes. They decided to stop at Fast Eddies to cool down. The small-town bar had been open for almost a century and had become a popular destination for the underprivileged. The menu was very cheap, and the Cajun décor inspired an 'old Louisiana' atmosphere. More importantly, the bar was blessed with fully functioning air conditioning.

As they parked up, Medgar was not surprised to find the carpark already half full. Like them, most labour gangs would have been sent home by now.

'I'm buying,' said Stokely with a smile.

'I'm not arguin' with that.' Medgar grabbed a couple of cleanish 'Ragin' Cajuns' college football shirts from behind his seat and threw one over to Stokely. 'You better put this on. You know how upset Fast Eddie Senior gets about people being bare-chested.'

They pulled the shirts over their sweating bodies and wandered into the cool confines of the shaded bar. The crowd was the normal mix of labourers and some out-of-place Ph.D. students from Lafayette University. Everyone was happy not to feel like they were melting. Stokely and Medgar soaked up the ambiance of the room, singing along to a vintage classic on the jukebox while they waited to get served. After a few minutes, an attractive waitress with a dark brown complexion and a room-grabbing smile approached them.

'Hi, guys. What's your poison?'

Stokely smiled broadly. 'Good afternoon, ma'am. I'll take two Old Squares. Thank you.'

'Two Old Squares comin' up.'

The cocktail was a classic from the French Quarter of New Orleans. The alcohol was subtly swapped with a synthetic alternative, called Alcosynth, since global warming made the raw materials to make beer and spirits impractical to source. Alcosynth was a derivative of a chemical that was used to treat anxiety disorders. It was an effective catalyst for conviviality, but everyone still desperately missed old-school ethanol.

The waitress returned, pausing only to drop a couple of reusable chill cubes from the fridge into their drinks. 'There you go, guys. Enjoy.'

Stokely paid what felt like a ransom for the cocktails.

'Thanks, Stoke.' Medgar stared down at the grey, granite cubes in his tumbler. 'I miss ice cubes.'

'I miss fridges, Med. I'm using a clay pot like the Egyptians.'

Medgar laughed. 'You're lucky to have anything to chill. My sister keeps tellin' me not to come home hungry.'

'How are they doing since Emmett died?' Stokely asked.

'She's tryin' her best, but I find her cryin' when the kids are in bed.'

Stokely shook his head in sympathy. 'Do the police have any idea who killed him yet?' Emmett's beaten body had washed up on the banks of the Mississippi River near Caernarvon. He had been shot in the head and wrapped up with an old metal fan to weigh him down.

'Several people came forward and accused a white shopkeeper. They said Emmett was talkin' to his wife when he made a delivery drop. Her husband got all jealous and threatened him with a gun. The sheriff's office doesn't seem to be tryin' too hard to follow it up.' Medgar took a sip of his drink. 'What do you expect when it's a Black man, shot by a white businessman inside city limits?'

Stokely gritted his teeth in anger. 'That's why it's worth fighting for our civil rights. There's still time to get justice in this country, Med.' Stokely was tired of going to the open-casket funerals of his Black brothers and sisters.

'Maybe you're right, Stoke. If I'm going to die young of heatstroke or drownin', I would at least like to die a first-class citizen and not an afterthought. It's not like we could face any more police hostility than we do today.' Medgar straightened up to his full height and finished his drink. 'I'll talk to Ruth tonight. She was talkin' about protestin' outside the Municipal Court buildin' to raise awareness for his case.'

Stokely licked his top lip and nodded, as thoughts of revolution fired up his focus. 'We should also take a posse of our own to boycott the shopkeeper's premises. Shame the suspect, until the sheriff gets off his fat ass and takes the investigation seriously.'

The waitress returned to refill their empty glasses, or politely shepherd them out of the bar. 'Hey guys, you ready for another round?'

'Yeah, same again please, ma'am,' Medgar said, enthusiastically.

'Hey, are you guy's fixin' to rob a bank or something? You both look awful serious.'

Stokely looked her in the eye. 'No, it's much worse than that. We're going to make a name for ourselves.'

The waitress looked at them with a confused smile and then shuffled off to refill their glasses.

Contra
Elle Boyd

Rodney looks up at the sky. It is blue, impossibly so, with a few wisps of cloud overhead. He raises a hand to his forehead to shield his eyes from the bright sun. He guesses it is about mid-morning.

He looks around him. To his right, a snow-capped range of mountains stud the horizon. Rodney has never seen real mountains, only photos in the few soiled magazines his mother keeps hidden inside her mattress. To his left, perhaps thirty feet away, there is a corn field. Or what appears to be a corn field. Again, Rodney has never seen one himself, just a picture of one. The stalks are taller than he is, and the husks look ready to be picked. His mouth waters at the very thought of eating corn – fresh corn, not the two-year-old cans he sometimes finds while out gathering – and he turns away.

He can't pick this corn.

Underfoot is tall grass interspersed with a few patches of flowering weeds. He recognizes dandelions, and guesses a cluster of purple weeds must be thistle. He is bare foot, and the warmth of the earth makes him smile. *I don't care how dumb I look,* he thinks, and lays down on the ground. The blades of grass prick the backs of his exposed arms, and it feels wonderful. He closes his eyes, hears the distant buzz of bees - or are they flies? – and the chirp of a small bird. He hasn't heard or seen a bird other than the odd crow since he was a small boy, before he and his family were moved to the Inner Core. At least when they'd lived in the Outer Core, the occasional tree still stood. There was even an old cemetery where he and his sister used to play hide and seek.

But the Inner Core – Inside – is nothing but poverty, overcrowding, desperation. Black markets, noise, and filth. Rodney has never stepped foot beyond Outside, but he recalls seeing videos of Tier 1, back when they had legal internet. What he's seen of Tier 1 is street upon street of townhouses, lots of bicycles, a few subcompact cars, and lawns the size of postage stamps. Still, they have lawns. Cars. Bicycles.

A neighbour had once drawn a map of the city with its concentric circles: Inside was the bull's-eye, surrounded by Outside, then Tiers 1 through 3. He described Tier 3 (Rodney still has no idea what Tier 2 may be like): detached houses, big trucks, big trees, big lawns, privacy. The neighbour's eyes had shone as he talked, and Rodney wasn't sure he should believe him. He'd wondered if the guy had been smoking something. 'No one lives like that,' Rodney had said.

'You're too young,' the neighbour had replied. 'You only know this life. It wasn't always like this. Inside is growing. Outside is growing. Tier 1 is shrinking. More change is coming, and it won't be good.'

Rodney pushes the neighbour's prediction out of his mind and concentrates instead on the feel of the grass and the sound of the bees. But he can no longer focus.

He stands up and brushes himself off. He hears a rustling sound coming from the cornfields. He freezes, fear prickling his chest. If his friend has found him already –

But he hasn't. It's Miranda. Miranda steps out of the cornfield. Rodney holds his breath without realizing he's done so. She is wearing his favourite outfit, the one from Page 124: knee-high black leather boots and pale pink leather jacket with the black V-neck tank top underneath. Rodney likes this outfit better than the long trench coat that hides her rail-thin body. He bites his lower lip; her brick-red mouth curves into a half-smile. She is so beautiful she practically glows.

Rodney wonders if she's still modeling, if she's still young enough to model, which Tier she lives in. He frowns, refocuses. Miranda's smile wavers, then she beams, perfect teeth on display as she approaches him.

'Hey,' he says.

'Hey yourself.' She stops in front of him. In her heeled boots she's easily three inches taller than Rodney.

'Take those off,' he says, pointing at the boots. Without a word she pulls them from her feet, dropping them on the ground. Her toes disappear into the grass.

Rodney fingers the fabric of her tank; it is buttery soft. His own clothes are permanently stained, jeans with worn-through knees, sneakers with the soles hanging on for dear life. She looks – smells – clean, unsullied. Too good for Inside. He half expects his hands to leave smudges on her clothes.

'I don't think we have too long,' he says. He grabs both of her hands in his. 'I need you to know I love you, okay? I just had to see you one more time.' He leans close and buries his face in her blonde hair, inhaling the scent of her shampoo; *Is this what coconut smells like?*

Miranda sighs against his neck. 'I love you too.' Her floral print skirt flutters against his jeans.

He kisses her forehead, her hands. 'Your skin is so soft,' he says. She smiles, waiting. After a moment she brings her lips to his. Her lipstick tastes odd, almost coppery. He wraps his arms around her waist gently, as if afraid she will break if he applies pressure. She breathes into him, and the sensation sends a lick of electricity through his body. He brings a hand up to her neck and grabs a handful of her hair.

'Rodney!' He hears someone calling his name far in the distance. Miranda pulls away, wipes her mouth with the back of her hand. Something shoves his shoulder; he stumbles backward. He reaches out for Miranda, starts to plead for one more moment, but then the headset is ripped away and she is gone. The cornfield is gone, the grass, the mountains. Everything.

'What the hell are you doing?' his friend shouts. He rams the headset into an old grey backpack, burying it down in the bottom, all the while angrily scolding Rodney. 'How could you be so stupid? You know VR is contra. You trying to get us put away?

What if a patrol came in?'

Rodney props himself up on his elbows. 'I—'

'And you damn near drained the battery. Where do you think I'm gonna find another one? Huh? You think they're just lying around here? You know how much this one cost me?'

Rodney is sitting on the floor of his friend's bedroom, which he shares with his brothers. One double bed for three teenagers. One of the brothers usually sleeps on the floor, using an old couch cushion as a pillow. Their father sleeps on a love seat in the living room, feet protruding over the armrest. They are a family of four in a one-bedroom apartment with threadbare furniture and an ant problem.

His friend is shaking his head as he continues his lecture. Rodney closes his eyes and tries to remember how Miranda felt under his hands, how her hair smelled, how her pale feet were invisible in the grass.

His friend smacks his shoulder. 'Wake up! How can you try to sleep with all this noise?' And it is noisy: the woman upstairs stomping around and what sounds like furniture scraping across the floor; downstairs the young couple is playing some sort of bass-heavy music; they can hear a baby screaming in the bachelor unit next door. Noise is constant Inside; it is chronic. It is the background to every day, every night. Rodney wonders if these old buildings will one day collapse under the weight of so many people.

Suddenly the music stops and there is a brief lull; the power has gone out again. Then the scraping and the screaming resume. Rodney pushes himself up from the floor. His mother will be angry if the outage has ruined another dinner; their next grocery allotment isn't for another three days. Government is scraping the bottom of the barrel already – another sanctioned famine may be looming for Inside.

He apologizes to his friend, promises to find him a new battery on the black market, and goes down the hall in the dark.

After a cold dinner, after his mother and sister argued themselves hoarse, after the power is restored for at least a little while, Rodney enters the bedroom his mother and sister share and fishes the magazines out of his mother's mattress. He takes them back to his room. He tosses the nature magazines aside and flips through the ones with Miranda, the fashion magazines. The front covers are long gone; many of the pages are half-torn, wrinkled and stained. His mother had found the magazines stuffed behind the fridge when they were first moved Inside a year ago, into this awful building, this awful apartment.

Upstairs it sounds like a patrol visit: the stomping of heavy boots, demanding male voices, the sound of furniture being knocked over as they search for contra. Rodney misses Outside, where at least 'fashion' and 'nature' and 'art' are concepts permitted to exist, albeit in a limited capacity. But once his mother had been laid off, patrols had trucked the family Inside. All it took was one late rent payment. His hand tightens on the magazine, further crinkling the pages.

He flips through to page 124, where Miranda poses in his favourite outfit, a field of corn in the background. He lays back in his cot, tries to block out the sounds from above and below, and instead pretends he can hear the buzzing of bees and the chirping of small birds.

The Sweetness of Water
Fiona Ritchie Walker

Edward is dreaming about water. He's ten again, paddling in the river, stones rough and unsteady under his feet. He loses his balance, slides so that his body falls back, submerges. But it's not the cold mountain rush he was expecting. He's in a warm fragrant bath, surrounded by bubbles. Someone's hand – nanny's? Which nanny? – is swooshing water over his shoulders.

Edward gasps in air and blinks himself out of the dream. He looks round the bedroom, but doesn't want to wake up, find himself back in this new world with its absence of water.

It's never the sound of rain or a running tap that stirs him from sleep these days, just the noise of Maria sweeping in the courtyard below, as she does every morning. Edward yawns, stretches, and pictures her downstairs, petite back bent over as she hurries the dust from dark corners with her swish, swish, swish.

Sometimes, when Maria serves supper, he says that this drought is all her fault, she's used up all the water rinsing rice.

'Me? Ah, Mr Edward, you are mistaken.' Always the same reply, an exaggerated frown furrowing her face, pulling her fine eyebrows together so they almost meet.

Last night, she'd not only frowned but pointed a sharp-nailed finger in his direction. There was even eye contact, the hint of a smile.

'It is you, Mr. Edward, who has drained this country of water, with your love of baths and endless washing.'

A bath. How he longs for a soak below soft, fragrant bubbles. It had been easy when he was a boy, the huge bath filled each night by the thundering taps.

Eddie - ready? His favourite nanny, Margaret, had such a

sweet voice. She arrived just when he was at an age to appreciate her nightly offers to soap him down. And an evening bath was a ritual he stuck to as an adult, even when the UK bathing ban began. Then those bloody meters were made compulsory and he could no longer turn up the radio to drown the sound of the tap running from his London neighbours.

Not that he would have needed the camouflage of music up here in the Scottish Highlands. Moss Cottage. What a ridiculous name. It's like a palace compared to his flat, or compact apartment as the estate agent called it, when he was trying to sell. Still on the market when he left, along with thousands of other homes as people tried to follow the water.

Now he wakes in one of the cottage's four bedrooms on the first floor, while Maria chose the converted attic, which she said was five times bigger than the house she grew up in. So it isn't really a cottage and there's a definite lack of moss. As a child, coming up to visit his aunt during the holidays, he'd been desperate to find moss. He'd even tried to persuade his aunt to change the name, but she told him that would mean she'd never receive any post again. He wonders what she would have made of the place now, the garden and any traces of moss destroyed by the terrible rise in temperature, lack of rain.

The nearest house is at the end of the lane, although since the family left - such a hellish situation with young children - there would be no-one to hear if he did get out of bed, head to the bathroom and turn the taps full-on. If, of course, there was any water.

Edward rolls over in bed, pulls the sheet across him. Not for warmth. It's always too bloody hot these days. Sheets are what he uses to soak up the sweat from his body.

Hard to imagine he used to stand, shivering, when he got out of the bath, couldn't wait for Nanny to smother him with a warm towel, even better when they had an ample bosom, like Margaret's, to rest against. What he wouldn't give for a bit of shivering now. If only his parents had taken him with them on their travels. India, Tanzania, Thailand. It might have prepared him for coping with this endless Scottish sun.

'It's just not right,' he mutters. Southern England scorched. The Highlands in a never-ending heatwave. 20 degrees on Hogmanay and people crowing about the drop from 25, which only lasted two days. Hoo bloody ha.

Edward rubs the sheet under his armpit - oxter as his aunt had called it - and sniffs. More feral every day. Is it right that the more of them you eat, the more their smell comes out through sweat and skin? Will there come a day when he'll stop noticing it?

He lies still and listens. The sweeping has stopped. Why Maria bothers, 8a.m. on the dot, he'll never know. When he suggested that the rulebook (her words) or the list of duties agreed at the time of employment (his words) could be well and truly ripped up in their new circumstances, Maria shook her head. Told him that sweeping was peaceful for her, letting the rhythm of the brushing take over. Something she had done since she was four, her job in the family home every morning.

'I like it, so I will keep doing it,' she'd told him when he asked why she continued when it was only the two of them and no-one would ever visit.

Edward tilts his head. Today's sweeping has stopped. Whatever dust gathered in the last 24 hours has been safely disposed of. Maria will have wiped her hands on her apron and gone into the kitchen to prepare them each a cup of tea.

He's never been one for hot chocolate. While his sister, Anna, gulped down a Peter Rabbit mug of the stuff, Edward always had tea. The best nanny for tea was June. Creamy milk, just enough sugar. The only thing that spoilt it was losing the soft aftertaste when she insisted he brush his teeth after the bedtime story.

The door creaks open and Maria appears. 'Your tea, Mr Edward.' She is carrying a tray with two mugs on it. Edward smiles. So she's finally decided it's acceptable to join him after all. Maybe one day she will drop the Mr, call him Edward as he's been asking her to do since she began working for him. He pats the side of the bed, but she ignores the gesture, waits until he's propped himself up, then hands him a mug, places the tray on the table by the bed and carries her tea to the window seat.

Well, perhaps things are changing, Edward tells himself. At least she's stayed in the room. After they moved from the city, she stuck to the old ways, the rulebook that he had never written. House cleaned, meals cooked and served, drinks delivered. Then her half-bow and she was back to her room in the loft, even though he'd offered her the pick of the other bedrooms. The heat must be stifling.

Edward thinks back to the day she arrived at his front door, letter from the agency and a pile of other paperwork in her hand - *you must know that I am legal* - and how her eyes glistened when she saw her new surroundings. A palace, she'd called it. Not like the previous one. Katia? Kara? Stayed five minutes. Never did make him a decent cup of tea.

Edward sips from the mug Maria brought him. Of course, there's been no milk for months now, and their supply of sugar, which seemed so plentiful when they arrived, has been diminishing. But this cardamom malarkey isn't too bad. He can see that Maria's watching him.

'It's a very clean taste, hint of sweetness,' he tells her. 'I like it.' Over the months, he's tried to detect when she's blushing and is sure she's doing it right now.

'The same cardamom pod all week,' she says. 'For both of our drinks. Next week I will bruise it, release more flavour.'

Cardamom. Whoever would have thought that he'd be drinking this fancy concoction at his age, after nearly six decades of milk and two sugars. Tell the truth, he really quite enjoys it. They sit in silence, sipping their tea. I wonder, Edward thinks, if this is what life would have been like if I'd taken a wife. He considers, for a moment, his choice of words. Yes, it would have had to be all his doing, for no woman would have chosen him. He has never risked the ridicule, the inevitable refusal, opting instead to employ women to meet his household requirements. Other needs - really, he should class them as desires - were unrequited and then gradually disappeared. He hopes that every one of his housekeepers - even the Katia or Kara one - will remember him as a good employer.

Edward thinks of the day he found Maria with the small brush and plastic shovel. It was in the city flat, a few weeks after she'd moved in. He'd been working in the study, distracted by the frequent tapping coming from the other side of the wall.

When he popped his head round the door, he saw her in the corner, curled up like a mouse, the plastic edge of the hand brush sounding out a thump each time it met the skirting board.

'Easy with that or the paint will start chipping.' He regretted it the moment she turned round and he saw the shock on her face.

'Oh, please, Mr Edward, if there is damage, I will pay. It's just —' And she began a long explanation about brushes and how, in her country they had the softest brush ever, with no need for plastic, the broom so wide and flexible it reached into every corner with ease.

'So much better than...' Her voice tailed off as she looked at the hard blue handle in her hand.

What happened next? Edward can't remember if he said anything. Did he reassure her there would be nothing to pay, no money docked from her wages? What he does know is that within minutes he'd found a supplier online - how he took the internet for granted then - and placed the order in her name. Had to look up her surname in the paperwork she'd brought with her, make sure the spelling was right — always his weak point - but it was worth it to see her face when the parcel arrived. Two bloody household brushes. Who knew that would make anyone so happy?

They'd not been able to carry much when they moved north - Edward knew that a lot of the basics would be at the cottage already - but Maria had carefully packed the brushes in her case, as if they were best china.

Edward finishes his tea, hands Maria the mug. They really were fortunate with all the supplies left in his late aunt's house. Just as well she lived to ninety-six and he'd not had time to sell it as planned. Her wartime attitude, inherited from her parents, means that he and Maria will be enjoying morning tea for a long time, providing the water holds out.

It's a shame about the trees, leaves falling, not returning, but their dead and broken branches mean wood to burn. He'd been worried about the lack of electricity, but Maria took it in her stride, told him that in the country area where she grew up, many people still cooked on wood.

'And the taps, they were always dry, so it was my job to walk the one mile there, one mile back to the well,' she said.

Edward remembers how her head dipped at that point, to hide her tears. They still had radio then and the world's searing temperatures, rising death toll had been dominating the news for weeks. Maria had tried phone, internet, letter while they were still in the city and services were running, but got no replies.

'That was, as usual, delicious,' Edward says as she puts the mugs back on the tray, heads for the doorway. They have decided, to save on fuel and food, to forego breakfast these days. It was Maria's suggestion and Edward was quick to agree, but some mornings, like today, he dreams of fluffy egg, scrambled, a sprinkle of black pepper, grilled tomato. Hadn't he heard somewhere, just before they moved, that now the only tomato seeds remaining were at Kew? Although there had been so much speculation and panic it was hard to know what was true these days.

'Lunch?' He may as well ask, though he already knows her reply.

'Rice, with a little seasoning.' She pauses in the doorway.

'And tonight, Fergus will be joining us.'

Edward claps his hands. 'Wonderful!' Thinks how, before they moved here, he would have been nauseated by the thought. Maria closes the door behind her and Edward rubs his eyes. Reading? No. Writing? No. He'd like to do some painting but even with the lids firmly shut, the tubes have dried solid. Maybe he will get a sharp knife, slit the metal sides and ease out the pigment, add a little precious water. But not today. Instead, he will take paper and pencils into the lounge, sketch the view from the window. Just another way to fill another day.

When Maria rings the bell for lunch - another of her habits which he finds endearing - he has added another sketch to the pile. Edward glances at his aunt's faded watercolour on the wall. The loch dominated the view from the house then. Today his pencil has recorded the latest, lowest level. He and Maria have already spoken of how, sometime soon, if the well dries up, they may have to make a plan with buckets and the like, although the long walk back in such heat will take its toll. He used to see water tankers, small as the model cars he once collected, arriving at the far shore. Lack of fuel, lack of people - something has led them to stop coming.

Edward makes his way to the dining room. Two of the window shutters are closed to try to keep the room a little cooler. He remembers a family Christmas in this room, the agony of tweed prickling his skin, fire roaring, the icy chill at the far side of the laden table.

Maria has set two places. His heart flutters. For the first time she will be eating with him. Two bowls of rice are brought, and he waits for her apology. Too dry, too stiff, too cold.

'Nonsense.' He lifts a spoonful to his mouth, feels the pepper fire his nostrils. 'What you do is absolutely bloody marvellous.' He chews the rice, which is indeed too dry, too stiff, too cold.

He is amazed they are both well, after all the scaremongering stories over the years about the dangers of storing rice at room temperature, the risks of reheating. Although the kitchen is Maria's domain, Edward knows she cooks up a batch of rice once a week. Every morning she boils water for their tea on the log fire, saving the extra from the kettle in the Thermos flasks. At lunchtime, she pours a small amount of water over the solid lumps of rice to ease the grains apart, ready for serving. In the first weeks they ate it with soy sauce, but now they are down to pepper and even that is low.

Edward swallows another dry mouthful. Rice pudding. Oh, how he'd love a bowl of it right now. Margaret made the best rice pudding of all the nannies. Just the right amount of nutmeg. She must have added cream. And oh, the slightly burnt skin on the top, his favourite. So many fights with Anna over it.

He places his spoon in the empty bowl, knows Maria will add them to the stack beside the scullery door. Thank goodness they have a house full of crockery and cutlery. Thank goodness for Maria. What would he do without her. When she has cleared the table, he rises up, places his linen napkin back in the silver ring.

Yes, he knows what to do now. He will go up to the study, take a sheet of his aunt's headed paper, write a new will. Goodness knows if his old one still exists. What was it Mr Godwin said? The safe lined in lead - even the end of the world won't destroy it. At this rate it will outlive everyone at the solicitors, if the business is still going.

In his old will, he'd left everything to Anna, apart from a rather fine nib pen, mother of pearl, which had belonged to his father. That was to have gone to his aunt, but as he opens a drawer to pick a pen from the vast selection she collected during her lifetime, Edward feels it may not have been appreciated.

Last Will and Testament. The letters stand out on the thick paper. Edward adds his name. Everything to Maria. He thinks she must be twenty, maybe twenty-five years younger than him, but age is so irrelevant these days. Even looking ahead to next year, any planning for the future beyond merely existing, seems frivolous. Edward pauses. Will the document be legal without witnesses? Will anyone find it, be around to ensure his wishes are met? He signs it anyway, checks the calendar on the desk, remembers turning the dog-eared cards to December 25, Anna scolding him - a day too early. Now he makes sure he changes it every morning. Even with all the seasons gone, just this relentless heat and no rain, he likes to know what day of the month it is.

Date added, he leans back, studies what he has written. Folds it carefully and puts it in an envelope, addresses it to Maria, then adds *or whoever may find this,* but realises if it's not her who opens it, then the whole exercise will have been pointless.

For a long time he remains seated in the leather armchair, looking out of the window. No birds, butterflies. No midges. He wonders how the changed weather has affected the west coast swarms. He wonders if there are still fish in the shrinking water of the loch. Last week he held the old binoculars close to his face until the cracked eye-rest made it too painful to view. He scanned the surface, left, right. No movement.

Edward tries to think of something else, tries to dismiss the image of fish, smell of fish, texture of fish from his mind, but today it's not working. Nanny's voice is back in his head, the white slop in front of his closed eyes. White potato, fish that is so uncooked it lies translucent in its white sauce sea. There's not even the crisp cheesy topping that Margaret used to make, to coax a few mouthfuls between his lips.

He remembers his cheeks warming, tears falling. That awful roar that came out of his mouth. His sister's saucer eyes. A rare occasion when his parents were back in the country but of course, even then they were out. A theatre, play, dinner - no matter where they were, they had abandoned him to nanny's cold hands, her impatient voice, the starched white of her apron.

A whimpering noise brings Edward back to the present. It's coming from him, his chest rushing in and out, as if he's been running. That's the problem. No contact with the outside world, or what's left of it. All his thoughts are in the past.

Now what to do? Maybe a little reading. He needs to think about something else, anything. He's about to pick up *A Tale of Two Cities* – such a favourite - when the gong sounds. That time already? Another afternoon gone. Is it wrong that he feels relieved?

Edward takes his place at the table, releases the serviette from the ring and places it across his lap with a flourish. Maria brings in two plates and he smiles. So he won't be eating alone. There's white rice on the blue and white china and in the centre, dark chunks steaming.

'So how is Fergus this evening?' Edward asks.

'Braised in a little oil. Off the bone as usual.' Maria picks up her fork.

Edward nods. To begin with he'd worried about disease, read too many pages in the old encyclopedia he got down from the study shelf. Rattus. Rodentia. He'd worked his way through the list of diseases that they carried. Black Death, foot and mouth. He learned that a group of rats is called a mischief, that they are opportunistic survivors.

Edward's first thought when he saw the flash of tail and fur in the courtyard was elimination, but Maria explained that in many countries, it was a poor man's protein - sometimes even savoured. She knew good ways of catching them.

He'd retched the first time, that roasted shape on his plate too familiar, but now, deboned with Maria's skilful filleting, he finds the taste and texture quite agreeable. An empty plate in front of him, a satisfied stomach below his clasped hands. Maria smiling. He doesn't even crave a glass of wine.

'And now.' Maria rises, stretches out her hand. For a moment Edward isn't sure how he should respond. Shake it?

144

But before he has time to ask, she grasps his fingers, and he's up, following her through the doorway, placing his feet one after another to trace her steps upstairs.

'I am being bold, assuming,' she says, opening the bathroom door. In the large, empty bath are two plastic washing up basins, a small metal saucepan. Edward notices that although the white enamel is dry, the plug is in place. A towel and his old dressing gown sway on the back of the door.

There's a folded flannel on the edge of the bath, on top of it, a bar of white soap. It's only after taking all this in that Edward notices the large green plastic barrel behind him. He lifts the lid, sees halfway down his reflected face. Edward turns to Maria.

'Just something I've been saving,' she says.

He looks again at the water. Drinking and cooking only, they'd agreed. Until there's a cooling in the weather - who was he kidding - and they can walk to the loch shore. The worst bit for him had been when the toilet stopped flushing, but Maria didn't see it as a problem. 'Here,' she'd said, handing him a shovel, instructing him to dig a hole at the back of the house. She'd begun digging on the other side of the shed. One for him, one for her. Maria gathered ash in old flowerpots and got two silver serving spoons from the kitchen, showed him how to sprinkle it over, after using a page of an old telephone directory as toilet paper. Had told him: 'Now there's no need to miss flushing.'

Edward peers in the green barrel again, sees a starchy film on the surface of the water, a piece of rice floating. He turns to look at the saucepan and the basins.

'This is how I washed when I was very small.' Maria lifts the saucepan, begins to scoop water into one of the basins. 'Let me show you how.' She takes the dry flannel, holds it close to the water then pretends to rub it across the soap. 'And then you become lovely and clean. Stand in the other basin please, so that I may collect and use the rinse water after you.'

There is a lump in Edward's throat, so big he cannot

speak, so hard it's bringing tears to his eyes. Maria waits. When he doesn't move, she undoes the top button of his shirt.

'Maybe I can help you,' she says. 'I know it's a little strange when you have been used to baths with such deep water.'

Edward nods, tries to find a smile. He's thinking of uneaten fish pie, hard words, the threat of bed with no bath. His hot tears. Legs running, hands opening the door.

'I shall have a bath, I shall, I shall!'

Steam from the hot tap. He didn't register the silence of the cold tap next to it. His body, deep in scalding water. Someone crying. His own voice, screaming.

'I'm afraid,' he takes Maria's hand to still her fingers. 'Not a pretty sight.'

He watches her eyes take in the start of the scarring, a shining pink that he's been careful to hide from anyone else's eyes for all those years.

She smiles. 'Ah, such a history.' Unbuttons the rest of the shirt in a swift movement, moves to unzip his trousers.

Before Edward realises what's happening, he is standing, naked, with his grubby feet squeezed in a plastic bowl. Maria is behind him, softly humming a tune he doesn't know. He hears water trickling, feels cooling wet, like a delicious shiver on the back of his neck, the softness of the cotton flannel, back and forth, smell of soap, clean, in the air.

Maria pours water over his shoulders. The soapy puddle grows. His toes disappear.

He thinks of her own small body under her apron and dress. Her dusty legs waiting to be washed. Trickles of water are cool on his forehead, run over his closed eyes. He is no longer dreaming about the roar of a river, the long-ago bath time that went so wrong. He's alive in this moment. Nothing else matters, just this sweetness of water.

The Coming End
Boshra Rasti

Hermando woke up and grabbed the top of a tree to steady himself as he stood. Below him he could see sparsity in the forest floor where they had landed to emancipate them. He bent down and flipped the two trees off the top of the home he had constructed for them - those that had survived. They huddled, shivering in a corner of this habitat. Some of them squeaked in an unintelligible jumble of sound and syllables too foreign to make sense of. They huddled, pushing against each other until Hermando picked one up with his thumb and forefinger.

How depraved and hairy they were! The tops of their heads like mops of brown seaweed or the sinewy stuff of spider's webs, feet dangling like miniature matchsticks. Hermando lifted one up toward his nose, sniffing softly as not to startle him anymore than he already was. The smell was terrible. A musky, dark smell; rancid and cadaverous. It must be his health; teetering between life and death, a compass needle out of calibration.

I will take him to Esperanza, he thought, placing the boy on his shoulder and marching off into the Amazon River, stepping over brown waterfalls, where their horrible excrement had washed into and poisoned. They must not know, Hermando shook his head with disappointment. Such waywardness comes with depravity. Hermando could not speak their language, if it could be called such, more squeaks and whines than delicate chords. But Hermando understood that they were ill. The whole lot of them. How could they not be with the poisoned rivers, jellyfish ridden oceans, and rising sea waters? The fruit they ate were all the same shape and size, outwardly perfect, but plastic - no variance which is needed for nature or health or science. Those who knew had been decimated, doing away with goodness. Allowing the most sinister to rule from behind screens that sucked the life out of them - first weakening their eyes and twisting their minds. Dummies clicking for a dopamine flash.

Hermando stopped as the fellow gave a shrill cry and jumped off his shoulder. Ricocheting to the ground, innards splayed on the branches and body tumbling gutless to the river below with a slight splash. The pink-tinged brown haloed outwards.

Did he not sense Hermando trying to help? Why, he could have just pinched him between his thumb and forefinger if he wanted to get rid of him. They must not understand. Illogical and backwards - scared of those who have come to save them from themselves.

And so it went on, day after day. Hermando would place one on his shoulder to take deep into the Amazon, to get them medicines; to heal them; to teach them his language; to restore the gentle balance that was so gravely oscillating; to save them from the sickened earth, long weary of them. But each day another one would take its own life until there were none left.

Hermano felt ashamed. How could he face the other gods? Esperanza - what would he say to her? Perhaps smelling the first one was what startled them into self-annihilation every time he'd place one on his shoulder, trying to take them to the band of beings deep in the Amazon - the ones who were closer to saving. The Amazonians were not afraid but welcomed their coming. Peculiarly, they seemed to know that the earth was at an inflection point. They waved their smokey wreaths as the gods came closer to landing.

Even the aftershocks of their landing had not worried them, even though many had died as a result. It was almost expected. But the others, the others who were designated to Hermando, pale and unnaturally placid faced, were different.

Once they realized that Hermando would take one of their own and not return him, they had tried bullets and other rudimentary artillery, but this just scratched his skin, not even producing blood.

It was with these annoyances that Hermando walked toward the Amazonians. Esperanza had done better with them, she sat down in the middle of the village, smiling broadly in meditation with the little beings circling her, touching her, speaking unintelligibly.

Esperanza opened her eyes as she felt Hermando approaching. 'He's one like me', she said as the beings walked towards him offering smoke. They seemed to take great pleasure in her voice, foreign to them though it was. It was impossible that Esperanza had taught them their language, not with what she had to work with; simple and depraved beings who had laid violent and unrelenting siege on their own home for centuries.

'How do you influence them?' exclaimed Hermando.

'They knew we were coming, that it was only a matter of time. Where are yours?' Esperanza's eyes squint as if trying to identify the miniature creatures in Hermando's beard or hair.

'They were afraid, they all died from fear.' Hermando sat down on the forest floor crushing the sparse and half-deadened trees underneath him as he sat. 'Or perhaps it was prejudice. They could not reconcile differences in their small minds.' Esperanza nodded her head solemnly, knowing that prejudice had conjured the fear.

'Have you told them?' he says.

'No. I can't bring myself to.' Esperanza looked down at her lap, displeased with the reality that at some point she would have to.

'They'll find out soon enough.' Hermando tried to dispel

Esperanza's sorrow with the dire reality of the situation.

The Amazonians hollered together to get their attention. They pointed to a drawing on the dark soil of the forest floor. The image showed the giants planting seeds.

'They want us to restore their forest,' Hermando muttered.

'But the seeds we have are only fit for our world.' Esperanza said, watching as one pointed to her. 'They must know this.' But the hands waved frantically, begging and pleading that they plant their seeds.

Into the evening Esperanza and Hermando planted seeds and the Amazonians circled the mounds of soil, each as high as boulders.

The next morning a small bud had sprung, cracking the earth around it. A few of the Amazonians had wandered close enough and fell into the crevices in the ground, down, goodness knows how deep. Hermando stuck his index finger close to the base of the bud, scratching at the dirt, but this only covered the crevices, burying the poor fellows deeper. To the miniature beings, these buds were like the rainforest trees being restored, both in size and height. They danced around overjoyed, despite losing a few of their compatriots.

Did they know that these were only seedlings and that in time, trees larger than Hermando and Esperanza atop each other, would tower above from the earth?

On the second day, the seedlings had become taller, the Amazonians beat their miniature drums and sang into the night. Did they know the natural cycle of things, and what must come from the ground to aerate it?

Esperanza resolved that she would warn them. She drew pictures, showing them that the trees would become too large and would separate one miniature being from the other. They did not heed her pictures, they were too enraptured by the seedlings which reminded them of their ancient forests, taken from them by corporations and greed. How short-sighted, Hermando thought. This earth is afflicted by short-sightedness; even he was becoming prey to it. Had he not brought his finger down, those poor souls might not have been buried.

On the third day, the seedlings had now sprung forth further, creating mountains where the ground curved up to the stem. These separated the miniature beings from each other. Great effort was expended for one to get to the other. No amount of drum beating or shrill screaming could carry the sound from one being to the other. The seedlings had grown large enough to separate them. They cried out, waving their matchstick arms as Esperanza made it her job to brush aside the new leaves to find the beings and to move them all from one place to the other, reuniting them.

Hermando whispered at night into Esperanza's ear, 'Do they not know what will spring forth from the earth in time? They brought this upon themselves, asking you to sow our seeds.'

Esperanza blinked in the dark, 'My lot is not like yours. They welcome me. They knew of our coming. They hadn't divided themselves from the earth, living in cement blocks, in crowded cities, expending the irreplaceable wealth of water, sky, and earth'

Hermando held Esperanza's hand as she lay silent. She was tormented.

'Remember what they say in our world, my dear Esperanza, when fire comes wet and dry burns together.' It was a proverb that spoke of the great law of existence; that once irreparable damage had been done to nature, destruction would unfold, regardless of who was faulty or faultless.

But Esperanza refused to agree. 'There is still time... there is still time', she repeated, lulling herself to sleep.

Esperanza was awoken by ten beings stomping on her nose. Her eyes narrowed in on them and she suppressed the urge to shake her head. Instead, Hermando rolled over onto his side, his left hand under his head and plucked the beings off Esperanza, one by one. Once on the ground, they scurried to their people who lay lined just beyond Esperanza's feet. They waved their arms in a fury running to-and-fro. Esperanza arose and looked down at the ground below, meters away, she could see where the seedlings had grown taller. One of the little beings was running as an earthworm ten times its size squiggled along. Blindly diving into the soil and up again. It moved quickly compared to them and as it dove in and out of the soil in the direction of Esperanza, she noticed that some beings were devoured with the dirt into the earthworm's mouth. Horrified, they ran to her feet, holding onto her toes.

'Hermando, quick! Pick them up!'

Hermando furled his eyebrows. 'The last time I did that they jumped.'

'Maybe that was your lot, mine aren't that stupid,' Esperanza said in a frenzy, picking up the little ones and putting them on her shoulder.

'We can't do this forever, Esperanza - the earth is becoming hospitable to us. It has taken our seeds, and now there is no recourse for them.'

Despite half-believing what Hermando said, Esperanza's soft heart could not accept this. 'Let's walk towards the other gods.'

Hermando frowned but followed Esperanza towards the mountains in the distance. The miniature beings held onto the hair flowing from Hermando's beard and those on Esperanza's shoulders pointed emphatically at the mountains. When they arrived there, Hermando plucked them from his beard and laid them on the peak. This seemed to please them greatly. Esperanza's miniature beings also pointed down to the mountain peak, holding hands and dancing excitedly. From their vantage point, they could see the beautiful trees which Hermando and Esperanza grew, growing larger and larger, higher than the mountain peak on which they stood.

Suddenly, the grounds shook as the other gods approached, some crying bitter tears. The miniature beings danced again, others beat drums and blew into their conches. Welcoming the shaking earth. The gods would stop and the beings would moan out loud, beating their breasts until the gods moved again and once they did, they resumed their merriment. With each step the gods took, the earth shook and the beings fell from the peak, like droplets of rain, until the very last miniature being raised his hands in praise, blowing his conch and then receding into a cave in the mountain never to be seen again.

'Where did he go?' The distraught gods cried to Esperanza.

'He went to his ancient cave, where the tablets of the end of time were written.'

'Why did they rejoice?' Hermando questioned.

'Because we planted what they could not - our giant trees. In time the earth will recover, but not for the miniature ones.'

'Then for who?' One of the sobbing gods asked.

'For us - but we must learn from their mistakes and never neglect what has been given to us.' The gods sat for a while in silence, meditating on the sadness of the ending and the hope of new beginnings.

The Sun in My Belly
Shrutidhora P Mohor

In my own dark world, I see everything through her eyes.
She tells me there is a fire outside.

I remain seated here through the day, every day. I can sense the
world happening around me. There is nothing that I can do in
it, neither is there anything that I wish to do. It rolls past me like
a huge drum, on which the beats caused by the drummer are
anticipated and monotonous, unable to cause music, unwilling to
solicit attention of the absent-minded listener.

On days when I am hungry soon after waking up in the
morning, I fall asleep. It is easy to sleep, for in my world it is
forever dark and the dead of night reigns supreme.

I wake up only when she arrives at the door of my hut and
the tinkle of her glass bangles reaches my ears.

'*Utho ab, khaana laayi hun.*' Her standard sentence, every
time she brings me food.

Food is a rarity in my world. Yet it is one of the most talked about
things. At those times when I am awake I hear conversations, or
monologues, on food. Tones of despair, anger, helplessness, mix
with food-words to make them tastier, more so because as the real
food gets scarce, the words about food become precious, more
numerous.

Wahaan pe khaana mil raha hai. Food is available there.

Main kahaan se khaana laau? From where shall I get food?

Ma, bhukh laga mere ko. Mummy, I am hungry.

Kuchh khaaye ho ji subah se? Did you have anything since the
morning?

Khaana, khaana, khaana, khaana, nahi hai khaana ghar pe!
Food, food, food, food! There is no food at home!

When she brings me food, I generally don't ask her from where she has got it. Instead, I shove my hand in and dive into the meagre spread on the plate. My fingers mostly touch shifting, lightweight puffed rice, a few of them flying off the plate before I can catch them. In anxiety I keep moving my hands in circles around the place where I am seated, anxious to catch even one morsel that might have escaped my plate. If I think there is one which I can't catch, I cry out, like a child, complaining that she has not laid out the food for me as well as she should. On some days she gets me rice, cold, sticky, fat. On a few days I have a feast when I discover that there is boiled potato alongside rice, or some roots of vegetables, sprinkled with salt, tossed on a pan with dry red chilli. These meals are memorable; I lick my fingers and run my tongue over my unwashed lips for minutes after I have finished the lifetime meal experience.

Today she is late. I know that because the longest possible spell of my sleep has come to an end. My dark world gives me no indication though. I guess the time from the sounds around me. An incessant clanking of metal buckets next door tells me that all of them are checking out to see how much water they have and if that will last the night.

It must be evening now.

Glass bangles kiss each other as she arrives at the door.

'Why are you late?' I grumble.

'Shhhh, quiet!' Her suppressed voice comes close to me. Her breath is on my face.

A few seconds of arrangement as she pours some water from a pitcher to a tumbler, spreads the collected food on the plate and then the much-awaited '*Lijiye. Khaana.*'

I grab the plate from her hands and throw my fingers in. They meet with things not familiar. Rounded soft items, spongy elongated ones, rubbery square pieces.

'What food is this?' I ask with a frown in my voice.

She lowers her voice. 'Have it fast. They must not see you.'

I am still suspicious. 'But it smells good too. What is this? Where did you get this from?'

She keeps quiet. I understand she is reluctant to share details. Finally she says, 'There is a food festival near the highway.'

I bring the plate close to my face and take a deep breath in. Appetising smells of food I have never even dreamt of waft through my big nostrils. 'What are these called, Moua?'

She snaps at me. 'I get the food for you, you blind old man! Isn't that enough? Be content with that. I risked my life to get it from there and you think I'll memorise names for you! *Paagal!*'

My big bad hungry belly is rumbling. I waste no further time. For the next thirty minutes or so, I lick clean the surface of the plate much after the food has gone down the food pipe into the stomach. My fingers move in and out of my mouth. My tongue is tired from all that work. I sit back when I am certain that there is nothing left on the plate, nothing at all.

I hear Moua throw a mug of water on the plate, rinse it briefly, then another half mug to wash off the soap. A little later all is quiet inside the hut. But I know she has not left.

The lingering taste of food never known until then has made me dreamy. I think I can see the stars in the sky outside. I hold my face up, pretending there is a cool breeze caressing my duck-mouth and bear-ears. But there is none. The air is as still as the bodies of the debt-ridden farmers in the next village who killed themselves when there was a bad monsoon last year. Thrice in a row. There is nothing like a bad crop... a sure and effective way to reduce the population on this planet... I chuckle aloud. *Saala, yeh bhi koi zindagi...?* To hell with this life... Shitty, shitty, *saala...*

'Moua...?' I call out, her name slipping down my over-worked and half-drowsy tongue.

'*Kya?*'

'Moua...'

'*Arre, kya?*'

I move my hands over my belly. 'How old are you?'

'What will you do with my age?' She pauses and then adds in a different tone, 'Will you marry me?'

I wonder if she is smiling. Her tone appears teasing but in my forever dark world sometimes intonations can be misleading.

I smile, assuming that she is too. Then I remember something relevant. 'Moua, you said a food *puja*...?'

'A festival, actually.' Her bangles jostle with each other to correct me.

A festival... But...

Tonight there are words inside my stomach, buried under the mound of unnamed delicious food. I must pull them out if I want to speak.

'But Moua... didn't the *Pradhan* say that there is a terrible shortage of food? That the government is considering declaring a famine in several districts here?'

She does not answer. I know she has heard me. At last she says, 'That's for *us*. A famine here in the villages does not mean that they don't have food in the *city*. The sun here has become a fireball. It is burning us every day. There they have machines to cool the sun down.'

Around a week after that one day she is unusually irritated while she tidies my things in the hut. I am seated in front of the door, waiting for her to share all the news of the village and the surrounding areas. When she does not begin her commentary, I enquire if everything is alright. She does not reply. Once as she passes by me, I manage to touch her arm.

'Moua?'

She pulls her arm out and continues to move around, creating more sound than on other days.

A few minutes later I ask, 'Is something wrong?'

She is putting the utensils in place. There... that is the sound of the sheet being thrashed clean and then being spread out over the bed. A metallic gong... she is moving the bucket and the lock-chain away to the other side...

I pull my fifty-odd year-old body up and move towards where she is. As I slightly bump into her, she makes a mild sound of annoyance with her mouth. 'Move,' she commands.

I don't. 'What's the matter?' Before she can reply I ask for some water.

'There is only half a pitcher left.'

I am unable to follow her. 'So, you will have to fill it up.'

'That's not going to be easy anymore. The river has dried up almost entirely, and whatever remains of it is muddy and poisoned.'

'Poisoned?'

'The fly-ash from the factories on the outskirts of Kalyanpur.'

'Oh.' I pause and add, 'Then?'

She does not reply to this either.

I sniff the air.

The nauseating smell of charcoal is close by. How did it arrive nearby?

'But the factories are far?' I look for an explanation.

Now she stops at one place inside the room and says, 'I am leaving soon. My father is aged and unwell. My child is starving. If I continue to stay here, they will die without food. I shall have to leave this village in a few days.' Her tone is cold and formal.

Her words play around in my ears for some time before they make complete sense. My mind goes back to that time many years ago, I don't exactly remember when, she had taken up the responsibility of looking after me. In my permanently lightless world she had initially been only a news giver and had gradually grown into a caregiver. She had brought mobility to my stationary existence. Since my family had got scattered over the years she had become one of my own. Unable to accept what I have just heard I demand an elaboration.

'But what could have happened to drastically worsen things? The rains have been less, I know. There is a shortage of food too. But why do you have to leave the village? Everyone manages through hard times.'

She raises her voice now. '*Everyone* is leaving. Do you have an idea how hot it is outside? Do you know how many of us have died of heat stroke and hunger in the last one month? One can't step out of the home without getting burned. It flashes into our eyes, it scorches our skin. The river is unusable. The *haat* is empty. There is nothing to eat, nothing to drink. Can you imagine how I have to procure food to keep myself alive? My son alive? The food that I get for you... do you know how I manage to get that?' She stops. I can hear her shaking in excitement, her breath heavy and irregular.

Inside my large body I too am shaking. In fear, in insecurity. I can't control myself and blurt out, 'What will happen to me if you go? How can you be so selfish?' I want to see her expression... oh god... give me light in my eyes... so that I can see... is she reconsidering? Is she remorseful? Maybe she will stay back and manage something... god... some light please, in my eyes... I want to see her change her decision... can the fireball sun not spare a ray for me... can I not have a bit of the light that is blinding all others... some light, some light for me...

My body is twisted, and I fall to the ground. I am having convulsions. The violent vibrations are sending shockwaves through the ground. Will she not come and lift me up?

Days pass. I haven't heard human voices for the last four-five days.

Hungry... I am hungry... there is no food anywhere... I need to eat... why is the pitcher empty... Moua... Moua... bring me water... my chest is about to burst of thirst... Moua...

In my own dark world, I see nothing anymore.

There is a fire inside my belly, while a shooting sun is blazing away outside.

Wherever its rays fall concentrated, the interiors of my body get cracked up into a million fissures. I guess they look exactly like the fractured field in front; dry, lifeless, barren.

Glossary

Utho ab, khaana laayi hun = get up, I have got food for you

Lijiye. Khaana. = here is your food

Paagal = crazy/ insane, mostly used indulgently in the subcontinent; informal use

Kya = what? (literally); interrogative common word in India; signifies a question

Arre, kya? = an expression of mild impatience, common in the colloquial tongue, accompanying the question word

Puja = the word for Hindu forms of worship

Pradhan = the head of a body, in this case of the rural local government bodies called *Panchayat*

Saala, yeh bhi koi zindagi...? = literally, is this a life worth living? *Saala* specifically is a common abuse/ slang

Haat = rural marketplace

Harsh Winter
Heather Mills

Heavy boots crunched as they sank into the snow, before lifting out of the deep hole and creating another. The woman lifted her gaze from the endless white desert to the large building in the distance. It was the last place in the country with real meat, the flyer had said so.

It had been six years since Vanya had seen an animal, seven when the snow started falling and never stopped. The cold, starvation, or people had killed all the animals they had thought, as well as a large population of people. Two years ago there had been a rumour amongst travellers that an old radio station had received a call from some station in the states, the message they sent spread despair across the country: *The snow mass has doubled, the temperature keeps decreasing and is impossible to survive in, everyone is dead, I'm all that's left, all hope is lost. God bless you all.* Then the gunshot rang across the airwaves as the last American took his own life. The message left anyone who heard about it without hope, wondering how long until the inevitable came to them too.

Vanya slowly made her way towards the building, seeing the torches by the doorway. Finally, she approached the door, knocked lightly and slowly opened the door and stepped in. A man smiled as she entered, appearing to be in his forties with a full, scruffy beard and shaggy hair under a tattered beanie.

'Welcome! I'm Mica,' he said warmly, approaching Vanya and offering his hand out towards her. She hesitated for a moment before slowly extending her own hand into his and shook gently. She looked down at the flyer in her right hand and cleared her throat.

'I…I saw the flyer saying you have meat? Is that true?' she asked quietly, turning the flyer for him to see it, resulting in a large grin breaking out across his face.

'Absolutely it's true! I ran a farm before the world went to shit and kept all my animals safe, and I knew how to breed and slaughter so I've been providing meat to anyone that can find their way here, as you can see!' Mica explained, leading Vanya through to a large hall, filled with men, women and children, all sat at tables or gathered by the large fire pit in the centre, eating various cooked meats from plates.

Vanya's eyes widened as she saw the sight, before beginning to tear up seeing the rumours were true. Mica smiled at her and placed his hand on her shoulder. 'Come, let's get you a warm plate and something to drink,' he said, his friendly demeanour helping her to relax.

Vanya followed him to an empty seat beside a gruff looking man and a malnourished boy. She was amazed at seeing a child, as most had not been able to survive the harsh, endless winter. The boy noticed her stare and smiled at her, before taking a bite of his food and staring off into the distance. Mica waved at a girl in the corner who was beside an open fire cooking different cuts of meat on a grate. The girl smiled at him and grabbed a cooked chunk and stuck it on a plate, bringing it over to the two of them. She placed it in front of Vanya and the smell of the cooked pork filled her nostrils, causing her mouth to water and eyes to mist up, remembering all her friends and family who died of starvation. Mica stood behind her and watched as Vanya took the first bite of her meat and smiled to himself, happy to see her able to eat. He turned and made his way back over to the grill, leaving Vanya to warm up.

The sun fell and most people began to leave, making their ways to God knows where. Vanya pushed her hand through her hair and stood, wrapping her thick coat around herself, preparing to go out into the cold to find somewhere safe to stay. Mica approached her once more and smiled at her.

'You can stay the night. You look exhausted and I can't let you go in the cold in this state,' he offered, which made Vanya realise just how tired she was. She hesitated for a moment, but glanced towards the happy looking woman who had been cooking and thought to herself: *Just one night, I spent days getting here, I can stay one night.*

She smiled at Mica and nodded to him, allowing him to lead her through the back to a room with a few beds. Each one was warm and inviting, with the cleanest bedding Vanya had seen in years. She took her coat off, laid it over a bed and closing her eyes for a moment breathed a relaxed sigh. She began to pull back the covers to collapse; before she felt something heavy make contact with the back of her head.

Everything went black.

Vanya's eyes slowly opened, a ringing headache causing her eyes to be unable to focus. She tried to move, but felt something tug on her ankle. Squinting in the dark at her feet, she reached down and felt around. Her body froze as her fingers felt the cold metal cuff, before her hands ran down the chain connecting her to a long bar. Slowly, her eyes began to adjust to the poor lighting in the room, and her worst nightmare came true. She was in a cage, big enough for her to stand but not comfortably. Looking around, she saw there were other cages in the room.

'Hello?' she called out, but she was met with moaning as a response. Vanya strained to peer into the cages, seeing what was without a doubt a human torso, missing their arms and legs, deep lacerations in their incredibly thin torso.

Suddenly, a bright light turned on, triggering Vanya's severe headache to be even worse than before, and after a moment her eyesight managed to adjust as heavy footsteps descended down some stairs. Her breath caught in her throat as she could clearly see the room around her. There were more cages than she thought, each with people in different conditions, and the cage beside her with the person she was trying to examine caused a terrified scream to leave her lips. The man had been near flayed, with his muscle and even some bones clearly visible as chunks had been removed from him. He looked at Vanya with tears in his eyes, sitting in his own filth. He opened his mouth, trying to speak to her but could only groan. She realised his tongue was missing, but could see pity in his eyes, as if trying to communicate what happened to him would soon happen to her.

Mica stepped into the room and smirked at Vanya, approaching the cage beside her with a large cleaver.

'Don't look at me like I'm a monster. You enjoyed eating Markus here, and I did tell you when you arrived, fresh meat that I breed and harvest myself!' he stated with a chuckle as he opened the cage the man was in. Mica grabbed him by the hair, dragging him out and towards a bloodied table before Vanya.

Mica raised the cleaver and glanced over his shoulder at Vanya. 'Unlike Markus here, you get to choose to be bred or harvested at least,' before the cleaver came down on the poor man.

There Were Nine Children Left
Lucy Grace

Orla stepped hard into the snow, lengthening her stride to deceive them. If they were even bothering to look. They would, as a matter of principle. She wore a man's boots. From which man, she didn't know, but they weren't her father's, she didn't know what he was wearing. The paper she had balled and stuffed into the heavy toe-capped ends was now sodden and cold, blotting up wet slush through the gap between sole and upper. She could no longer feel her feet, but she trusted them to keep moving. Sticking white flakes fell, covering everything.

She risked a backwards glance. The distance between each print was shortening as she tired. She breathed hard, digging in to find the last energy, striding out. Bracing her shoulders against the pressing sky, she kept on.

Waking, she stretched and cracked like a frozen twig. Her thin knees dug into the rough branch of a tree, a rope around her waist holding her above the ground, twice tied. She was not going to take risks now, not when she was halfway there. Was she halfway there? It was too dark to see the horizon, but she could feel the pull of direction, she had the magnetism and the bones of a bird. Below her she had left a myriad of boot prints, to and from the tree, circling and leading off in multiple directions before turning back on themselves and looping around. The impression was that of a rendezvous, a hunting party lost and found, the tree as a marker. This deceit had taken her a long time. There were no clues she had climbed high. The few trees here stood desolate, empty of foliage, dead black markers in the landscape. Her tree had a violent scar where it had shed a bough in a storm. It was against this injury she took shelter, twenty feet from the ground.

She rubbed her cheek against the lip of the wound, felt the bark change beneath her skin to smoothed wood. A planed kitchen table, hall floor. Sudden tears came but she quickly brushed them away. There was no time for feeling.

She coiled the rope like a farmhand before feeling her way down the trunk, slithering and rushing the last six feet. Falling hard on her back she lay still, surrounded by cold as though in her grave. The snow was deep, it cushioned her limbs and cradled her head, comforting and soothing her with its sameness. Lie with me, it said, stay with me, let me. For a moment she was tempted, and her mind swam with the dark. The iced earth was freezing, feeding stultifying damp into her muscles and bones. A tiny, lit part of her shouted. Get. Up.

Summoning everything she had, she rose from the ground in a single movement like a strung puppet, snow falling from her clothes and hair like ash from a flaming newspaper. Feet heavy in her man's boots, she set out.

After two more sunrises and sunsets the landscape began to change. Still the dirty snow, the ice and the grey, but now there were rocky patches in the landscape, scattered like scabs. When the lifeboat had landed this was the shoreline they saw. She remembered the suck of the tide and the roughness of the rope as they drew the boat as far as they could up the beach, and shivered. There was little colour, bleached marram grass clung grimly to the dunes and the wind blew continuously. It was bleak, endless ocean and sky pressed together in the thin grey line of horizon she had stared at for so long on the boat. There had been just the nine of them on board, including her. She was neither the oldest nor the youngest.

When the wars first started, the Islanders thought they were safe, nestled up high. They were smug, smiling at each other in the way they did when summer tourists came over on the ferry and stood in the only shop, marvelling they could buy bootlaces and washing powder, dubbin and bacon, knitting needles and barbed wire. The Islanders could also buy bullets, but didn't tell the tourists that. Instead they nodded graciously, smiling at the 'Gee, we sure could live here,' and the 'You people have everything, it must be great to be away from it all.' Islanders didn't discuss the long, numbing winters or the repeated darkened days that rolled across the peat like a suffocating fog. Instead they looked to the end of the holiday season, when the walkers and birdwatchers thinned out like a drop of dye in water, until eventually no-one new stepped off the ferry, and their protective grey sea stretched out, deep and still once again.

Five families lived on the island, plus old Mrs Marriott from the far edge and the farmer from the Peak. No-one used his name. Orla wasn't sure he even had one. People just called him Farmer. Four of the families had always been islanders, knew no different, but the fifth family had brought their primary-aged, primary-knitwear-coloured children from the Mainland seventeen summers ago and, against all odds, they stayed. The Islanders didn't trust them, these New Folk, and exhausted by the pervasive and continual scrutiny, their two children left for university in their late teens and never returned. At least, the Islanders supposed it was for university. No-one asked. The parents remained, clinging grimly to an existence at the eastern end of the island, offering bed and breakfast to visiting tourists each summer before hunkering down when the clocks changed. Rumour had it he was a painter and she was a writer, but no one had evidence of either. The Islanders didn't need to believe it or not.

Now there were nine children left, and Orla was one of them. They were supposed to go to school each day in the little hall room on the harbour but rarely bothered unless the authorities from the Mainland came to check. Their island was the furthest north, the last in a broken necklace of rocky outcrop trailing from the top point of the country. School inspectors had to be dedicated to make it all the way across the sea. Realising this, the mother of the first family, who had put herself forward as the teacher, made the most of a termly phone call, explaining in detail to the inspector what the curriculum consisted of, how lessons were taught, which exams were sat. Some of it was true. It helped that the children of the New Folk had gone to university. They must be doing something right up there, the inspector said to her colleagues, and signed off the report, 'Authorised'.

The internet connection had always been patchy, but now the link became jittery, stuttering like the terrified, stopping and starting without rhythm or reason until the Islanders could no longer trust it. When they lost overseas contact altogether, life became simpler and older; people lived by light and dark, wind and tide, hunger and thirst. They pulled together when the ferry stopped running, pooled resources and efforts, waited it out. It wasn't until Farmer commented that the nights were now drawing out and stores were low that they made a plan. It was decided that the Fathers from families Number Two and Three should go with the Ferryman to the Mainland to see what was happening. The Islanders didn't wave them off at the jetty. They weren't the type of people to make a fuss.

More than a week later the boat returned, sailed only by the Ferryman, paled and wordless. After a warm at the fire and three slugs of amber whisky he found enough words to make broken sentences describing the endless sea, more water than before, a new shore, dragging the boat up, a makeshift camp, starving people, ill people, desperate people collected up at the end of the world. He met no-one's eyes as he described how he had pulled on the sleeves of the Island Fathers, begged them to leave now, right now, this will not end well, but the Fathers were Fathers, they were well-meaning, stubborn, disbelieving. The Ferryman stared into the fire as he told of the Fathers going into the camp, sleeping there for the night, how he returned alone to his boat and slept underneath it, crawling out in the morning like a creature from a shell. He was barely audible as he described how his stomach growled when he smelled a wonderful smell from the camp, of fire and food and roasting meat, of how he stole to the edge of the ridge and saw the spits, two of them, and the charring, and the grease dripping from the chins of the starving, and at this one of the Mothers retched onto the stone flags and the other rubbed her back and nobody spoke. It was then that the children were gathered up and shown the door, and the nine walked up to the headland together and looked out at the sea.

Cold and empty, Orla crawled up the dunes on her belly, waiting for dusk. There had been no dunes on her island, only stones. She was thinner than she had ever been, the flatbreads and biscuits stuffed in her pockets had run out a couple of days ago; she was nearly finished. It was three weeks since the nine had landed the lifeboat and there had not yet been a complete moon cycle nor a high tide. She needed the high tide, needed the physical world to help, to stand alongside her small girl's frame. She slid over the gritty ridge feet first. Her clothes were damp and cold, the wind cut through them. Now, standing on the beach, she began to lose faith. She had no weapons, no food, no water, no flame. No plan, no family waiting to receive her, only the map in her head and her father's voice. Her bird-bone wrists poked out of the sweater knitted by her mother and she folded her arms across her flat chest. She had only herself. She was enough.

Her ankles hurt in the man's boots. She was still glad she had worn them; her own shoes would not have been strong enough for the journey she had made, and the smaller imprint from the sole would have given her away if they were searching. She thought of those she had left behind, the eight left here and her family left there. Especially her family. They hadn't deserved it, to be left, but she knew it would not have been long until they did. People became more themselves when their normal world fell away. It had started with the Islanders already; the Eldest had noticed. He had the idea to take the lifeboat and escape, to be

169

heroic, to be first. None of the other eight wanted to go at the beginning, they wanted to stay with what they knew, but when the Mother from Family Two dropped from the church lintel, eyes staring, and the Mother from Family Three stepped outside of her mind and stopped speaking altogether, some children wavered. Then the Eldest made much of being orphaned, of the benefit of fresh starts, of creating a new family; he scared the youngest with tales of their own Fathers and Mothers disappearing, of the starving camp people coming to the island at night to find them asleep in their beds. Children are much easier to catch. When, finally, all but one had agreed to flee, he terrified the last and youngest child with the smells of spits and burning and dripping meat, until a plan was agreed. They were to leave secretly together on high tide, in the lifeboat, with supplies, and set up a new home, a hidden home. They would return for their parents and the Ferryman and Farmer and Mrs Marriott when they were established, after a tide or two, he said. Together, the nine would save the island, and he would lead them.

Orla hadn't believed him. She saw the glitter of deception behind his eyes, his poorly disguised desire for power. He was promising an escape that didn't exist.

Her father had told her that people could walk to Denmark from the island, many years ago, before the North Sea rushed in and filled the gap. Maybe the nine had reached Denmark, in their lifeboat, and she was in Denmark. Denmark, or Norway. Did Norway still have trees? She knew Iceland didn't, never had. No matter.

She remembered the maps her father had shown her. Not the school maps, or the impossibly folded walking maps the tourists grappled with, but the thickly creased and rolled sheets kept under his desk, marked with generations of oiled fingerprints where routes and facts had been measured and checked, retold and shared. The schoolteacher Mother had sought safety in the already printed word; classics, the history of dead white men told through long poetry. Most adults avoided questioning conversation about current events, some things were too difficult to think about. But Orla's father had not stopped her from knowing, he was different. Instead, he answered her every question. He unrolled leathery maps to show her seas and forests, the mainland and the tides. He took her into the dark to teach navigating by the stars, he tested her knowledge as she buttered toast, poured milk, cleaned her teeth. Her mother told him to stop, there really was no need, she was only twelve, they were going to be fine up here on the island, they were self-sufficient, but Orla's father replied quietly that the danger would not come from running out of flour or eggs, and her mother's face tightened in her reflection in the window.

In the gloaming Orla saw the lifeboat ahead. It was perched high on the beach, still upright, facing the waves like a watchful bird. Seaweed and debris clustered in a sparse line near its hull showing the beckoning of the previous tide. She clambered inside, stumbling painfully against one of the wooden plank seats, hurting her ribs. In the gloom on the floor of the boat she lay curled up under the seat, exhausted. She slept. When she woke it was fully dark, and a bright moon was rising. The sea swashed against the pebbly shore, a regular and predictable heartbeat, comforting. Last night the moon had been almost full: tonight, it would be high tide. It would mean she was visible, but who was there to watch her leave? Resting her chin on her chest, Orla pulled her knees in tightly, and waited for the sea.

34 to 1
Grace Choi

Each day, she thought the world got a little brighter. The dimness of the hallways seemed less persistent, less cloaking of the dark corners of her room. She could see the rusting rivets embedded in the walls with less strain as she counted them nightly, the flakes of browned metal peeling away like blooming flowers. She imagined them popping out of the walls, ricocheting around like loose rockets. They'd pepper themselves in a collage, hammering the metal of her walls so thin she'd see marvels of marine life on the other side, wonderfully unhuman. She'd seen a penguin once drift past through the porthole – her only glimpse of the outside – a shock of white feathers against the blackness of the sea. When it twisted in the stream, she'd realised it had been sucked clean out of its skin like a morbid variation of a plastic bag, empty of everything that had once animated its short life.

Perhaps she was just trying to convince herself that the stagnancy of the submarine they called home was dissipating. Or maybe that it wasn't true energy was running low; if the lights were shining brighter, then the nuclear reactor must still be firing away, locked behind impenetrable cages of lead. Two weeks of the emergency lights hadn't been completely terrible. They were mercifully softer than the usual overhead lights that washed everyone out with their impressive white blandness. At a stretch they were even atmospheric, although their eerie green tinge imposed a different type of sickliness on the residents. No one complained. That sort of superficiality was frowned upon nowadays and even her parents' clothes, real life artifacts from aboveground, had long since been repurposed into the same shapeless garments thrown together by people who'd never had to learn to sew. They'd taken everything worth saving with them in huge trunks that sat useless by their bed.

The textbooks she occupied her days with had certainly been harder to decipher at first under the one allocated lamp. She'd been afforded a limited education based on her parents' distant memories of school: reading, writing, mathematics – although she got the impression that they hadn't been very good at it as they fumbled their way through equations. When she was younger, she remembered sitting on her mother's lap and scrawling with coloured pencils, wearing them down to shavings before they'd been gently plucked out her hands and stored away. Out of sight, like all their precious possessions.

She hadn't been afforded an education in science, but she understood what no more fuel meant. The last scientist on board had broken the news to the outdated glasses in his shaking hands rather than to them, eyes downcast as he laid out their options. They could sustain themselves for a little longer by cutting energy elsewhere (the first thing to go had been the lights) but nothing would divert the ultimate end: surface or sink.

And now the only thing not shaded green on the submarine was the board of red numbers above the dining room table, a fluorescent counter of the number of people left in their little community. The 34 washed their heads in bloody neon.

The next community meeting – probably the last – felt pointless. Dull. There'd been a revival in extravagant clothing and accessories as people hauled out their stashes of earthly possessions for a grand runway show, sitting in a mismatched fanfare of furs and glittering rocks. Her father draped a scarf around her neck. She thought the colours were wasted in the low light. Every time the 34 flickered off it felt like a threat – an omen of the times to come.

They attempted to distract each other with meaningless

snippets of knowledge. 'Do you know the origin of the word submarine?' Her father supposedly had a degree in etymology. 'Submarine. Sub meaning below, and marine meaning of the sea. Both derivations from Latin.'

The pointlessness of the statement irked her, a waste of time in their last hours together. 'A dead language. Very fitting for the occasion.'

Her mother's mouth twinged in displeasure and she thought that she was going to chastise her, but then she leaned over and trailed a tender hand through her hair. 'I'm sorry for bringing you into this existence,' she whispered. 'I wish you could have seen the world. It was really quite beautiful before... everything.'

'Why can't we?' She thought that her greatest regret would be not knowing. The stories of wildfire, drought, and rising sea levels had once scared her even far removed from danger in their submarine, but they didn't matter anymore. Her father had sold the last house they had to buy their place onboard. She wanted to know if it had been worth it.

It wasn't difficult to persuade the remaining residents to spend the last of their fuel charting the course to the nearest surviving port. They were lethargic, too withdrawn to their private mourning to make a real protest. She stood waiting under the hatch cover, bracing herself against the jolt of the submarine as their sudden buoyancy burgeoned around them. Just a few minutes in case you can't handle the climate, her mother warned her, and she reluctantly agreed.

And then she was rising, rushing towards some unknown end. The submarine groaned around her, great metal walls creaking in an ancient protest, dissolving into an imitation of whale song until they burst through in an explosion of seaweed and vapour, shuddering in the water. The hatch cover thudded open, extending a sunny beam towards her, and she climbed with eager hands, surfacing from the dark tube into a halo of sun.

It was light.

Painfully light.

Blues and whites danced across her crimson vision, spotting polka dots onto her eyes. Hands guided her off the top of the submarine, tripping along the cold metal until she staggered down onto a rough ramp, water gathering around her ankles. It gave way to pliable sand, grains shifting under her soles as she took another step. Her skin blistered and crawled in the heat, unlike any of the cool dryness at home. She wondered if she was glowing.

'That's a nice boat.' There was someone on the beach. She nearly missed them, sandy robes blending into the ground, but his voice was unmistakable. He spoke with the dry snapping force of years of desert and fire. The simmering air rasped and caught in his throat, clawing its way through burnt lips. 'I never thought I'd see one of you back up here,' he continued. His words were salted with derision. 'I always thought you'd found some lost city under the sea and turned part fish when you bought those from the navy. Got the better end of the deal.'

'This is my last day alive.' She saw the sunburn on his face and his threadbare clothes and briefly wondered if he would have traded the rest of his life for brief comfort. Or if she would have done the opposite. But that musing could be saved for the journey back down, not wasted on her only moments in the sun. 'We can't survive up here and our submarine's out of fuel. There's nowhere left to go.'

He faltered at her predicament, his face screwing up with

sympathy and disagreement. 'It's not all that bad on land. There's not much food most places anymore so we have to move around a lot – take what we can get. But it's definitely liveable.' His coat was a patchwork of faded clothes when she looked closer, all sunbleached to the same beige. She spotted half of a logo – bits of letters all stitched together. Memorabilia from abandoned cities.

'I didn't even know people still lived on land,' she confessed. She took in the beach turning grey under the waves. Behind them the sand blended into miles of orange jigsaw puzzle, cracked into pieces. They'd seen a video of a nuclear explosion once and she thought it looked a lot like the horizon, a blinding supernova of white doming above her. She wondered what would be better. Eternal entombment in the tube she'd called home for years, or being simply blown to nothing in a nuclear blast, disintegrated into molecules and scattered into the scars in the ground. He noticed her looking.

'The land's all the same as this.' He'd seen it a thousand times before and there was no reverence in his voice, only flat observation. He eyed the submarine bobbing at the shore. She wondered if he was imagining the cold decks beneath, dreaming of shade from the aboveground. Water swelled around the great black marine body. 'Are you really dying after this?'

'Don't feel too bad about it. I've had a while to process.' Two weeks had rolled out into an eon when she'd had nothing to do. The bulk of the existential contemplation had passed her by without panic and she'd decided that deep down, underneath all that numb acceptance, she was vaguely irritated. Not at the thought of dying itself, but at the fact that she'd wanted to choose.

'We have to go.' Her parents' voices beckoned her back towards the submarine and she brushed the sand off the tops of her shoes, watching it clump into the laces and stain them yellow. It stuck deep under her fingernails, a lasting souvenir of the beach.

She offered him a smile and then, after a moment's thought, unravelled her scarf from her neck and held it out to him. Maybe he could add it to his coat and she could leave a little piece of herself up here, one lasting memory travelling over the world in her stead. His hand grasped hers, hot through the silk, pity welling on his face.

'You could stay up here. There's space with my family and we take in people who've been stranded.'

'I'm not stranded.'

'All the same – it doesn't feel right to let you go to your death,' he said stubbornly. His grip tightened. She could see her parents on the top of the ship and she felt time stretch under their silent insistence, anchored to the beach by a determined hand.

She took another look at him. What she could see of him was dusted in a fine layer of sand. He could melt into the earth like a chameleon, hiding in a veil of his clothes. His concern, though, was clear. It blazed through the weathered sunspots on his face and she knew that despite the brevity of their exchange, she didn't doubt the sincerity of his offer. Would she live in a tent? Survive off unfamiliar plants and animals, roaming from place to place whilst never really settling in a house? She allowed herself to dream not of a better life on land or even life itself, but a beginning. Decisively blank slated with the freedom to take an alternative. She gave him a nod.

Then she was splashing through the water, wading to the submarine and throwing herself as far up the curved walls as she could reach to say her last goodbye. 'I want to stay.' Cold fingers reached down and grasped her face. They were wet, salty with sea spray.

She tried to burn her parents' features into her eyes in the hope that once she closed them they'd still be there, illuminated imprints of their smiles on the backs of her eyelids. Their lips moved, murmuring farewell and good luck. A necklace slipped over her head and a flask of water pushed into her hand, their last gifts to her. She hoped they could tell there was no regret within her for any of it, least of all the life they'd given her underwater. Their touch was understanding.

And then they were gone, sliding back towards the submarine. She heard the heavy clang of the hatch door through the throbbing in her eardrums and the sea bubble and heave as they pulled away and down. The surge they left in their wake pooled into her watery shoes. Her tongue was already thick with dryness in her mouth as she turned away from the beach onto firm, flaking ground. She might yet waste away in the heat, withering away like a plant deprived of hydration, or fall victim to a fire and shrivel into a brittle shell of herself. Crack into pieces and peel.

But deep below the waves, before the red counter fizzled into the darkness of the seabed, it flashed a final hopeful number.

One.

The Seeker's Story
Shabnam Ahsan

We used to hear tales of the time before. A time when rivers flowed, and lakes rippled; when the rains fell like mercy from the skies. When the waters of our lands teemed with life. When there was no desert without an oasis, if you only knew where to find it, gleaming in the sunlight like a green jewel in the dust. A promise of the blessings of Paradise. A time of innocence. A time before the Fall.

My ancestors were fishermen. They lived on the banks of the rivers which were their livelihood, the stores from which they nourished their families. Their tales were passed down from generation to generation, until they became the stuff of legend. The boats our great-great-grandfathers would steer over the rushing waters were light and graceful. The songs they sang were swelling and rhythmic, like the currents they paddled over. They knew which fish could be caught in which season, and the exact times and spots where the most fish were to be found. The crops were lush after the rains. Water was life.

In the rainy season, fat drops would scatter the dry earth, bringing relief from the intense heat of the weeks before. At first, everyone would go out, arms outstretched, faces turned up to the sky. Then, the welcome showers would turn torrential, thundering on tin rooftops, pouring off the ends of banana leaves, swirling and eddying in ditches. The roads would turn to mud, slippery and dark. The swollen river would rush past, its waters opaque and foaming. Sometimes the river would burst its banks. The water pooled on the streets, rising higher and higher, until it washed away carts and homes, flimsy pole-and-thatch dwellings. Belongings floated away, and people had to push themselves around on boats to get anywhere. Drinking water would be contaminated, livestock and food stores ruined. Starvation, disease, and homelessness were everyday truths. Many people were taken by the river, no longer nurturing mother but vengeful goddess. And so we learned, water could also be death.

When the rains ended and the water receded, began the business of assessing the damage, counting the dead and rebuilding lives again from the bottom up. At least the soaked earth left behind was fertile ground, in which to plant. Until the next year, when it would all happen again. People got used to the cycle, the fragility of life, the transience of possessions. Survival was all anyone thought of. That, at least, has not changed.

But then the rains began to grow heavier. Over the years, the floods became worse. It rained out of season, so that nobody was prepared. It took longer for the waters to recede. The river ate away at the land, a fierce serpent taking gigantic bites out of the shoreline. Our land dwindled until eventually, we were left a nation of nomadic sailors. The boats became our homes, a precarious shelter among the waves. Here, babies were born. Parents tied ropes around the middle of their infants, to secure them while the vessel rocked and tilted. The children grew up in the spaces between the fishing nets and the cooking pots, married and moved onto boats of their own. The money they earned from fishing was spent on food and necessities. Any little wealth they could save was worn by their women, as gold rings piercing their earlobes and the sides of their noses – the safest places to keep your savings, when you live on a boat. The land-dwellers knew them by the ornaments they wore; they looked down on the river-folk, and their rulers gave them no rights or protection - even though the river folk were land-dwellers too, once.

Then, the fish started dying. Those who had knowledge said the seas were rising, and the river water was turning salty. All we knew was that there were soon too few fish for us to make our living. We knew the story of the prophet Noah and the Flood, how it was a punishment from God. Our world was flooded once again. But nobody heeded the warning, and now we are in Hell.

It grew hotter each year. Slowly, the ponds and lake dried up. Then the smaller streams and finally, the rivers. The heat made our existence unbearable. We moved inland, seeking refuge. The people took us in, but grudgingly. Our boat-building, net-mending skills were useless now, and we were simply extra mouths to feed, leeching off their generosity. But we held on to our tales and songs, and our pride, even as we were driven to the cities, the rich still sheltering in their machine-cooled homes, far above the streets where we scratched out a living by picking through waste. When deadly disease began to kill us, some of us left the slums and fled to the empty land beyond the city walls, never to return. Our ancient skills were all but gone, like the rivers that once sustained us, but somehow, we survived.

We are still nomads, like our forefathers. I am a Seeker for my tribe. Or should I say, I was, for it has been many years since I went on ahead of the group, seeking out the next place we should set up camp. It does not make sense to move everybody – the children and elderly – before we know where we are going. So every time a child comes of age, they must take the test which tells us whether they possess the gift. It sounds like magic, but it is not really. Over time, some of us were born with sharpened senses and the ability to read the earth for signs of water. Those who have the gift are rare, only coming along every other generation, if you're lucky. We are called Seekers, and we are invaluable to our people. It is serious work, dangerous – but the life of the tribe depends on it.

When we find a source, it is usually shallow, and we stay near it until it dries up. When our stores run out, we move over the parched earth again in search of water, the soles of our feet cooking on the stones. There is never enough shade. When the sun is at its height, the only hope is to burrow deep into a cave or mountain, if you are lucky enough to be near one. There, the air is cooler, and the sun's rays cannot scorch you. Some go out at night to forage and go about their business. But if you cannot hide, that is when you feel that there can be nothing worse than living on this earth, where every breath is a struggle.

It is a harsh existence for all of us, but most of all for the weakest among us – the very young, the very old, the sick. And yet you must go on living, trying to survive. But there is sometimes a price to pay, and each must decide for themselves whether the cost is too high, or whether it is worth the consequences. Here, at the end of my life, I think of the young ones I leave behind, and of the life they still have to face. A life of growing uncertainty and hardship. I think also of the high price I paid on one, terrible day, and whether the choice I made was worth the consequences. It weighs on my heart like a stone, and so I unburden myself of it now, with you as my witness.

One day long ago, in the first years of the Great Drought, when I was much younger than I am now, my tribe had settled briefly in a place where we had come to the previous year. Then, there had been a pond with several thin-limbed trees hanging over it. Now, the trees were dying and the pond had shrunk to half its size. It was obvious we could not stay here for long. We had already trekked for miles over weeks to reach here, and many of us had lost loved ones along the way, myself included. We arrived heartsick and grieving, and I could not bear to be around other people whose pain only reflected my own.

After two days to rest and strengthen myself again, I had gone on ahead; this time striking out in a different direction to the one we had taken last time, looking for the next stopping-place, alert for all the signs I alone could discern. The sun was high overhead, and the air in front of me shimmered. There were only a few precious drops in the water-skin I carried, and I moistened my lips now. Still weak from our long trek, I was beginning to think I ought to turn back, and to take another chance tomorrow, when it came to me: a faint waft of dampness to wrinkle my nostrils, followed by a barely discernible gurgle echoing in my head, and a delicate tremor from deep in the earth, making itself felt through the soles of my feet and rumbling its way up and into my bones. From the strength of the feeling it seemed there was a spring not far off, south of where I stood. I took a breath and began to move forward again. The sun was directly in my eyes now, and I shaded them with my hand in order to be able to see ahead.

As the sun continued to dazzle me, I made out a dark smudge on the horizon in front of me. I thought they were trees, tall and thick-trunked, with broad, spreading leaves throwing shade over the ground. They stood like sentinels, standing guard over what seemed to be a sparkling stretch of water. I thought I must have been hallucinating, for surely this was something we only told each other about in stories: an oasis. But the rushing in my head told me that the water at least, was no vision. As the knowledge gave me strength to go on putting one foot in front of the other, I suddenly became aware of another feeling, humming on the edge of my hearing like a warning, and it filled me with dread. Someone was there before me – another Seeker.

Crossing paths with other tribes on our journeys is usually a good thing. It makes us feel a little less desolate. We can talk, hear each other's stories, and, if we are lucky, trade for much-needed goods and resources. When it is not a good thing to come across others, is when you are headed for the same stopping-place. You especially do not want to arrive at a place, and find there are others already there. The water-sources are scarce and far-between, and usually shallow. Most of the time, they are barely enough to sustain one group, let alone two. When this happens, the unwritten code of the plains dictates that the newcomers should move on and search for another place. If the ones who were there first are decent, they will allow a little respite; perhaps they permit everyone to have a drink, or at the very least, the weakest. But once that is done, the newcomers must leave.

The burden of leading those I had left behind, into safety and comfort, lay heavily on my shoulders. If I was not able to lead them somewhere we could stay in the next day or two, we would lose more of our people. So the last thing I wanted to see at that moment, was another person. Another Seeker meant more people would follow, and more people meant competition.

As I stepped into the shade of those spreading trees, I glanced all around me, but could see no one. It was a tiny grove, much smaller than it had looked from the outside. I could see through to the patch of sunlight at the other end. There were a few smaller fruit-trees here and there, bearing golden-coloured spheres the size of a child's fist. It was still better than anywhere we had stopped, in years. I moved cautiously toward the pool in the middle of the grove; it was not deep, but it was cool and clear. I dipped my hand into it, and drank deeply, splashed water over my face, and refilled my water-skin. Then I stood and wandered between the fruit trees. I picked one of the pale fruits and sank my teeth into the soft flesh, tasting the sweetness on my tongue. I was about to take another bite when I felt again the sensation of being watched. I looked around, and again, saw no one. Then, a rustle, and a figure dropped down in front of me from one of the trees. The figure was a little shorter and slighter than me, and was dressed in the same loose robes we all wore. The face was wrapped in a scarf, but the dark eyes above stared at me with an expression I could not name. The hand pointing at me now, held a knife.

'You must leave, now,' a low voice said.

I had no wish to leave the peace and the shade so soon.

'Why must I?' I demanded. 'I am a Seeker, like you.'

The eyes blinked, and the hand holding the knife gestured towards my chest.

'Because if you do not, I will kill you.'

'Why can we not both stay here? There is room enough for both our tribes.'

The stranger scoffed. 'Surely you know that if both our tribes stay here, we will be forced to move on in half the time. My people cannot endure that.'

Neither could mine, but still, I hesitated.

In that second of hesitation, the stranger lunged towards me with the knife-arm still outstretched, the tip quivering inches from my throat.

At that moment it was as if my vision went dark. The sound of the water rushing in my ears was replaced by a high whine; all I knew was that the thought of my people going back out into the heat and glare of the sun, was unbearable to me.

I do not remember what happened next, but suddenly the two of us were locked in a furious struggle. My opponent was lithe and fast, but my desperation gave me a strength I did not know I had. The knife slashed at my cheek, drawing blood, and then found its way to my arm, and my shoulder. Clenching my teeth against the pain, I somehow managed to sidestep and trip the other Seeker to the ground, pinning him down from behind, knocking the knife from his hand. He struggled, but I was bigger, and heavier, and fuelled by something beyond fear or desperation. I pinned him like that with my full bodyweight, I do not know for how long. When I came to myself again and rolled away, something about the way the form lay still on the ground, filled me with horror.

I crept closer. As I reached out to touch the figure, my hand brushed the scarf away from the head, revealing a heart-shaped face, and those dark-lashed eyes, fixed and staring. It was a young woman.

The realisation of what I had done washed over me, taking the strength from my limbs, as I thought of her tribe, waiting somewhere for her return; I had taken so much more from them than the life of their daughter or sister. They would wait the three days that was customary, and then eventually set out on their own, forced to navigate the world now without their Seeker.

I buried her, and her knife, in a shallow grave beneath a tree at the far end of the grove, digging through the earth with a branch. Then I returned to our camp, and led them back to the oasis. They never asked about my wounds, and I never spoke about what happened. We stayed there until it was time to move on; the others savoured the fruit and the coolness and the water, but to me, the shadows hid ghosts, the fruit held no flavour, and every mouthful from that clear, cool spring tasted bitter.

The Stars Will Keep
P D Anderson

"And the moon rose over an open field."

Paul Simon – America

Her children would live on the moon. Of that she was sure. Leonanna took a deep breath and plunged her spade into the wet, viscid soil at her feet.

She turned over a solid clod. It oozed a treacly liquid. She smiled to herself. This was what she wanted; the precious material known as Sable.

She was digging at the boggy edge of a shallow pond, one of many, laid out around her like the rice paddy fields she had seen in old books from way back in the 2020s, when the staple foodstuffs could still be grown on Earth. The moon, almost full, was rising just above the horizon, where high hills marked the edge of the vast prairie where her little hut and ponds lay.

The sods of overturned soil, black as pitch, wet and sultry like warm tar, were slowly stacking up behind her, waiting to be moved to the main drying area.

It was good to be out on the ponds again, working towards quota. For the last few days she had been trapped in the hut as one of the regular, climatic storms – with their noxious, sulphurous winds – had blown up.

After a while, breathless, she paused her digging and glanced across the water. The lampreys that filled the pond glistened on the surface of the water; they were certainly busy tonight, their writhing backs glinting pale yellow in the moonlight. Known to everyone as moonfish, the lampreys had been genetically modified so that they could live off the thin and exhausted prairie soil on the bed of the ponds and excrete deposits of the super-nutrient rich Sable.

As the moonfish grew to maturity, Leonanna would shepherd them from one shallow pond to the next, letting them work the bed until she was ready to drain it a little and then start to the dig out a new batch of the precious deposits.

This was her life now, tending the lampreys and digging and drying clods of processed earth for the quota. All across the vast prairie thousands of others were working their own ponds. No one grew wheat here anymore. No one had managed to do that in half a generation. Not since the collapse.

Something stirred in the scrubby bushes just beyond the wire fence that marked her patch. Checking the rifle strapped to her back, Leonanna scanned the horizon, her eyes narrowed.

Deer most likely, nibbling at the thin pickings of the stunted and failing scrub. Or scavenging stray dogs. But it could be those bastards, the rustlers; criminal gangs who stole the lampreys and could be relied upon to do worse to the women.

She felt exposed, now that she was having to live alone out here. She double-checked the rifle and then crossed herself and recited the benediction of all the pond dwellers:

'To the moon, the stars will keep.'

*

Kane skirted the ponds, keeping his profile low behind the scrub bushes and fencing that surrounded the property. He could see Leonanna in the near distance, bending over at the edge of a pond, digging. It had been several days hard marching, but finally he was back at his old home. He ached to run over and speak to her. To touch her. To remind her that he existed. To tell her the terrible truth he now knew.

*

Leonanna returned to her digging, satisfied that it was just animals. There was much to do if she was to reach quota. Soon, the inspectors would be coming to assess the quality of her latest batch of Sable, now drying in a huge pile of clods behind the hut where she slept and cooked.

She was hoping this would be her final inspection. It had been a long couple of years of grinding work delivering one batch after another and the last few weeks of working alone without Kane had been especially hard. Exhausted and lonely, with her back playing up, she was praying she was near the end and that the inspectors would pass the quality of the latest batch. Finally, she would hit quota.

Only those with quota went to the moon.

There was another rustling noise from the edge of the property; louder this time. She dropped her spade and fingered her rifle, silently thanking her father for teaching her to use a gun.

Leonanna was pretty sure it wasn't Nadia, her immediate neighbour, working her own set of ponds just nearby. She always signalled before coming.

She enjoyed Nadia's visits. They would sit on the edge of her hut and sip some of the dwindling tea stock and talk about their lives before all this. Before climate crisis. Before crop failures and eco-system collapse. Before what everyone now just called 'ecogeddon'.

Swapping spade work techniques, they would show each other the raw skin and the calluses. How soft their hands once were! Back when they lived in cities and had jobs and lives; touching things for pleasure rather than brute work. It all seemed long ago.

Nadia always asked about Kane.

No, he's not likely to be coming back.

No, there had been no word.

Yes, it was over three months now.

'It's a shame, he was a fine young man.'

Leonanna would nod and sip her tea, and stare into the distance. And ignore the hole in her heart, which, week by week, was slowly turning into a black star of boiling anger.

In recent months, Kane had started to question things. He was always fretting away at details and nagging about little inconsistencies with arrangements. He had, she had decided, an overly suspicious mind. Funny how she hadn't noticed this when they lived together in their previous life. Too busy with other things, she expected.

His incessant 'why?'s began to feel like she lived with a toddler. He seemed incapable of accepting the situation as it had been explained to them by the authorities from the Government of the Reconstruction. Their names had been selected by a lottery process to be among those given the opportunity to work towards going to the moon to start a new life. Allocated a set of ponds on one of the great prairies, they would be given a batch of lampreys and expected to work towards quota.

A light caught her eye and she looked up from her rifle. In the distance, beyond the high hills that formed the boundary of the prairie, something bright and burning flared into the evening sky. The monthly rocket being launched! Another set of pioneers with their quota of processed Sable heading to their new life.

She did not know the details. No one from the authorities had explained exactly how it all worked, but somewhere up on the moon a whole new civilisation - a second Earth - was being carved out of the moon rock. Each pioneer was allocated a space for a new farm under some kind of gigantic artificial umbrella where an Earth-like atmosphere had been recreated. With their own quota of nutrient rich material they would begin again, growing what increasingly could not be farmed on this world.

If she made quota at the coming inspection, she might well be on the next flight. As would Kane have been, had he not left. Only the young and fit of childbearing age were in the lottery. Why could he not just be grateful at this one chance to escape the dying Earth and start again?

On and on, Kane went, asking how lamprey droppings could be sufficient for a whole new life on the moon. Who was picking the stuff up? Who were these people who came and measured their quotas and tested the chemical structure of the fresh material? Why didn't they have government uniforms on? It was exhausting. They were the officials, overseeing a complicated process, why had it become so hard for him to just accept things and knuckle down?

Then, one day, Kane started on about why they had never heard from the ones who had already made quota. That nice Finnish couple two patches down from theirs who had regularly come to dinner and played their accordion. They had got to know them really well, Kane argued, and they've been gone six months and yet we have not had a word from them. The Internet still

191

worked, despite all the chaos, so why no messages? On and on he went about the bloody Finns as they worked together digging earth and shepherding lampreys. Leonanna felt she was going to scream by the end of that day. And then, as they cleaned off their spades and nets, he suddenly announced that he was going to watch a rocket launch.

'You can see them from here,' she had said, 'you know that. We watch one every month.'

'No, I mean close up. I want a proper look at what goes on.'

'But it's, I dunno, a hundred miles away. How will you get there?'

'I will walk. Shouldn't take more than a week or two.'

And with that, the next day he was gone. A small rucksack thrown over his shoulder, marching across the edges of the irrigation dykes and ponds and off into the distance. She had watched until he was no more than a dot in the flatness, lost between their home and the distant hills.

Leonanna found that she was relieved. She could concentrate on the work in hand and not listen to the incessant querying and worries. It was like the relief you got when the noise of incessant beating rain on the roof finally stops and the sun comes out.

*

At the edge of the property, Kane sneaked into one of the drainage ditches. He was exhausted from days of walking and he lay his head against the side of the ditch and looked up at the evening stars that were beginning to shine through.

He knew the truth now. No one was going to the moon. No one had been to the moon since 1972.

After he had left, Kane had walked for several days across the endless flat prairie, heading for the far hills from where the rockets were launched. He had passed countless miles of ponds and hundreds, maybe even thousands, of people, who, like Leonanna, were working their moonfish and building their stores of Sable. Some stopped to talk to the odd fellow who was stomping purposefully across their land, but most viewed him with suspicion, fearing rustlers, and waved him away with guns and upraised spades.

At last he made the hills at the end of the prairie and headed up roughly in the direction of the launching rockets. After a long climb through dying pine woods and boulder-strewn clearings, Kane made it to a high point. Looking back at where he had come from he could see the endless flat plain of ponds and huts stretching into a hazy distance. In the other direction, he could only see woods and more hills: there was no sign of any place where a rocket could be launched.

He considered turning back and heading home to Leonanna, but he had come this far and his curiosity and suspicion drove him on to begin a systematic search of the woods. It would take some time — the woods stretched in all directions — but he was determined to see a launch at close quarters.

One afternoon, weeks later, after yet another fruitless search, laying down for a rest against a tree, Kane opened his eyes to find a man in a simple brown smock and straw hat standing over him.

There was a long silence as each man regarded the other.

'Every so often there is one who comes seeking the truth,' the man finally said, before introducing himself.

Kane had heard about the Hermits of the Extinction, men and women who had turned their backs on society years ago, just as it was becoming clear that ecogeddon was approaching. They had opted out, living a lonely, scavenger life in various wildernesses, awaiting the full fall they were convinced was coming.

Many were dangerous religious fanatics, placing all their faith in a pantheon of animal gods and spirits of extinct species who would return to the living world when it was finally cleansed of humankind with a great purging fire.

The hermit beckoned him to follow, but Kane was initially reluctant. Stories and rumours were legion of hermits and their shamanic rituals and sacrifices to the animal gods.

Yet, old and a little frail, the man seemed harmless enough, and his cryptic comment about the truth had rekindled Kane's curiosity. They headed further into the pines and before long came to a cave, where the stranger had set a small fire.

Over a simple meal - Kane's first cooked food in weeks - they talked of the hermit's life in the woods, the ponds and the collapse. Finally, Kane could no longer contain himself and asked the hermit what he knew of rockets for the moon.

'It is all illusion,' he replied, 'like so much in this benighted world.'

Kane said that he had seen the rockets launch from these hills with his own eyes.

'Only from a distance. It is a giant optical trick; a clever projection. All you can see from your little homestead out there on the prairie is a hologram.'

By the end of the meal, Kane knew the full truth. No pioneers went to the moon. No Sable had ever been near a rocket, let alone the moon. Somewhere deep in these woods there was a site where equipment projected the vast illusion that lit up the sky once a month.

The hermit talked on. Banging a stick on the stones surrounding the fire to emphasize his points. The full deception was even more incredible than Kane's suspicious mind could conceive. Sable, rich in nutrients after its processing by the lampreys, did not go to the moon. It was taken from the ponds when the quota was reached and sent to the Crystals, the giant glass shards in the desert where the technology billionaires had retreated as the Earth's collapse had taken hold. He had seen these places with his own eyes said the hermit, shaking his head in anger, gesticulating his disgust. The plutocrats lived under those towers in unimaginable luxury, sustained by all that could be grown and made from Sable, and working on their plans to send themselves to a new life in the stars.

The whole business of people working patches of ponds to create quotas with the promise they would start a new life on the moon was a lie. A terrifying ruse to keep people processing the precious material without even realising they were in a giant open prison. It was slavery, said the hermit, banging his stick repeatedly, without guards.

Finally, Kane asked the question he had been dreading posing. What happened to the people? The ones who reached quota and came to these hills with their load ready to go to the moon.

'They are also processed.'

And then silence fell, and Kane stared into the campfire, knowing he must return to their home and try and warn Leonanna.

*

Leonanna had finished her digging and had waded into the pond to begin shepherding this particular batch of lampreys to the other side. She deftly wielded the landing net, carrying the squirming moonfish over the line of submerged plastic fence that lay across the pond. The light of the moon, silver and ethereal, danced across the water on the little waves she made.

She had always been a huge optimist. Many had lost faith in the future; she was not one of them. She believed. She had no doubts. She had lost track of the friends and acquaintances she had lost along the way. Unable to face the future on the failing planet, they had died by their own hands. But she and Kane had been gifted a future and it lay on the moon. Her anger flashed up again.

There was a sploshing sound in the near distance. Ceasing her work with the lampreys, Leonanna again pulled her rifle around from her back.

*

Kane lay low in the ditch and tried to figure out what to do. Having returned from the hills bursting to tell her the awful truth, he realised he had no idea what her reaction to seeing him would be. She had been angry enough when he had left. He had been gone, what, nearly three months now, and all that time she had been working their ponds hard and alone. Judging by the pile of drying earth by the hut, she was near to making quota.

He knew she was a fine shot. She wouldn't miss if she

caught him in her gunsight. The bodies of two rustlers buried at the end of this ditch – unlucky enough to be caught in the act by Leonanna – were testament to that.

He had to get close enough to speak to her. Tell her what he knew; before it was too late. A few moments should be enough. But first, somehow he had to distract her from the rifle. She might mistake him for a rustler, or just want to take a shot at him anyway.

At the edge of Leonanna's ponds, several ditches, pipes and streams for the water irrigation met and flowed in from Nadia's property. Keeping low, Kane skulked his way to this meeting place. Here, the water flowing into the various ponds was controlled by a series of sluice gates and flow valves.

Kane briefly looked up to check. Leonanna was standing in the centre of a pond, rifle up close to her face, scanning the edges of the property for movement. He ducked down again and began opening sluice gates and turning valves on water pipes. Pushing on further up the stream, he made his way, as quietly as possible, to the edge of Nadia's ponds and opened a twin pair of gates, diverting a huge flow from her ponds: anything to try and get water flooding faster through the system.

This seemed to do the trick, and a wall of water suddenly began to race through the rest of the irrigation system, sloshing and broiling its way towards Leonanna's main ponds.

He risked another quick peek above the ditch. He could see that she was slowly lowering her rifle and starting to look concerned as water quickly began to rise over the sides of the ponds around her.

Kane took his chance and pulled himself out of the ditch, pushing his way through the bushes at the edge of the property. He began to run down the side of a pond, towards Leonanna, his feet slipping in the mud and brackish water as the levels rose on all sides.

Standing in the pond, her rifle partly held down, she watched as water started to pour out all around her, flooding one pond after another. Something was very wrong. The irrigation system seemed to have been wrecked. The lampreys, sensing something was amiss, were thrashing around wildly.

She heard a shout and looked up to see a man running towards her waving his arms.

Sensing disaster, she turned and looked in horror at what was happening by the hut. Rising water was starting to lap around the drying mound of Sable. If it rose too high, much of her quota would be washed away.

She looked back at the figure, now rapidly moving closer towards her, shouting and gesticulating. Lifting up her rifle to her face, she lined the man up in the sight.

Kane.

He was running towards her; bounding over collapsing irrigation ditches and splashing through waterlogged ponds. She could see him clearly now, washed stark in black and white in the moonlight.

He had gone mad. He must have opened all the sluices. What was he thinking? All her work of months – her final quota – would be ruined.

She glanced up for a moment from the gunsight – and the moon, bright and yellow and on the rise – caught her eye. She was going there.

Something primeval made her briefly lower one hand and touch the gentle swelling in her belly. *They* were going there.

She returned her eye to the sight.

Kane would not stop her.

He was close now, and yelling something about 'lies' and 'rockets' and 'hermits'.

Raving.

She let her finger rest gently on the trigger and, then, for a moment, everything in the world seemed to freeze. Bathed in lunar light, she was suddenly struck by the beauty of it all and a haunting sense of loss.

She hesitated, unsure. Titanic anger seemed to be bearing down on her crooked finger, resting on metal.

She took a deep breath and then suddenly found herself repeating the words of the benediction; hoping that somewhere, in the simple meditation, an answer could be unearthed:

'To the moon, the stars will keep.'

Lunar Security Forces
Zilla Jones

Everyone looks the same in a space suit, thought Nova. When you put one on, the privileges of skin colour, gender, weight and age all disappear. 'We're spending so much time on the treadmill, and all those hours won't even show under these bulky things,' Prunella C. had complained at one of their training sessions. There were so many Prunellas and Priscillas and Mauds on this mission, all born between the mid-2020s and the mid-2030s when the fires and the virus tore through the former cities, and new parents looked to the past for hope.

Nova believed that her own naming had been an act of rebellion. By choosing a moniker that meant 'new,' her mother had tried to bestow a future upon her baby girl. But she couldn't have predicted that Nova would grow up to settle on the moon: she fell victim to the Theta 2 wave long before that was a possibility.

'We won't have to wear the suits in the pods,' Margaret had reminded Prunella C. 'But we can't buy any new clothes up there until they stock the Lunar Stores.'

Annoying as they were, Prunella C. and Prunella O. and Margaret, Gloria and Maud P. were the closest Nova had to family now. As she looked around the airlock, everyone was a stranger behind the glass bowls of their helmets. She craned her neck, hungry for a glimpse of Earth. Not as the first astronauts had seen it, but with more blue and less green. A planet where oceans replaced deserts and seas spread over prairie grass, and where the hot, carbon-filled air was laced with endless variants of a virus that thrived in greenhouse gases and buried itself in lungs already weakened from decades of breathing smog. A planet that the mission's Director of Psychiatry had told Nova over and over again might never again be her home.

The airlock opened, and the exit chute gleamed under the

laser flare lights. Nova had practiced this slide hundreds of times, but her legs sagged at the thought of actually touching lunar soil. She inherited some of the fear Neil Armstrong had experienced almost a hundred years ago when he faced this same descent. He had not known if his feet would burn, if he would sink into intractable mud, if inconceivable monsters would rise up to attack him, but he also knew that he was only a visitor. There had been a planet to return to then.

The air glowed greenish with the artificial lighting, but Nova knew that it was really darkness that surrounded her. An eternal void, pricked through with the silver of the stars. A deadly beauty that could cause you to despair if you dwelt on it too long, said the psychiatrists, but you must remember that Earth is still out there, still orbiting the sun as it always has.

A Warden, in a green space suit, flashed a message to Nova's Watchphone: *Pod 3*. Written communication was the only kind possible here, unless you were inside a building that replicated Earth's atmosphere, so Nova wore the newest model of SoftApple Watchphone. The Watchphone 33 had impeccable security, as all members of the Resurrect Mission were guaranteed privacy in their communications. 'You will go through many emotions, and you must be able to speak freely about them to your supports,' the Director of Psychiatry had said.

As Nova followed the Warden, she adopted the awkward bunny hop she had practiced on the stimulated surface of the Resurrect Mission Training Centre. She bounded past the Blue Moon hotel, erected during the tourist boom of the 2030s. The yellow curves of its legendary one-lettered sign announced the moon's first fast-food restaurant, and Nova longed for French fries and a coffee, but with ovulation approaching, she knew it was not a good, even if this was only a test cycle.

On the landing pad, the shuttle's thrusters glowed and its engine revved. Nova fought a desire to run after it and bang on the doors. 'I made a mistake,' she'd say. 'Take me with you.'

But then her memory flashed back to Aunt Jennifer in the Covid Centre, her cracked blue lips moving behind the hermetically sealed plastic.

'Promise me you'll get off this planet,' she'd said between coughs. 'Stay away until they clean it up.'

Even if Nova returned to Earth, Aunt Jennifer was dead now, claimed along with the rest of Nova's family in the fall of 2058. Nova herself had spent three weeks in the Covid Centre, where she had been one of the 15% of patients who still reacted positively to the serum treatment. Two years later, that percentage had tumbled to less than 5% and most governments had stopped providing it.

The Warden scanned them into Pod 3 and showed Nova her cabin. Her suitcase had been placed on her bed, and she sat down next to all that remained of her life on Earth. She removed her helmet and breathed in the manufactured oxygen. She shook her head and felt the tiny bots in her hair grafts tunnelling into the skin overlaying her scalp. She squelched the guilt she had felt when, just a few days after getting them installed, she saw on her Update account that the hair follicles came from Covid patients in the Slavic Union states, sold to buy the serum and its slim chance of recovery.

The comms screen above her dresser lit up, and when Nova activated it, Dr Pires' face came into view. 'Hello, Nova,' she said. 'I just wanted to review your job responsibilities as part of the Reproduction Team. The hormone monitors have been installed in your vein and will transmit to your Watchphone, which is synched to our system, so we can see what your cycle is doing in real time. No one but the Reproductive Team will have access to this data. You need to complete three test cycles to gauge how things are working in the lunar atmosphere. Then we will begin our first attempt at infusion.'

Having a baby was one of the most prestigious occupations there was, and for months, Nova had imagined how she would watch her belly swell as her home planet waxed and waned in the sky, how Earth's future would grow below her heart, how all her beloved dead would rise again with this new life.

Dr Pires said, 'As you know, this endeavour is not without risk. We are hoping to roll out reproduction robots in the next few years, but it is not a certainty, so we want to know how pregnancy and childbirth work on the moon in human bodies. We are not sure if it is safe. And we want the children who are born to be cared for by people who love them, to preserve our human culture, which is a problem we have not yet solved with the robots.'

Nova nodded. She already knew all this. 'Finally,' Dr Pires said, 'you understand that we aim to replicate a cross-section of the ethnic heritages and mixtures of people on Earth, and you have been placed in the mixed-race division. You, a Black biological female, are to be infused with sperm from a white male donor.'

'I know,' Nova said.

'Don't forget, we're here to help. We understand that childbearing is a very difficult profession, and so Psychiatry is on call twenty-four hours a day.'

'Thanks,' Nova said. 'I appreciate it.' She longed to be alone, but as soon as Dr Pires disconnected, the comms screen beeped again, and Prunella C's face beamed into the room.

'Isn't it *lunatic* up here?'

'I haven't really seen much yet.' Nova unzipped her space suit.

'Oh, I know, but it's so *busted.*' Prunella giggled. 'Just wait till our separation ends, and then we'll go to Mare Desiderii, you know, the nightclub, Sea of Dreams.'

'Should we, though?' asked Nova. 'Staying up late alters your body temperature.'

Prunella giggled again. 'They won't have to monitor us as much if we decide to do it the traditional way. If we meet some males up here.'

Nova said, 'But they still have to qualify. If their sperm's been damaged by Covid-'

'Yeah, OK, I get it.' Prunella pouted. 'We're here to save the human race, not to have fun. You don't have to rub it in.'

Nova reminded herself that Prunella was only twenty-six, eight years younger than Nova. She had only been Mature for a year.

'We can have fun, Prunella,' said Nova. 'When it's safe. When it's time.' People had been telling Nova that all her life, but it was never safe, and it was never time. Now, almost 400,000 kilometres from everything she had ever known, perhaps those hopes could finally be realised.

The next day, Nova lay in bed and watched Earth's continents roll past her window, waiting for the Liberated Allied States to appear. Finally, she recognized the parts of the old United Kingdom that still remained above water, and then, scrolling west, the half-finished Atlantic Bridge. Then the former Canada appeared, brown earth spreading into its melting north, above her birthplace in what had been the Independent Eastern Seaboard States, before they were moved westward into the old fly-over country. City lights went out and then sprung up again somewhere new as people tried to outrun the twin dangers of water and air. *Everyone is a refugee now*, Nova told herself. *Any home I had is long gone.*

She forced herself to get up and organise her room. She was still shuffling things around on her dresser when Prunella commed her. 'I'm so bored,' Prunella said. She had atom-waved her hair and used enhancers on her face. 'What are you doing?'

'Just organising,' said Nova. It was good to have someone to talk to, even someone she found irritating. 'You look nice,' she told Prunella.

'Can I see your clothes?' Prunella asked. 'I've only ever seen you in a space suit.' Nova activated the laser eyes of her Watchphone and directed them to the clothes rack. Her wrist swept over the dresser and Prunella said, 'Ooh, who's that? Is that your love bug?'

Nova covered her wrist. She had not anticipated having to explain this story to the likes of Prunella C. 'No,' she said. 'He's just a friend.'

It was a lie. Cornelius wasn't a friend anymore – he was nothing and nowhere. Their relationship began after Nova turned Mature and was finally allowed to date someone up to five years older. But only a year later, Cornelius was dead – not due to the virus, though. He was shot by police at a traffic stop, and the rally that was planned to protest his murder never happened, because the weekend it was supposed to take place, the Upsilon 5 variant emerged and was determined to spread fastest outdoors.

'He's *cooked,*' said Prunella. 'You should have just had a baby with him.'

She should have. But with egg extension therapy so readily available, there was no real rush. It wasn't until Nova herself was thirty that human fertility began its extreme decline, when the virus began attacking ovaries and testicles. She didn't want to talk about any of this. She walked over to the clothes rack. 'Want to see the last dress I bought before I left Earth?'

'Ooh, *fetching,*' said Prunella. 'They moved better stores to Philadelphia-Minneapolis than we got in Tampa-Little Rock.'

The transplant of the cities began when Upsilon 5 receded, but in the middle of the move, police in the former Oklahoma shot an eight-year-old child, and protestors from what became the Free African States blocked all transportation routes. The provisional government had no choice but to capitulate to their demands, and as a result, there had been no police in the Liberated Allied States for the past seven years. Too late for Cornelius, but at least Nova's child would never see the flash of red and blue lasers or hear the words 'Hands in the air.' They would never lie before her with a dark pool rippling out from under the head she had kissed only moments ago.

The Warden appeared on the comms screen to invite everyone to Orientation in the Gathering Hall. It was their first time outside since the walk from the shuttle to the pod. Nova and Prunella stopped by Pod 5 to pick up Maud and Margaret. Nova watched their messages flash on her Watchphone, but she didn't contribute any. She fixed her eyes on the rim of Earth rising behind the buildings.

The Head Warden conducted the Orientation, and Nova only half-listened until he said, 'We introduced a new space suit colour yesterday. Black. It belongs to the Lunar Security Forces.'

Nova typed her question into her Watchphone, and it flashed across the screen behind the Warden. *Why do we need security? What do they do?*

The Warden raised his hands, palms up. 'They're just here to answer questions and help direct people where they need to go.'

Nova wrote, *I thought that was what Wardens were for.*

'They can perform crowd control, enforce any curfews or restrictions we may need to bring in, and control traffic and land use.'

Are they armed?

'They have standard defensive weaponry.'

Relax, Prunella typed to Nova. *It will be fine.*

Nova dropped her arm. The Watchphone felt like a rock around her wrist. What did Prunella know? She was young. She was white. Nova pushed her resentment aside and forced herself to think rationally. Lunar Security Forces would surely not hold the kind of power that the police used to have. There was no need for it here. Everyone on the mission had gone through extensive background checks and screening. And in any event, she imagined that bullets could not fly far in the dead lunar air.

Nova lifted her wrist and pulled up Prunella's picture with her chin. *Yeah,* she typed, *it will be fine.*

After the orientation, Nova headed to the Mare Desiderii nightclub with her podmates. They hung their pink spacesuits up at the atmosphere-controlled entrance and fixed their hair in a row of mirrors. The club was decorated like one from the set of a vintage *Star Wars* movie, what was then a fantastical vision of a future in space. Nova walked past glass walls flashing with green and purple laser lights, statues of imagined aliens, a floor spangled with chrome stars and planets.

At the sight of the kitschy décor, Nova's tears began flowing. She excused herself to go to the bathroom, and she cried even harder when, on the way there, her Watchphone beeped the message, *Pre-ovulatory. No LH rise detected.* A baby was her only purpose, and if she screwed that up, there would be nothing left for her. She remained in the bathroom until the crying fit passed, and on her way back to her group, she glanced over to the bar and saw a man sitting there in a blue spacesuit, the colour worn by the Technical Team. A man with skin as dark as hers. She tried to look away before he noticed her, but he smiled and patted the stool beside him. A finger of curiosity poked her, and she walked over.

'Hi,' he said. 'I'm Sebastian, but everyone calls me Seb.'

'I'm Nova.'

'Where are you from?'

'Philadelphia,' she said, and then, 'I mean, Philadelphia-Minneapolis. And you?'

'Birmingham,' he said, and by his accent it was apparent he meant the one in the former United Kingdom, not the one in Alabama. She smiled at the newness of their two nations now being joined, and the fractures of her parents' United States mended back together again. There was strength in numbers: the rising nation had won control of the moon in the Second Space Conflict.

'What Team are you on?' he asked.

'Reproduction.'

'Traditional or assisted?' He leaned towards her as if the

answer was of great importance.

'Assisted.'

'Next question,' he said. 'Age.'

So he was interested. 'Thirty-four.'

His eyes clouded over. 'I'm forty-three,' he said. Forty-two was her statutory maximum. Then he grinned. 'Wait. Earth's laws don't apply up here. We get to make our own Lunar Codes by consensus, and I'm going to suggest that we do away with the rule that only people of certain ages can socialise, or that you have to be twenty-five to date.'

Nova said, 'Even on Earth, people of any age can talk.'

He winked. 'I'm hoping we won't just be talking.' He leaned closer. 'Have you been crying?'

She shrugged. 'A bit.'

'What's wrong?'

Nova was not embarrassed to talk about her delayed cycle. Being on the Reproduction Team, she had spent the past year discussing the functions of her body with dozens of medical professionals. They had instant access to view everything that happened in her body and everything that came out of it. Fertility was a public good and widely discussed everywhere. But she recognized that her sadness ran deeper than what she felt in that moment. 'I miss everything,' she said. 'We weren't meant to live here. We had a beautiful planet, and we -' The tears returned and she turned away.

'We didn't do anything wrong,' he said. 'Our generation did everything we could to fix it. We gave up oil, we popularized renewable energy. It's just that the generations before us didn't do enough.' She felt his hand extend, hover, and land on her shoulder. 'But we're the ones that are going to fix it. We've elected the very best representatives of Earth's governments to the Lunar Council. And people like you are giving your body to preserve humanity.'

Nova wiped her eyes on a cocktail napkin and blew her nose.

'How about a drink?' Sebastian asked. 'Non-alcoholic, of course. I don't want to interfere with your work.'

The following evening, Nova met Sebastian at the viewing platform. It was encased entirely in glass, with atmosphere control, and a large comm screen at the far end. They lay beside each other in the soft leather recliners and it was all she could do not to rest her head on his shoulder and press her face into his chest. They didn't speak at first, until Earth turned its face to show the emerging Atlantic Bridge. 'I worked on that,' said Sebastian. 'Before the terrorist attacks.' He took a deep breath, and said, 'You may as well know. My wife was standing right where the first bomb fell. Some days, it's still a lot to carry. I think that's mostly why I signed on to the mission.'

Nova felt her sternum expand, her diaphragm lift. She told him about Cornelius. About the shooting, but also about the great well of grief that had opened within her, and had never been filled, not with another relationship, and not with academic work. 'I did my PhD in Extraterrestrial studies,' she said. 'I wrote my dissertation on the ways humans viewed the moon before and after the first moon landing. We used to see the moon as a goddess. A smooth pristine surface covered with lush vegetation. But now we know it's just as imperfect as Earth. It's no more than a cold, rocky place.' She didn't want to cry in front of him again. He had enough sorrow to bear.

Her Watchphone flashed. *Time for bed. Regular sleep and waking times are essential for successful reproduction.* She switched off the notifications.

Sebastian asked, 'Do you want to have a baby?'

In all her interviews with the Reproduction Team, she had insisted that she did. Because she needed to. She had to. She hadn't allowed herself to think of what she wanted; what she would want if she wasn't living in the midst of a perpetual crisis, what other dreams she might allow herself. 'I don't have a choice,' she said. If she was not pregnant within eighteen months, she would be returned to Earth and a new team member would take her place.

The door to their compartment slid open and two figures in black spacesuits entered. On their waists, they wore atomic carbines, non-defensive weapons that had been outlawed by the Abolition of Police Act for any non-military use, and certainly not to be carried by parties providing security or peace-keeping.

The figures walked over to Nova and Sebastian. 'Identify yourselves,' one said. Nova held up her Watchphone, and the figure checked it. 'Reproduction Team members should be in bed now,' said the figure.

'We were just leaving,' Sebastian said.

The Warden leaned across her desk. 'We have a report that you've been spending time with a member of the Technical Crew.'

'Just a friend,' Nova replied.

'Perhaps,' said the Warden, 'but we are concerned about violation of your contract.'

Nova thought of Prunella's earlier comment. 'I could reproduce with him if I want, couldn't I?' As soon as she spoke the words, she wished them back. She had just met Sebastian. This was an acceleration of their relationship before it even began.

'Absolutely not!' The Warden pulled up a document on her Watchphone and flashed it to Nova. 'You are in the mixed-race division. I understand that this – person – is Black.'

'Well, couldn't I just switch to the Black division?'

'They already have enough members. The Free African States are responsible for selecting those participants, and they will be arriving on the next shuttle.'

The excitement at meeting more people who looked like her was eclipsed by the finality of the answer.

'You must follow your care plan to the letter. Clause 5(1)

(b). We're adding some new elements, as Clause 11(3)(g) permits. A tighter curfew and an earlier bedtime. Responsibility for enforcement will be handled by the Lunar Security Forces.' The Warden dismissed Nova by jerking her head towards the door.

Nova's Watchphone pinged. It was Sebastian. *Sea of Tranquility. One hour.*

Don't worry, Sebastian's comm said. *Once you have one baby, your future is secure. Then you are free to do what you want. Reproduce again with whoever you want.* Nova felt the same rushing pressure she had felt in the Warden's office. It had been the same on Earth. With the planet either burning or drowning and its reproductive capacity narrowing, everyone with whom you had coffee was a potential lifeline. Until people began thinking twice about having children. They asked: if you were just going to leave them orphans, was it ethical? Maybe Earth needed a break from human consumption. Maybe humanity needed to dwindle to almost nothing, until the waters receded and the ice returned.

So you don't care if I have it? His answer was a most precious thing.

It's your job, he replied. *I can be stepfather, can't I? I'll rub your feet and hold your hand when you go into labour.*

The stars around them gleamed more brightly than they ever had on Earth, with no laser flares or solar lamps to obscure their light. Nova cleaved to the idea of a baby moving inside her and Sebastian squatting by her birthing stool, his eyes filled with wonder.

That's why we all came here, said his next message. *To preserve hope, to believe there is still a planet worth saving and people to save it for.*

He was right, of course. Nova's Watchphone beeped. *Increased heart rate*, it said. *Increased pelvic blood flow.* Her Watchphone screen flashed orange and a message appeared. *Attention! The curfew times have changed to take effect immediately. Lunar Security Forces require you to return to your pods right away.*

As they walked, Nova noticed two other people traveling in the same direction. When she scanned her Watchphone at the door of Pod 3, Prunella slid in behind her, pulled her helmet off and giggled. 'I went for a walk with that *cooked* Warden from Pod 8,' she said. 'Who were you with, that engineer you met at the club?'

The Warden appeared in the hallway. 'It's bedtime,' she said. 'Hurry up now.'

The minute Nova was in her cabin, Prunella commed her, as Nova knew she would. She longed for privacy, to think on Cornelius, dead eight years. The grief would always be with her, but she was ready to peel it away just a little. She half-listened as Prunella babbled.

'My dad didn't let me date, even after I was Mature,' Prunella said. 'But up here, I can do what I want! We all can! Isn't it *wondrous?*'

You *can do what you want*, thought Nova. An ocean of salt rushed over the parched land of her heart. The Warden from Pod 8 was white, so Prunella could apply for traditional reproduction. Nova thought of how the Black History Act had mandated that all students in the Independent Eastern Seaboard states in the 2030s and 40s participate in simulated 4D recreations of the civil rights protests of the 1960s. Despite the immersive technology, the experiences had always seemed foreign to Nova, but now they reached across a century and snared her with their blistering tongues. *You thought you were safe from this*, they jeered. *We weren't allowed to have interracial families, but you are forced to.* Not forced, Nova reminded herself. She had chosen this, and that made it worse.

Before the weekly dinner at the Gathering Hall, Nova's Watchphone flashed green. *Ovulation imminent.* She pressed the screen to her cheek and savoured the return of the heady feeling of possibility. As soon as she arrived at the hall, she saw Sebastian sitting with the members of his crew. He patted the stool beside him. She wasn't sure if it was the sight of him or of the long line of Lunar Security Force members spread out across the room that made her throat constrict.

A serving robot approached with a tray of appetisers and drinks, and Sebastian selecting a glass of wine and a glass of grape fizz. He introduced Nova to his Team, but as they began to chat, Nova found herself looking longingly at Sebastian's drink.

Just a little couldn't hurt...' She lifted his glass for a quick sip.

Immediately her Watchphone beeped. Sebastian swivelled in his chair towards the sound.

Words appeared on the screen: *Fertility protocol: no alcohol permitted.*

'It's never done that before,' Nova said, turning her wrist to show Sebastian. 'At the end of the day it tells me what I've consumed and makes suggestions of where I can be healthier.'

'They must have reprogrammed them.' Sebastian took the glass of wine away. 'I suppose you'll have to stick to the fizz.'

The comm screen lit up and the Head Warden addressed the group. 'Good evening, missioners. You may have noticed that reinforcements for our Lunar Security Forces have arrived.'

Nova's Watchphone flashed. Sebastian's comm read: *Because the shuttle of Black people is on the way.* She felt her stomach churning, the way Earth's seas did below her window.

Heartrate rising, chirped her Watchphone.

Want to take a walk? Sebastian asked. She slipped off her stool and zipped up her space suit.

The laser flares and flashing signs overwhelmed the moon's pale glow. Nova wondered if all these alterations would change its essence, if its core would someday rebel. Sebastian slipped his gloved hand into hers and squeezed. She squeezed back before letting go to concentrate on her bouncing gait. They headed toward the observation platform. Inside, Nova pressed against Sebastian and tilted her face up to his. Their lips met.

The comm screen on the wall beeped and the faces of two Lunar Security Force members appeared. 'Violations,' said a voice. 'One, Age of Consent violation. Two, violation of reproductive contract in progress.'

They were watching. Horror strangled Nova. Her Watchphone chirped. *Heartbeat rising. Blood pressure increasing.*

'Nova Stewart, your physiological responses are counterproductive to your employment responsibilities,' said the voice.

Nova tried to stay calm. She breathed in and out. 'I thought that only the Medical Team had access to my biological data,' she said.

Sebastian added, 'And I thought the laws from Earth don't apply here.'

'The entire legal framework of the Liberated Allied States was adopted this afternoon by the Lunar Council,' came the answer.

Nova got up. 'I'm going back to my pod.' Sebastian followed her to the entrance. The Lunar Security Forces members stood in front of a black Lunar Rover, their atomic carbines pointing upward.

Nova's Watchphone delivered the message. *Nova Stewart, you are being placed in medical isolation.*

What is that? she replied.

Her Watchphone pinged. *Breathing irregular. Heartrate rising.*

A treatment centre, read the response. *To stabilize your biological phenomena.*

Sebastian looked down at his own Watchphone. He threw his arms up, and then he ran. Nova debated whether she should follow, but there was nowhere to go. She tried to slow her breathing as her phone lit up. *Heartrate rising. Blood pressure rising.*

The bullet was soundless, and it flew from the carbine more quickly than any bullet on Earth. Nova's scream was soundless too. She stopped screaming only when she realized that the Security Forces were inexperienced in shooting into lunar gravity, and their bullet streaked over Sebastian's head. The sight of it was enough to cause him to stop running. To adopt the pose that had not been seen on Earth for seven years. Hands in the air. Kneel. Do whatever they say.

Nova and Sebastian were placed in the Lunar Rover, wearing handcuffs big enough for their puffy spacesuits. The Rover rattled over the craters, past the hotel and stopped at a building behind the still-empty Lunar Stores. Nova was led to a small room, painted white. It held a bed with equally white sheets and nothing else. The door clicked and locked and she lay down. She pressed the button to activate her Watchphone, but a message flashed: *Communications disabled.*

The room had a window just big enough for Nova to see a blue corner of Earth as it turned and turned on its axis. Nova imagined she could feel Earth spinning, that she was rotating with it, until her vision blurred, and she almost believed that she had whirled off into the glittering, aching emptiness that surrounded her home planet. All that existed outside this window were the dark and the stars and the stifling cold, and in that great expanse, she was utterly and terribly alone.

The Seeds of the Tree
Rona J Firth

Transplanted flora and fauna over hundreds of years, altered in the soils of our new worlds. All original species are now unrecognizable, yet still it was our duty to rescue them from the decimation of climate change. I'm sure each and every one would thank us if they were able.

NEW EARTH 2.01986

HALCOURT MINING COMPLEX

'One rule,' old Clyde, the store's owner, yelled from behind his counter-top when his metal door clanged shut and his little mechanical replica of a dachshund started to yap. 'One rule – You steal anything, you're dead.'

The *One rule* announcement made Pongo sweat, his stumpy fingers scuttling into the safety of his jacket pockets.

'That's right, fat boy,' Clyde yelled. 'Keep those hands where they can't misbehave.'

The *One rule* announcement didn't have the same effect on Abe by Pongo's side. He strode forwards, holding out a battered piece of paper.

Clyde looked at it; his coal black eyes two cigarette burns in a face as shabby as a threadbare carpet. 'Looks like you've been trying to read that poor thing into pulp, boy.' Clyde leaned his scrawny chest over the counter, peering harder at the paper and the red and yellow logo across its top. '*Premier Gang* headed paper, eh? Set you a little challenge, have they? All set to try to join the Gang and earn some privileges, are you?'

Abe raised his chin proudly. 'Yes, sir.'

'The good jobs on the best machines. Drink and parties and impressing the girls.' Clyde made it all sound inviting enough. 'You two pups will be men in no time, won't you. So - what d'you need?'

Clyde's store - lines of metal cages like rows of teeth - was aisle-on-aisle of low-tech items: boots, overalls, toilets rolls, all mingled in with every high-tech gadget and gizmo you could think of. You wanted something, you rooted around in the mess for it, because hell if Clyde would remember where he'd thrown it.

Abe brushed dust off his top lip, both his face and his work clothes heavy with grit from the mines. He studied the piece of paper intently. 'Things aliens are scared of,' he read. 'One: loud noises. Two: strange smells. Three—'

'Guns,' Pongo shouted out, feeling the shake of the heavy wattle of flesh under his chin

'Guns aren't allowed,' Abe said sharply, staring down at Pongo by his side with a curled lip.

'Who says?'

'The Gang does. You don't mess with the *Premier Gang*. We're nothing but a couple of stupid kids to them right now. We don't want to stay that way.'

Pongo nodded, feeling his cheeks starting to burn. 'I'm not stupid.'

'Prove it, and shut your mouth.'

Pongo scowled. He and Abe had arrived on planet

together, been processed together, been deloused and had their heads shaved together. They'd found Ridge Town about as visually stimulating as a prison cell. A tin can town on a colony planet; long walkways of steel sheets with wire mesh ceilings and floors stretching between buildings encased in more metal. Everything was closed in, everybody locked in tight. They said, deep down as they were, the mines were safe. Nothing else was.

'Noise and smells.' Clyde grinned; his mechanical dachshund barking as if its metal ears had caught the tagline of a joke. 'Little kids' screams might do.'

'We're not little, we're sixteen,' said Abe.

Clyde raised grey brows. 'Sixteen is little to me. Little boys always stink of fear. You know what's out there?'

'They gave us a picture.'

The name *Gielanga* underlined the roughly drawn sketch at the bottom of the gang's instructions. Pongo peered at it over the top of Abe's arm. The alien had a ridged back, a wide mouth, and lots of teeth. It walked upright like a man - if that man had a broken back.

'Big teeth. Big claws.' Clyde raised his hands, curled his dirty bitten nails into his palms and snarled. 'Seen a man ripped apart by one once. He wanted to join the best work gang too. They sending you up to the big tree out there?'

'Yes, sir,' Abe said.

Pongo felt sweat slide down his back, the old man's intense gaze enough to strip flesh from bone. 'How fast can you run?' Clyde asked him. 'The slowest man gets eaten. The slowest man always does.'

Pongo's stomach flip-flopped. 'Abe's my friend,' he said

218

with a glance to Abe's skinny-rig of a body. 'Abe wouldn't leave me behind.'

'Course he won't. Abe's a hero.' Clyde winked at Abe. 'You boys best go low tech for *noise*. Batteries might fail; you might drop something and break it. A bucket and a metal spoon - how's that grab you? Stink is easy; got loads of fresh chicken guano out back I collect from the coop for such occasions. I'll make up a special mix with some extra grease to bulk it out a little. Smear yourselves with it, it'll disguise any human twang.' Clyde's gaze raked over Pongo's bulk again. 'You never know, no matter how meaty you are, grease yourself up right you might slide free.' He pointed at Abe's piece of paper with a cocked finger. 'You read the last part?'

'Aliens have fur,' Abe said. 'Says here, aliens are scared of non-fur.'

Clyde smiled. 'Non-fur, eh?'

'I don't know what it means,' Abe confessed.

Clyde's drawn-out chuckle sounded like an engine refusing to start. 'It means you go out there naked. Those aliens think our bodies are weird. No hair shocks them. Still, there's no need to be fools about it. You wear the grease and the chicken poop and disguise yourselves any way you can. You don't go up that hill towards that tree brazen-like, you sneak up there fast so you've been and gone before anything out there cares. Those aliens know that tree, they know the games we play, likely they'll be waiting for you.'

'We'll take the buckets and the spoons and the rest.' Abe's words were a sudden squeak. 'And we'll need *clearance*.'

'Damn right, you will,' Clyde said. 'The authorities don't like you opening outside hatches without the right paperwork. I can get you that. I can let you out. I'll even stand by with a gun in case you get into trouble. I'll fire only from the hatch mind; I'm not coming out there after you. North hatch, midnight, is the normal set-up. There'll be two clear good-sized moons tonight so you'll be able to see without falling over yourselves. I take it you'll go tonight?'

Abe nodded. 'Yes sir.' He glanced to Pongo who forced himself to nod.

'I'll want the full amount in cash,' Clyde said. 'I take it you've spent your first three full days working here getting enough funds together to finance this little venture?'

Pongo heard Abe's throat click. 'Yes, sir.'

'Well then, I'll get everything together and we'll see if you can afford it. Nothing's cheap in Ridge Town. Nothing but the skin on your back and the thoughts rattling round in your heads.' The old man walked around his counter, laughing his machine-gun rattle laugh.

'I can't run fast,' Pongo said as Clyde foraged through the store's metal cages looking for two buckets and two thick metal spoons. 'I'll be the slowest and I'll die.' Abe glared at him from under his dark brows as he always did when Pongo complained. 'Why can't we take a gun?'

'Stop whining,' Abe said in a low hiss, sneaking a glance at Clyde's slow rummage through another cage. 'We came here because Clyde's a *Premier.* You want your whining to get back to the gang leaders?'

Pongo didn't answer; he scowled instead.

'You need to be in a gang here,' Abe hissed out. 'So why

not be in the best?'

Whack. Clyde slammed a spoon into a bucket's side. 'Drum on the buckets only if you need to,' he instructed, returning to the counter. 'Otherwise just use them to gather up your trophies.' He banged the buckets down on the countertop, clattering two long spoons into each with a flourish of his fingers. 'I take it the gang asked for trophies?'

'The cones,' Abe said. 'The tree drops cones. They want us to bring some back, as many as we can carry.'

'So pile them into the buckets,' Clyde said. 'Then run like hell.' He took the money Abe offered and counted it slowly. 'Either of you have anybody you want me to write to if you don't come back?'

'We're orphans,' Abe said.

'That's best, that's always best. Nobody to fret over you, nobody to pine.'

Pongo gathered up the bucket Abe had left him. His bucket wasn't shiny like Abe's; his was a dull matt black.

'You know why you won't need a gun,' Clyde added, cocking his head Pongo's way, yellow teeth bared in another grimy smile. 'Because us Premiers don't want whining little cowards in our gang. That's why – Midnight boys, the North hatch. I'll bring everything. Don't be late. You don't show up I'll personally demonstrate what happens to cowards who mess with the Premiers.'

Nobody left Ridge Town on foot. Supplies came through the hatchways from the big trucks, and the big trucks, Pongo had heard, were always armed and manned by soldiers with guns and flamethrowers. It was ten minutes past midnight and he stood stripped to his waist in the night's chill, surrounded by the smell of shit. Abe stood smearing the acrid greasy concoction of chicken excrement and God knows what else across his back for him. The stench was all-consuming. It filled up Pongo's nose, this throat, his chest. He'd stopped believing other smells existed.

Abe stood naked. Abe wasn't shy about it; he'd already smeared the concoction across his chest and down his thighs, his smile bright white against the filth on his face. 'Hurry up,' Abe's words clouded the air. 'Get out of your clothes.'

'Aren't you scared?'

'Of seeing you naked?'

'Of going out there.' Pongo slid down his trousers then the shorts beneath. He shivered, trying not to look at his own body, trying harder still not to look at Abe's.

'We'll be fine. We'll get this done we'll fit in. You want that don't you? You want to be in the Gang, get the good jobs, get the extras?'

'Of course. Everybody here wants that.'

Old man Clyde stood by the hatch listening, a long lean cigarette lolling out the side of his mouth, Pongo all too aware of the weight of the man's stare on his back as he hunkered down to the bucket. He piled the heat-leaching slime onto his legs, across his buttocks and over the deep folds of his belly.

'Hate to rush you, but you both stink so bad my nose is running blood here, boys,' Clyde coughed out. 'Time to move.'

Clyde pushed his weight into the lever that opened the hatch, the mechanism squealing in protest. 'I'll be watching,' he said, pushing the door wide.

Pongo had never seen the world beyond Ridge Town's walls. He'd arrived straight from the dock in one of the blacked-out transport trucks, the truck backing up and unloading their human cargo like garbage through the hatchways. The darkness beyond the doors wasn't very dark at all. The two moons - one to the West, one to the South – were high and full, rinsing the land beneath them in soft yellow light. The tree stood at the crest of a long sloping incline. Tall and wide, it looked like a welcoming hand, its tapering fingers trailing off into the cloudless sky.

Pongo had to nip his bottom lip still, he was shaking so badly.

'We'll be able to see for miles,' Abe said glibly. 'There's nothing out there to hide behind.'

'Fast run up the hill, grab the cones and run down.' The cigarette in Clyde's mouth danced with every word. 'Simple, boys. Now hurry it up, the authorities don't like these hatches left open for long.' At Clyde's feet his little mechanical dog gave an encouraging yap.

Abe trotted out first, tense and animal-like, his head turning left to right and back again. 'Hurry, Pongo.' He gained pace, bucket swinging, the metal spoon in his other fist held out like a sword.

Pongo lurched into a jog, belly and chest jiggling, more private things joining in. He gave a yelp, the bucket's cold sides catching the meat across his thighs with a sudden thunderous slap. He glanced left then right, the land beneath his toes as furry as a dog's back, the thin, soft grass up the slope heaving to-and-fro in strange patterns with every whisper of wind. Pongo looked around again, then again, the motion frantic, Pongo trying to breathe, look and run all at once.

Already halfway up the slope, Abe spun about. 'This is

going to be easy!' he shouted. 'What were you scared of?'

Pongo shook his head. His cheeks felt scorched, his inner thighs already rubbing themselves sore; Pongo was sure invisible hands were crushing his chest tighter and tighter in their grip. 'What's that?' He jerked up his spoon and pointed, the sudden spasm of movement enough to make Abe jump. 'What's moving in the grass?'

Abe wielded his own spoon and turned around.

Things shifted under the fringes of the open: small dark things, lots of them swarming closer and closer to Abe's naked toes.

Pongo snatched a glance back to the town's steel walls, his own toes digging into the ground, his whole body telling him to turn around and bolt.

'They're the cones,' Abe bent over double for a closer look. 'They're the seeds of the tree.'

'But they're moving,' Pongo said. He saw roots as scarlet as fresh blood gripping at the grasses, hauling along tiny oval bodies packed with spikes that looked as sharp as pins. 'Run, Abe,' Pongo hissed. 'Please, Abe. Run!'

The rest of the swarm banked up against the lead cones so hard and fast they were thrown up Abe's legs.

Abe yelped but he didn't flee. 'It doesn't hurt,' he said. 'The spines aren't hard.' He plucked up a cone, holding it aloft by one long tendril of root. 'They're soft. They're soft all over. They can't hurt us.'

Abe dropped the cone into his bucket. He grabbed up more, each making a tinny thump as it hit the bucket's bottom. The trapped cones started to squeak like cornered mice, while

224

below in the grass the others started to flee in alarm.

'They're running.' Abe's grin was a flash of whiteness. 'I'm going to catch some more.' Abe ran after the fleeing cones, sweeping more into his bucket while the squeaks of protest in both bucket and grass grew louder and louder.

Pongo scooped up a straggler. It felt soft in his fist; so spongy he was sure if he squeezed too hard it would explode like an overripe fruit. He dropped it into his bucket, it landed with a soft plop then rolled about in panic, its high-pitched squeaks growing hysterical.

Not safe, we're not safe, Pongo reminded himself. He turned around, carefully examining the land, searching for movement, searching for anything crawling in the grass alerted by the cries of the captured cones. He heard a noise, a low grumble like an upset stomach, and glanced back to the tree. He squinted. He couldn't see Abe.

Pongo jogged as fast as he could up the remainder of the slope until he stood under the boughs of the tree. It looked so much like a hand, its palm lined and chapped, flakes curling off it like dry dead skin.

'Where are you, Abe?' Pongo wheezed out.

He saw a foot, pale and white, on the tree's far side.

'Abe?'

Abe lay in the grass, his head on a risen crown of earth, his body half twisted over. He stared skywards through the tree's branches. He stared and stared into the navy sky as if he could see into the universe and count every single star within it. He didn't move or say a word; he just lay peacefully staring into the heavens. By his side his bucket lay overturned and empty.

Pongo placed a hand on the tree's trunk to steady himself. He stared at Abe's chest willing his eyes to be mistaken - a trick of the night, a trick of his own terror. Abe was breathing. Abe was playing a joke. He had to be.

Pongo's teeth started to chatter, a sudden rush of warm urine splashing down his legs. He stood shaking, dripping in his own disgrace, realising the night was utterly silent now.

He sucked a sharp breath and every sinew loosened. He turned, breaking into a run, heading down slope. The cone bounced in the bucket he'd still had clenched in his fist. Its thin roots squeaked down the metal sides, trying to catch over the lip with every heavy recoil.

Pongo started to laugh, he laughed so loud he didn't notice the slow growl gathering from the earth beneath him, or feel the land quaking under his heels. He didn't notice much at all until he tripped, landing on his belly with a whoosh of expelled air. In front of him an enormous ruby-red tendril of root snaked into the sky. Up and up it went, soil and grass raining from its sides.

Pongo screamed. He flipped the bucket over, the cone inside rolling away. 'I let it go!' He pointed at the fleeing seed. 'I let it go!' He held his hands over his head waiting for the root to smash downward, waiting for his skull to break the way Abe's must have. 'Please. Please,' he begged the tree on the hill.

The root lowered, its whip thin end wrapped tight about his ankle and pulled. Pongo wriggled like a fat white maggot on a line. 'Help me!' he yelled towards Ridge Town. 'Somebody help me.' He could hear Clyde's metal dachshund in the distance, barking its laughing bark.

The root went skyward, heaving him up with it. He hung upside-down, struggling, hoping the root would break, hoping someone would hear his yells and come running. 'I let it go!' he screamed. 'I wasn't going to hurt it.'

The root yanked him backwards. Air whooshed past his ears, his fingers snatching at nothing, his eyes bulging as the stars whizzed past the moons. On the zenith of the root's arch Pongo's hot tears were cast into the cold empty heavens.

Then the tree threw him towards Ridge Town.

He flew, his scant seconds airborne the most graceful he had ever been in his life.

Ridge Town's steel walls caught him. They shattered him, pounding him into a misshapen lump of flesh and bone. He lay in the dirt, every breath, fire in his lungs, his leaden thoughts repeating slowly, *I'm broken. I'm broken.*

Clyde loomed over him chuckling, his metals dog's legs clicking with every footfall as it scuttled closer. 'You bounced,' Clyde laughed out. 'Fat boy, you bounced like a rubber ball.'

People laughed, they whooped. It sounded like the whole town had been watching.

It was all one big sick joke - like the alien in the sketch, the alien that never existed. Abe lay dead and they'd all stood and watched him die.

It's all broken, Pongo thought before his swollen eyelids closed.

The Ridge Town gossips said Pongo had lost his mind the day the mother tree threw him home. They said, when his head hit steel, bone had entered his brain, splinters like knives pushing inward, dividing Pongo cleanly from his sanity.

Here was more proof of his madness. Six months and seven days after Pongo had slammed into the metal, he limped out of the North hatch of Ridge Town in broad daylight, walking up the hill towards the mother tree. He didn't take a bucket or a spoon this time. He wasn't naked.

Ridge Town watched from every spyhole it owned. Townspeople with stilled faces wondering what the not-so-fat boy was going to do out there. Whether the not-so-fat boy just wanted to die, now he had only one hand and one working leg, now he had a dent in his forehead that caved into one eye socket. He was in the Premier Gang. He'd had extras aplenty. Food and drugs and even ladies of the night. He'd drunk himself into insensibility many evenings since the doctors had patched him whole.

The not-so-fat boy slogged his way up the hill on his mechanical leg, his metal hand held high as if he meant to welcome a friend and the tree - the tree loomed tall, waiting. When the soil at Pongo's feet quaked he stood fast. When the huge root rose up before him he didn't flinch.

I'm not the same boy you threw away. Perhaps the tree sensed his thoughts. She had chased others off the hillside the Premier Gang had sent her way since Abe's death. She'd sent them yelling and crying; she'd broken bones enough. None of the others had ever come back, none of the others had ever dared.

I'm not the same as them. I hate them all, Pongo thought, his broken mind a-whirl. *I can get you what you want. I know you want this world. I know why the trees lost another one now.*

This time, instead of winding a red whip of root about Pongo's ankle or sending a blow crashing down towards his delicate head, the tree did something she'd never done before. She hesitated and she listened to the heartache of a human seedling.

The Flooded Acres
Steve Wade

Once his limbs loosened and his stiffened eyelids parted, the first thing Carter Grayson did was to check in on his rejuvenating mother. Beneath the sepia-coloured light in her domed chamber, she remained asleep.

At one-hundred-and-seventy-three-years old, his mother already looked younger than him. And why wouldn't she? Since becoming eligible for the full revitalisation programme on her centennial birthday, her cellular and tissue structure had been put into reverse. So, for the five months she, along with three-quarters of the global population, were in hiber-bruma-estivation, more commonly known as 'the long sleep', her age had been decreasing from two to four years during every twelve-month cycle.

As a civil rights campaigner, Grayson's mom had spent her career fighting for the underprivileged section in society. Those unfortunates born into regions and circumstances which made them ineligible for certain basic human needs. The most pressing, the right to protection from the devastating winter months, when temperatures plummeted to minus one-hundred degrees Celsius. These people, known as the outliers, suffered huge mortality rates from October to March.

Because of his mom, Grayson, likewise, had dedicated his life to beneficial causes. But, where his mom dealt directly with the imbalance and unequal distribution of wealth and services to people, he concentrated on the conservation of the planet and its resources, to the welfare of wildlife and the habitats on which all things wild depended. This he did in a measured and calm way. Another trait he got from his mom. As she put it: *everything that exists or happens has a cause.* This was something he couldn't quite agree with. But he respected everything his mom said, did, and believed in.

No movement. His mother appeared as though still in the deepest part of her sleep phase. She ought to be twitching by now, her face muscles showing signs of loosening, her fingers curling. Grayson leaned forward; his face close to hers. 'I love you, Mom. See you soon.' Before leaving the sleeping chamber, he kissed the glass above her cheek.

Despite the gargantuan strides made in science in the past two centuries, particularly in the field of medicine, many things remained a mystery. One of them was whether the induced winter sleeper was conscious of outside stimulus. Grayson saw the faintest flicker on one side of her mouth. The suggestion of a smile. He smiled too.

Not long out of his own hiber-bruma-estivation, Grayson couldn't recall experiencing anything during his own prolonged sleep that suggested he was aware, at any time, of being in an induced coma. Anxious to see how the world had fared while physically absent for months, he worked his way to the living quarters and sat down.

To begin with, he needed to check his health. With his eyes closed, he pressed the thumb of his right hand to the centre of his left palm. The Internal-Net came to life behind his eyes. The first thing he noted was the date: February twelfth. This meant he had awoken a month early. Blinking five times, he scrolled down the red screen on the inside of his eyelids. The middle finger of his left hand he pressed to the health line in his palm. Apart from his blood pressure being slightly high - something which would adjust naturally now he was conscious and active – hard-wired reflexes were intact, musculoskeletal system functioning normally, cholesterol balanced, his eyesight needed minor adjustment.

Opening his eyes, he concentrated on the hologram portrait of one of his mother's historical heroines, the former fiftieth president of the United States, Yolanda Renee King. Unblinking, he remained locked onto the hologram for one minute, until Renee King's blurred features and lined face came into sharp focus.

With his eyesight fixed, Grayson could now view the different shoals of fish as they moved in synchronicity, glinting silver when they turned and caught the refracted light in the waters outside his winter home in High Street, long ago covered by rising sea levels. The family's winter dwellings, an inverted aquarium since before he was born, with the fish and other sea creatures on the outside looking in.

Too soon yet to remove the parenteral nutrition drip and take his first solids, Grayson put on a wet-dry suit, the type favoured by the outliers during the freezing months. The suit was made from fibres that mimicked the insulation properties of the eider duck's down. He then put on his amphibio gill mask and his rucksack and made his way to one of three pressure hatches. The significant rise in global temperature since the twenty-first century allowed him to enter the sea with little discomfort. Although being half a month in advance of March, the initial shock gripped him like an oversized frozen and clenched fist.

All about him the sea, teeming with vast and varied marine life, was as transparent and sunlit as a tropical reef. This owing in great part to climate change, despite the efforts by pioneering forefathers like Sir David Attenborough in the fight against global warming. Although that mission, to prevent the worst effects of the change in climate, didn't play out as originally envisioned, peoples from disparate backgrounds, cultures, and nations had put aside their differences and gained a control over certain conditions of life on earth. Enough to ensure the survival and continuance of many endangered species. Enough to keep the rising sea level at one that could be maintained. A healthy balance, but a balance that could always be improved.

Up to the surface he rose, past the vertical and self-sustaining gardens of different types of seaweed. On breaking the surface, the amphibio mask allowed him to take in his first gulp of undiluted oxygen in five months. Into his ears the sound of screaming gulls and calling terns mixed with the slap of waves against the façades of the higher buildings. Then, from under the sea, nose up, emerged a hoversubflyer hybrid. The pilot shot his craft into the sky, did a loop the loop, and brought it back next to Grayson. He then inched his craft sideways, and half submerged it, so that it scooped Grayson aboard.

'Picked up your signal,' the smiling taxi pilot said. He wasn't yet on official duty but was getting his craft ready for the working season. 'Didn't expect you people to be about yet.'

'Me neither.' Grayson laughed. 'Some sort of malfunction.' He recognised the taxi pilot's face but was certain they'd never met.

'It happens,' the taxi pilot said. He nodded. 'So, where to?'

'Upward and across.' Grayson chucked his chin in the direction of the city's central park. 'Islet PP65.'

While on the brief journey to the Flooded Acres, Grayson asked the pilot about the winter and how those who were ineligible for what should be mandatory for all had fared.

'Dropped to minus 110 at times.' The pilot compressed his lips, squinted, and shook his head. 'The figures were pretty high during the killing months.' Besides not having enough fuel to keep their basic shelters heated properly, the greatest challenge was keeping everybody fed, he told him. Unlike the privileged in society, who survived the Shutdown Period by having the required nutrition dripped into them while they slept, the outliers depended on food they had grown, raised, produced, or bartered and stored away during the less fallow period from March to September. Although they too, like Grayson's society, did their best to stick to a blue food-based diet, a huge contributary factor over the years in the reduction of greenhouse gas emissions.

'The problem is twofold,' the pilot said. 'Too many elderly folks to feed - despite the many we've lost - most of them too feeble to work. And with just a few babies born in nearly two generations, there just aren't enough hands to keep the system going.'

The low sperm count was an issue in both Grayson and the taxi pilot's worlds. Over reliance on certain plastics for hundreds of years had led to sperm counts too low to facilitate a normal and functional birth rate. In Grayson's society, this was countered by producing babies in laboratories. Each baby, in line with its genetic engineering, was then raised under the category of thinkers and doers. And these were further divided into artists, musicians, teachers, builders, engineers, philosophers, and so on.

'And your own situation?' Grayson asked.

The taxi pilot told him about his little girl. As happy and as bright a child as ever there was but she'd never seen her mammy or daddy's face. Blind since birth.

'I'm really sorry.'

'It's okay,' the taxi pilot said. But Grayson could see it was light years away from being so.

'I've read about you,' Grayson said.

'No doubt you have. That's why I'm piloting one of these for myself and not working for the controller.' The controller, the collective name of the outside government. Grayson's government.

'I remember,' Grayson said. 'They supplied you with the craft in exchange for access to you and your partner's medical history.'

The taxi pilot nodded. 'That's it. And then the media got hold of the story. *The Freak Birth Among the Outliers.*'

'I'm sorry,' Grayson said once more, wishing he could think of something to offer stronger commiseration.

'Me too. But, you know what? I'd give this machine right back to them if my little girl could see her own face reflected in a mirror.'

'What's her name?'

'Amyah.' The taxi man's face softened and brightened on saying his little girl's name. 'It's her birthday today.' He looked as if he was about to come undone. Grayson was about to shift the topic, but the Taxi pilot steadied his own course. 'Listen. On behalf of me and my people, I want to thank your mother. For all she's done for us.'

'No, not at all. I want to thank you and your family and your colleagues for your services. And all you have to go through.' Grayson held his hand out to the pilot. The two men grasped each other just above the wrist and tugged.

'Look at that,' the pilot said, as the Flooded Acres came into view. They shot forward and cruised above.

'Man, that is just sublime,' Grayson said. Inside his chest he felt his heartbeat speeding up, and in his ears a thrumming sensation.

Below them, dotted and spaced out among the one-thousand-seven-hundred-plus acres, the floating islands. Islands that were shifted about to allow an even distribution of sunlight to fall upon the waters to ensure photosynthesis beneath. The teardrop-shaped islands were the spring and summer homes of thousands. On others, circular-shaped, were housed animals and birds that would otherwise succumb to the extreme temperature drop in winter.

Replete with a geodesic dome house, the outer parts of the islands were planted with spruces, junipers, firs, and evergreen shrubs. Trees and plants that provided protection and further insulation when the helmet domes were deactivated. But the pink and white display below, which gave Grayson and the taxi pilot such a sense of wonder and marvel, were owing to the cherry blossom trees - one of several bands of trees planted for ornamental purposes.

Instead of going directly to his own home as originally planned, Grayson got the taxi pilot to transport him around the other islets. The ones that housed the animals and birds. Far too cold for winter visitors and equally cold in their historical destinations for those migrants that once left the shores when the colder months came, birds like the cuckoo, the swallow, martins, and the corncrake, were kept in specially designed islet enclosures. Spinning in a manner to imitate the world on its axis, the islets duped the birds into experiencing the same sensations they would were they travelling thousands of kilometres to Africa or across the Mediterranean Sea and the Sahara Desert.

The taxi pilot took great interest in Grayson's explanations about the workings of the system. Fascinated, he was, to learn that the swallow-like birds had already begun their six-week migration. The two men watched from the hoversubflyer the flights of birds, as they continuously and repeatedly circumnavigated their enclosures. The plant life in these heated enclosures were chosen to support and maintain the predominantly insect life upon which these migratory birds fed.

Once he had checked and surveyed all the animal and bird islets, Grayson decided he'd make a start on some of his mother's areas of interest. He invited the taxi pilot to be his guide, if, of course, he wasn't putting him out.

'You're my first fare since winter,' he said and winked. 'I'd be honoured.'

'Appreciate it, my friend,' Grayson said. And he assured him that, naturally, he'd be paid for his services.

The pilot shook his head in relation to payment but said that if he could help his people with some provisions, that would be all the payment he needed. Grayson tried to persuade him that feeding the needy was part of his mother's projects anyway, but the pilot pointed up that this wasn't due to resume for another few weeks.

'Can you fly a transporter carrier?' Grayson asked him.

'If it takes off, I can fly anything,' the pilot said.

'Good man. Let's get her loaded first.' He directed the pilot to one of the humming islets to land.

Next to one of the insectary buildings, Grayson deactivated the hanger cover to reveal the transporter carrier. Shaped like a manta ray, with three bullet-shaped pods attached to its undercarriage, the taxi pilot was into its cockpit before Grayson gave him the go-ahead. Within seconds he had the aircraft heated and the cargo pods freed. Then, with a voice command, two of the pods lifted a few inches off the ground and spun their way to the insectary. Another voice command from Grayson and the pods attached themselves to the porthole coverings in the building. The spiral openings triggered, and the pods shot down tubes, coming to a stop when half inside the enclosure. The tips of the pods opened.

The release of ultrasound and pheromones, along with white incandescent and florescent light stimulated the crickets, locusts, grasshoppers, cicadas, butterflies and moths, and other insects, pulling them into the pods.

With the third pod filled with plankton, algae, fungi, and seaweed, Grayson got them to stop off at one of the laboratories where his mother did some work. There he collected a number of vials. Not too many that they'd be overlooked, and not too few that they would be of little benefit. He stowed them away in his rucksack.

And while on the island that housed the science labs, he used his familial status to enter another laboratory, one frequented by his mother's colleagues. The genome security reader detected the requisite amount of DNA and granted him entry through the air door. But, once the taxi pilot drew too near, the sensor reactivated the invisible barrier.

Grayson took his time locating what he needed, which he put carefully into an inner pocket of his rucksack.

He and the pilot then took off for the inland parts of the country that had remained unaffected by the rise in sea levels. From above, the villages looked like crude and misshaped honeycombs. The original design, for reasons of space and heat efficiency, was successful, but at the cost of privacy. And packed so close together, the hexagon shaped homes afforded no escape from any outbreak of contagious illness or virus.

A community with its own social structures, every citizen watched out for his fellows. And with no disparity in social class due to equality in education and property ownership, the crime rate was very low. Those who did commit minor misdemeanours, such as food and water theft, were dealt with by the Citizens Syndicate. Their daily duties were increased, and their sleep entitlement rationed accordingly.

The taxi pilot landed his craft on a berthing port. Out of the tiny homes came curious faces. Not since summertime had a transporter carrier landed in their zone. On recognising the taxi pilot as one of their own, they broke into spontaneous applause. The taxi pilot told them that tonight they would all eat well. The crowd applauded harder and cheered louder. The chefs stepped forward and began discussing the different kinds of dishes they would prepare from the insect and blue food ingredients.

With part of the insect cargo safely transferred to the feed mill, the other to the almost depleted breeding insectary, Grayson asked for volunteer designers, construction workers, medics and nurses, to assist him with his project. As everyone had equal training in all areas, almost every hand was raised. Although every individual had their own daily tasks and duties to attend to, they welcomed the diverse stimulus. A lottery was organised, and the lucky winners chosen.

To begin with, Grayson needed a building they could work in. Agreement was soon reached that the long-ago defunct church would suit. As religion was no longer practised worldwide, the church had been preserved, originally out of respect and latterly for reasons of nostalgia. The designers and builders got to work on transforming it into a medical centre with the requisite laboratories.

Having worked on IVF programmes for native mammals like the badger, the fox, and the recently reintroduced grey wolf, setting up a similar programme for people wasn't very different. A smile came to his face when he envisioned the future media headlines about more 'freak births' among - well, he didn't even want to use the discriminatory term – among the taxi pilot's people.

That first evening of the two weeks Grayson took up the offer to stay with the pilot taxi's family, a communal feast was held in the biggest open space, the square. The taxi pilot introduced Grayson to his wife and to Amyah, his daughter. With long, straight black hair to her waist, skin as white as sun-bleached coral, and eyes as neon blue as a radiant blue angel fish, the little girl was a miniature of her mother.

Amyah held her mommy's hand as though the two were conjoined. Yet it was Amyah who seemed to lead her mommy from one group of guests to another, as the different groups wished her a happy birthday and gave her gifts.

To witness the diverse range of people together - people of colour, different appearance, and physical ability –interacting without any trace of prejudice or bias, Grayson wondered at the presumptive attitude of the society into which he was born. Great advances they may have made in so many areas, but they had yet to eradicate fully the unbending sense of entitlement by some.

'What's your favourite food?' Amyah asked Grayson when they were finally seated. Her mother had already told him of Amyah's love of cooking. He knew the dishes she had prepared.

'Honey and micro fried locusts,' he said.

Amyah opened her mouth in surprise and twisted to her mum beside her, a big-toothed smile on her face.

The first solid meal Grayson had had in months, his throat contracted as he swallowed in anticipation. The array of dishes bobbed about on the seawater tabletop. Cricket crackers were served as part of the antipasto platter. Atop a cracker he spread some of the aforementioned locusts. His first bite of the salty cracker sent through him jolts of piquant delight.

'Wow,' he said. 'This is so good.'

'You should try the plankton and algae dip,' Amyah said.

'I will,' Grayson said. But first he had a special birthday present for her. From his rucksack, he took a small coral pink case. 'Happy Birthday, Amyah. This is for you.'

The young girl received the case, her hands exploring its shape and texture. She asked her mother to describe its colour.

'Well. It's soft and sweet. The colour for a little girl just like you.'

'What is it, Mommy?' She held it before her and shook it.

'Open it and find out.'

Amyah repeated the voice command whispered to her by her mommy and the case opened. Grayson watched her concentrating features as her fingers explored its contents. Hesitant to put on the SuperSight goggles, her hands shook as she placed them on her face. Her mommy helped her. Grayson watched as the light transmitted through the lenses transformed into electrical signals to her brain. The signals then turned into the images before her. A process that took a fraction longer than it did in those born sighted.

The little girl held her own hands before her and twisted them about. She then turned her head up to her mommy's face, and brought both her hands to her own mouth, before reaching up and touching her mommy's cheeks. And she ran her fingertips down her mommy's smile lines.

'Don't cry, Mommy.' She wiped away the tears streaming down her mother's face, before using the back of her hand to wipe away her own tears.

While everyone continued to celebrate and enjoy the feast, Grayson went with the taxi pilot, his wife, and their little girl on a tour of their city. To watch her and how she reacted to everything – the blue sky above, across which floated altocumulus clouds, birds flying free, the colours of the homes, the shadows, the myriad plants and flowers, and everything he had long ago taken for granted, and to listen to Amyah's endless questions, filled a part of him he never knew had been empty.

Now Carter Grayson understood fully why he had awoken from the long sleep a month in advance. As his mom put it: *everything that exists or happens has a cause.*